Spook Anthology '23

Stage Plays and Monologues

DRAMATIC CHAOS PRODUCTIONS

Edited by Rebecca Holbourn

ISBN: 979-8-8658-1272-2

Dedication

This is dedication.
Yes, this paragraph.
Yes, this anthology.
Yes, every play written in these pages.
It is dedication.

This dedication is dedicated to the
dedication of all writers who have picked
themselves up, shrugged off the naysayers and
the rejections, sat in front of a blank page
and written something.

That's dedication, right there.

Dedication.

Contents

Play Title	Playwright	Page
A Housewarming in Hor'ton	Greg Lam	11
Arise and Prep	j. Snodgrass	26
Boogeyman	Dana Hall	36
Blackberry Fog	Christina Woods	42
Candlelight	Evan Baughfman	46
Champagne	Scott Younger	62
Crawl Space	Lee Lawing	78
Eisoptrophobia	Thomas Jancis	86
Flesh and Blood	Peter Briffa	98
Gluttony on the High Seas	Steve Duprey	104
His Face	Gerardo Rodriguez	114
Hold All Devils In My Heart	Thomas Jancis	119
In-terror-gation	Kerri Duntley	133
Kuchisake-onna	Marilyn Ollett	141
Lenore	Christine Emmert	147
Let The Dead Bury The Dead	Mike Brannon	155
Memento Mori	Donna Latham	170
Olly Olly Oxen Free	Jacquelyn Priskorn	187
Playwrights Versus Zombies!	Christopher Plumridge	197
Possessed by the Ex	Clinton Festa	224
Severance	j. Snodgrass	239
Silence in the Library	Benjamin Peel	252
Spa-mageddon	Scott Younger	265
Still Life With Grave Juice	Jim Moss	282
Sweet Ghoul Long Past	Christine Emmert	296

Play Title	Playwright	Page
The Bus to Nowhere	Cole Hunter Dzubak	300
The Dark	Janice Kennedy	314
The Demon Speaks	Rebecca Holbourn	326
The Ex-Files	Jamie Mcleish	332
The Frog Prince	Marzia Dessi	346
The Ghosts of the Doomed Circus Train	Joseph Galata	354
The Haunted Geese Goose Gift for Blind Brenda	Rebecca Holbourn	362
The Monster	Jacquelyn Priskorn	380
The Return	Abhisek Bhattacharya	387
Times Lost Forever	Roderick Millar	401
Voodoo Doll Syndrome	Clinton Festa	408
With Love, Your Ghosts	Mike Brannon	418

Monologue Title	Playwright	Page
An Audience At The Crossroads	Dominic Palmer	436
Claustrophobic	Emma C. R. Skinner	447
Ghost Whisperer	Melvin S. Marsh	450
My Friend Audrey	Greg Lam	454
Staring into the Portal	Katy Lever	456
Tell-Tale	Peter Dakutis	459
The Butler	Jamie Mcleish	467
The "Haunted House"	Ryan Vaughan	478
The Rescue	Debs Wardle	481
The Vanishing Texter	Peter Dakutis	492
Work-Life Balance	Emma C. R. Skinner	495

<u>Plays</u>

A Housewarming in Hor'ton
By Greg Lam

CHARACTERS
  TRISHA - *A new homeowner*
  MARTIN - *Her spouse*
  THE NEIGHBOR - *Their neighbor*

SETTING
  The living room of a nice suburban house,
  set up for a party.

                    MARTIN and TRISHA enter. They are in a
                    frantic rush, making sure the house is
                    ready.

TRISHA
  Drink cart… Charcuterie… Crudité. I think we
  have everything.
  …
  Ice! We need ice! Martin?! Can you fill the
  ice bucket?

MARTIN
  What, darling?

TRISHA
  The ice bucket! Our neighbors will be here at
  any moment!

MARTIN
  I'm getting the ice. Don't worry about it
  sweetheart.

TRISHA
  Please hurry. I do want to make a good first
  impression.

MARTIN
  Oh, I'm sure they'll be understanding. We only
  just moved in. In fact it's awfully early to
  be holding a housewarming party.

TRISHA
  It's just that this is the first house we've
  ever owned. Moving out to quaint small town
  America. Salt of the Earth, real people. I do
  hope that we can fit in.

MARTIN
  Relax. I'm sure that you'll fit in. I'm sure
  you'd fit in anywhere. If you could fit in in
  my home, you can fit anywhere.

TRISHA
I know that you didn't want to move all the
way out here. But thank you for doing this for
me.

MARTIN
Of course. I would do anything for you.

TRISHA
And this neighborhood is so darling.

MARTIN
That's what you said when you went around
putting invitations on everyone's doors.
Strange that no one was around in the middle
of the day. Not exactly the neighborly vibe
that Zillow promised.

TRISHA
Do you think they'll arrive soon? It gets dark
so quickly here in Hor'ton, even with the full
moon out.

MARTIN
Are you sure that's how it's pronounced?
"Hor'ton"?

TRISHA
Yes, it's one of those quaint regional
pronunciations, you know?

    A loud, powerful knock on the door.

MARTIN
What did I tell you? They're here!

TRISHA
Oh, I'm nervous.

MARTIN
Come on now, we can do this. Remember, we are
Good Neighbors. Let's put on our outside
faces.

They compose themselves with smiles.
Trisha opens the door.

TRISHA
  Greetings, neighbor!
     (pause)
  Strange. There's no one there.

MARTIN
  Are you sure?

TRISHA
  Yes, come look. See? Nothing.

MARTIN
  You're right. I could've sworn-

       Pause. They both shudder.

MARTIN
  My word, did you feel that?

TRISHA
  A great big chill?! Like someone walked over
  your grave? What's happening, Martin?

MARTIN
  I don't know. Look out!

                      SD - Plate smashing

TRISHA
  Oh! The tortilla chips fell. Salsa, all over
  the new rug. I'll clean it up.

MARTIN
  I'm beginning to think something is amiss.
  Between the knock with no one there and the
  toppled plate.

TRISHA
  It was probably just a gust of wind.

MARTIN
  A gust of wind?

TRISHA
  Yes. That gave us both a chill and toppled the
  tortilla chips. What else could it be?

MARTIN
  I don't know, but-

  A loud, powerful knock on the door.

TRISHA
  That gave me a start! Maybe now our neighbors
  have come.

MARTIN
  Unless it's another prank.

TRISHA
  Do you really think so?

MARTIN
  I'm beginning to have doubts about this
  neighborhood.

TRISHA
  Oh, Martin! You said you'd give it a try!

MARTIN
  I know, but-

TRISHA
  And you know we can't go back to where we
  were. Your mother was quite clear about that.

MARTIN
  I know. And I do like the house, but there was
  also that condo in New Jersey…

TRISHA
  Oh, please. Do not bring up New Jersey again,
  Martin. I-

    Another loud knock.

MARTIN
  Oh, not again.

    Martin opens the door.

MARTIN
  What?!

    *The NEIGHBOR appears, very dark and
    mysterious looking.*

NEIGHBOR
  Good evening!

MARTIN
  Oh, why hello there! Sorry for the rudeness. I
  thought it was another… Never mind. I'm
  Martin, and this is Trisha.

NEIGHBOR
  So wonderful to finally meet you!

TRISHA
  You as well. Welcome to our house!

NEIGHBOR
  Wouldn't miss it. I came as soon as it turned
  dark. We were wondering who was going to move
  into your home.

TRISHA
  We're in the town gossip already! I love it.

MARTIN
  Well, I hope we don't disappoint you!

NEIGHBOR
  Of course not.

TRISHA
  It seems like quite the tight knit community
  here. That's what we read online before we
  moved.

MARTIN
  So important to do your homework before buying
  a house. From what we've seen on Next Door
  this town really does seem to look after one
  another.

NEIGHBOR
  Yes, we all watch each other quite closely
  here in Hor'ton.

TRISHA
  You see, Martin! That is the right
  pronunciation!

MARTIN
  It'll take getting used to. "Hor'ton". Not
  like it's spelled at all!

TRISHA
  These quaint little towns! So much character.

                              SD - Chair falling

  Aah! Sorry. A chair in the kitchen fell down
  somehow. Darling, could you fix that?

MARTIN
  Sure.

NEIGHBOR
  Say, I was wondering. Do you think you might
  invite me inside of your wonderful home?

TRISHA
  Oh, well of course!

MARTIN
  Neighbors are always welcome!

TRISHA
  And you did get our invitation!

NEIGHBOR
  Yes, it would just make me more comfortable if
  you said something like "Please come in".
  Technicalities, you know?

MARTIN
  Oh, sure. C'mon in, neighbor!

NEIGHBOR
  Thank you.

        Neighbor enters.

NEIGHBOR
  What a lovely home! I don't see the inside of
  that many homes.

MARTIN
  Why thank you so much. We were so pleasantly
  surprised to see that this was in our price
  range.

TRISHA
  Our realtor tells us the previous owners were
  highly motivated.

NEIGHBOR
  I would think so.

TRISHA
  Would you like something to eat? Or drink?
  Mr…?

NEIGHBOR
  Oh, I'm not hungry. Perhaps I'll have a bite
  later.

MARTIN
  Fair enough. So, you're the first to arrive.
  Hopefully the rest of the neighborhood will
  come.

NEIGHBOR
  I'm sure they will. We're… kind of night owls
  out here.

TRISHA
  Really?

NEIGHBOR
  You could say that. You could call us
  creatures of the night.

MARTIN
  That is something we found when reading all of
  the reviews here. They say there's a vibrant
  nightlife for such a quaint little town.

TRISHA
  Yes. I like the quiet small town vibe, but
  Martin would prefer a bit more activity.

                                    SD - Crash

  Now the lamp in our bedroom fell off the
  table! What is going on? My nerves are all a
  fright.

NEIGHBOR
  Why it appears that Douglas has already
  arrived. He does like to come early.

MARTIN
  Douglas?

NEIGHBOR
  Yes. He lives on Birch Street. Well, not
  technically. He resides on Birch Street,
  usually. He's a mild mannered sort. Loves to
  nose around when you're not looking, and a bit

NEIGHBOR (Cont.)
  clumsy. You get used to Douglas. There are
  much worse here in Hor'ton.

MARTIN
  I don't think we want this Douglas nosing
  around our house.

NEIGHBOR
  But, of course, you invited him over.

MARTIN
  Well, now I un-invite him over.

NEIGHBOR
  You invited all of us over. It would be
  something of an offense to undo your
  hospitality.

MARTIN
  Yes. We want to be neighborly, but
  neighborliness has its limits. I'd say the
  only reason to move out into the boonies here
  is to get away from nosey busybodies.

TRISHA
  Oh, Martin. You promised.

MARTIN
  I know, I know.

NEIGHBOR
  "Nosey busybodies". Indeed.

        Another loud knock at the door.

TRISHA
  My word! Why doesn't anyone use the doorbell?
  I'll get it.

MARTIN
  Darling, wait! I should be the one who-

Trisha opens the door.

TRISHA
  Welcome to our-

Trisha screams.

MARTIN
  What is it- My God!

TRISHA
  What is that? And that! What is all of this?

MARTIN
  I see… Wolves standing on two legs. I see…
  Witches on flying brooms. And- And-

TRISHA
  Demons? Goblins? A family of Zombies? And
  dozens more creatures I don't know how to
  describe. All on our front lawn.

MARTIN
  Shut the door! Shut the door before they-

      The door shuts.
      Loud knocking begins again.

TRISHA
  All these… things! I never knew they were all
  real!

MARTIN
  And they're here at our house! Why?

NEIGHBOR
  Because you invited them. You invited all of
  us in.

TRISHA
  What did you…?

MARTIN
Look! Look at him! He's changing!

NEIGHBOR
Behold my true form!

The Neighbor has become a bat, flying around the house.

TRISHA
He… He's flying around. He's a… bat?

MARTIN
What is going on? Who are you? What are you all?

NEIGHBOR
All we've ever wanted was a place to call our own! A town where we wouldn't be bothered. A place that we wouldn't be judged and tormented for being what we are.

TRISHA
Is that bat… talking?

NEIGHBOR
But people like you always come, and invade our happy refuge. Newcomers.

MARTIN
Is this for real? This must be some sort of trick!

TRISHA
Who would play a trick like this?

NEIGHBOR
It's no trick, it's your new reality! Your new nightmare existence!

More intense knocking on the door.

TRISHA
  Martin, look!

MARTIN
  There are so many of them. Is everyone in this
  town a frightening, mythical, unholy creature?

TRISHA
  A whole town full of monsters?

MARTIN
  Not even a single normal human being?!

TRISHA
  My God!

NEIGHBOR
  I thought I was pretty clear in the matter.
  Are you not frightened? Are you not horrified?

MARTIN
  I'm… not. We're… delighted. Actually.

TRISHA
  How unexpectedly wonderful!

NEIGHBOR
        (*Turns back into a human shape*)
  Excuse me? What did you say?

TRISHA
  I am so relieved. Martin and I… Let's just say
  that we are grateful to find out we're amongst
  kindred spirits. We've had such a difficult
  time finding somewhere we would fit in after
  his mother threw us out of the kingdom.

MARTIN
  Yes, I in particular had reservations about
  this place, but I do say I'm pleasantly
  surprised that we're somewhere we can let our
  hair down.

TRISHA
  See, Martin? What did I tell you about this
  town? I told you I had a good feeling about it
  here!

MARTIN
  Yes, we probably wouldn't have found this in
  New Jersey.

TRISHA
  Now your mother can't hold kicking us out over
  our heads.

NEIGHBOR
  So, one moment. Out of curiosity, why aren't
  you terrified of us? Did you not see the flesh
  eating zombies?

MARTIN
  Oh, who do you take us for? I'm Martin, a fae
  of the Winter Court. You know, faeries?
  Mythical abductors of children and whatnot.
  Total exaggerations, of course. And my wife
  Trisha is a Banshee.

NEIGHBOR
  Really? Y'know, I've never met a Banshee
  before, nor heard her song. Would you mind?

TRISHA
  Oh, of course. One moment.

      Trisha screams very loudly.

  Sorry, out of practice.

NEIGHBOR
  No, that was marvelous. Sorry for all this
  rigamarole. We all like to put on a show when
  someone new moves in to scare away the rubes.
  Nothing like a couple of squares to bring a
  neighborhood down. You shoulda seen the dweebs
  who used to live here!

MARTIN
  Perfectly understandable. Humans are the
  worst.

TRISHA
  Yes, they say they're open minded, but one
  little thing goes wrong and then it's
  pitchforks and silver bullets.

  A loud powerful knock on the door.

MARTIN
  Speaking of unruly mobs…

NEIGHBOR
  Oh, right. Let me call off the dogs.
      (*shouts outside*)
  Hey, everyone! You can knock off the
  fireworks. These people are cool! Yeah, c'mon
  in. They have snacks!

TRISHA
  Oh, Martin. I'm so pleased that we've made a
  good first impression. See what I told you? A
  real community we can belong to. Forget the
  vegetable platter. Let's break out the good
  stuff.

MARTIN
  Yes, dear. I think we're going to like it here
  in Horrortown.

NEIGHBOR
  It is pronounced "Hor'ton".

MARTIN
  Right, right. I always forget.

                    END PLAY

Arise and Prep
By j. Snodgrass

CHARACTERS
  MELBA - *Female, mid 30s*
  JANE - *Female, mid 20s*
  BRYCE - *Male, mid 20s (silent role)*

SETTING
  Melba's Apartment.

BRYCE is lying on a table, dead, a scarf tied around his neck. MELBA is dancing around him with a knife. She must occasionally consult a book that's lying open on the table.

MELBA
The serpent circles, spirals, bites its tail.

Melba cuts her hand and presses it on Bryce's chest.

And blood, the blossom blooms toward the moon.

Bryce's chest begins heaving.

Now breathe my breath and rise, arise, arise.

She breathes into his open mouth.
Bryce groans.

Alright, hold on a sec.

She sprays breath-spray into her mouth.

And breathe my breath.

Bryce breathes in deeply.

Arise, my zombie henchman, time to… hench!

Bryce stiffly rises and stands beside the table. Melba hands him the knife.

Now take this blade and do what must be done.

She pulls a burlap sack from under the table, holds it up as if there's something alive inside, then puts it on the table and onions spill out.

And not too thick, just take your time, dice finely.

Bryce begins chopping.

No. NO! You bled on it!

She grabs the onion he was chopping and throws it.

Go slow! No blood!

Good zombie help is hard to find.

No, thinner!

JANE
   (*Offstage, banging on the door*)
Hello? I hear you in there, open up!

MELBA
   Oh shit! Go! Over there, and be a lamp!

Bryce groans, lurches to stage left, puts a lampshade on his head.

JANE
   Two seconds and I'm kicking in this door!

MELBA
   Hold on! Don't get your panties in a bunch!

JANE storms in.

JANE
   Well?

MELBA
   What?

JANE
   Well what the shit? I mean the hell?
   I've called your number fifteen times today!
   You swipe me straight to voicemail one more
   time?
   I'll kick your teeth in, sear your fingertips

JANE (Cont.)
   And dump your naked carcass at the playground,
   You'll never be identified--

MELBA
   Slow down.
   I haven't been avoiding you, just busy.
   I've got a lot, you know, a lot on my plate.
   What's up?

JANE
   Who's here, that you were talking to?

MELBA
   What? Nobody, just me. Me and these onions.

JANE
   I heard you.

MELBA
   Chopping onions, makes me cry.
   I use the time to talk through my emotions…
   It's cheaper than a therapist. In bulk,
   And pound for pound--

JANE
   And what about my pain?
   The loss, my brother, murdered, poor sweet
   Bryce…
   That's why I came to you to fix it! Well?
   You took my money, seven days and nothing!

MELBA
   These things take time! Revenge, it's not a
   sprint.
   The journey, right? Not just a destination.

JANE
   Don't mumbo-jumbo me, I want results!

MELBA
   I'm sorry, I've been swamped, neck deep all
   week,

MELBA (Cont.)
  My food-truck business fin'ly taking off,
  At last! So many maddening delays,
  The license, liability insurance,
  Competitors who threatened to-

JANE
  -Hello?
  Your problems don't mean shit to me. I paid
  you.
  To raise my murdered brother from the dead
  So he could take revenge on his two killers
  So I can sleep at night! Not hear the gurgle,
  Of his last breath, I hear it, bubbling,
  blood.
  Face pale with fear, the filthy bar-room
  floor.
  I see it every time I close my eyes.
  I haven't slept a wink, six endless days…

MELBA
  I get it. And I'm on it, right. Just saying…
  I didn't think this week would be so packed,
  And I can barely keep up with demand.
  If I don't get these onions chopped tonight,
  I'll miss tomorrow's lunch-rush-

JANE
  -Not my problem!
  You said you'd bring him back for zombie
  vengeance!
  So, try to weasel out of our arrangement?
  I'll cut you. Get me? Dead, and make it look,
  Like you had some weed-wacker accident.

MELBA
  …? Where do you get these mental images?

JANE
  My job. Obituary editor.
  I publish death. And I've seen this week's
  headlines.
  They say a grizzly bear is loose in town,

JANE (Cont.)
  And mauled three people, ripped out their
  intestines!
  But that's no bear, it's Bryce's walking
  corpse,
  He's out rampaging, mindless random violence!
  You said you could control him!

MELBA
  And I am!
  I mean- I will. It's not a perfect science.

JANE
  I gave you the addresses of his killers,
  The thugs who jumped him in that drunken
  brawl,
  And stabbed him with a broken bottle-neck,
  Then walked, scott-free, said it was my-- his
  fault.

MELBA
  He's getting there, revenge, he needs some
  training,
  A sensei, help him hone his zombie skills,
  You know, wax-on, wax-off and paint the fence,
  So he can take revenge with good, clean kills.

JANE
  I don't want clean! I clearly specified,
  I want those jack-offs folded, cracked in
  half,
  And choked to death on their own little
  peckers.

MELBA
  And that takes skill, conditioning, and
  practice.
  I'm training him. But what you're paying me?
  I mean, it's fair, in this economy,
  A lot, when I was unemployed. Last week.
  But all at once, my truck, a quantum leap,
  My lifelong quest is fin'ly building steam!
  Just days ago, impossible, a dream,

MELBA (Cont.)
    Deferred by obstacles, just out of reach,
    Red tape and paperwork, bureaucracy,
    Competitors with their hostility,
    But now it's happening, so suddenly!
    Goat curry, my own secret recipe,
    At last, its big debut out on the streets!
    But how can I keep up, this quantity,
    Without a sacrifice in quality?
    The magic's gotta come from here, in deep.
    I grind my teeth to dust, I weep, I bleed
    Into this food. Well, metaphoric'ly.
    And people, they can taste it, you can see it,
    Their glassy shining eyes, and bunchy cheeks-

JANE
    -And what the hell's this got to do with me?
    My- His revenge, so he can rest in peace?
    I've got more money, if that's what you need,
    An extra twenty. When the job's complete.

MELBA
    Not money, it's the time, the energy.

JANE
    And I need closure now, so I can sleep!
    So get on with this rash bloody deed!
    Two murders shouldn't take a freakin' week!
    He's on this willy-nilly killing-spree.

MELBA
    He's almost ready, really-

JANE
    Talk is cheap.
    I'm sure your other clients would agree.

MELBA
    My, um, my other clients… morally,
    They're pretty loose, so punctuality
    Is not a major a factor… usually…

JANE
    Wait, time out, cut, cut. Look me in the eye.
    Is this your first time raising up the dead?
    You are a licensed voodoo priestess, right?

MELBA
    Well, um… A course online, I've read some
    books,
    I sort of- It's a sideline gig, part time.
    The food-truck venture ran into some snags,
    So, yeah, my resumé, diversify-

JANE
    Your resume said "licensed voodoo priest!"
    With "devil-dancing in the pale moonlight
    And substitutiary locomotion!"

MELBA
    Well every resumé has little lies.
    You fake it till you make it, right? But
    still,
    I did it, raised your brother's corpse to
    life.
    I say the proof is in the zombie pudding.

JANE
    And where is he right now? Or do you know?
    Out butchering another health inspector-
      (Sudden realization)
    Oh!

MELBA
    No!

JANE
    He killed a health inspector!

MELBA
    Whoa!
    You said yourself, "a random killing spree."

JANE
    A licenser! A rival food-truck owner!

JANE (Cont.)
  I printed their obituaries!

MELBA
  Wait.
  This might look- To the untrained eye- I know,
  But zombies are irrational, haphazard-

JANE
  And you say you're a chef! Professional,
  But look, the clumsy cutting of these onions,
  It's like a toddler hacked them with a stone.
  Like when Bryce used to help me in the
  kitchen!

MELBA
  That's how I sensei, teach him self-control.
  Like wax-on wax-off, chopping onions,
  practice,
  And catching alley-cats, he's on a roll.

JANE
  But he's a freakin' zombie, not your intern!
  You're using him to kill your obstacles!
  And now you've made him your assistant chef!
  And stray-cat catching? I don't want to know!

MELBA
  It's just, you know, a crime, the price of
  goat.

JANE
  And meanwhile, those two greasy animals,
  Who murdered him are snoring in their homes,
  That guy with the disgusting, hairy mole,
  Like right there in the middle of his nose,
  Said "What' you lookin at?"
  He smelled so gross,
  "Well how the heck am I supposed to know?
  The love-child of a mushroom and a toad?
  Go back under the bridge, you ugly troll."
  He shoved me, and I threw my rum and Coke,
  And Bryce steps in, all manly and heroic,

JANE (Cont.)
　Like knight-in-shining-armor long-ago,
　And wham! And slam! He took it to them both,
　And then this flash of sound, a bottle broke,
　And suddenly the blood, he's gasping, choking,
　All wide-eyed like a fish out of its bowl…
　They'd killed him. And I swore upon his soul,
　His vengeance would be swift and horrible.

MELBA
　So it was you. His death was all your fault.
　You picked that fight and got him killed--

JANE
　What? No!
　You're twisting it, you nasty, skanky ho.

MELBA
　You killed him. And the guilt- You sold his
　soul!

JANE
　Tomorrow morning. I don't see results?
　You mark my words, I'll write an article
　About your 'secret recipe,' expose
　The alley-cats you sell as so-called goat.
　Then see if you can keep your dream afloat.

　　Jane leaves, slamming the door.

MELBA
　Awaken, lamp, be zombie Bryce. And go,
　That person who just left here is your goal.
　And stash the body down some sewer hole.
　Then swift, return… I can't chop these alone.

　　*Bryce emotionlessly slouches off after
　　Jane.*

　　　　　　　END PLAY

Boogeyman
By Dana Hall

CHARACTERS
  WHITNEY BRADWAY - *Female, pragmatic*
  MATT RYAN - *Male, charming to a fault*

SETTING
  A parked car.

The couple, MATT and WHITNEY, on a first date, walk to Matt's car.

MATT
  Wow, it's dark already. Guess the movie ran longer than we thought.

  Matt opens the passenger side as a gentleman does on a date.

WHITNEY
  Oh, thank you. I thought chivalry was dead.

MATT
  No, maybe on life support, but definitely alive and well with this guy. Get in before the boogeyman gets ya.

WHITNEY
      (*coy laughter*)
  As a kid, I taught myself not to believe in things like the boogeyman-

MATT
  -I thought all kids had that right of passage.

WHITNEY
  Not me.

MATT
  How'd you get around that?

WHITNEY
  Logic. If I felt something lurking in the dark, I'd turn on all the lights and check the closet. I'd repeat to myself it was just my imagination. That's what scares people the most, their own wild imaginations-

MATT
  -Well, I'd like to thank you and your imagination for a lovely first date.

WHITNEY
It's been so long since I went to the movies-
It's crazy isn't it-

MATT
-The cost of these damn tickets- yes, it's
insane-

WHITNEY
-No, that people go to these movies wanting to
be afraid.

MATT
It's exciting, it gives you a thrill. You feel
that rush of adrenaline around you. The Psycho
Stalker is a cult classic, and he's not a
slasher; he torments his victims methodically
by making them feel like they're going insane.
He knows everything about them and uses that
to build trust before he kills. It's
brilliant, really.

WHITNEY
Come on! We're supposed to believe these women
never see it coming?!

MATT
People are surprisingly trusting, or maybe
they just think they're smarter than everyone
else. Until they realize they've been
outsmarted, and then it's too late.

        Whitney checks her watch and sighs.

WHITNEY
Damn. Speaking of late, we should get going- I
have to be up early, and I barely slept last
night.

MATT
Why? What happened?

WHITNEY
It's silly- nothing- It's silly-I woke up, and
I felt like someone was watching me. I know it
sounds crazy-

MATT
-It's understandable- you do live alone. Did
you check it out to make sure?

WHITNEY
I turned on all the lights. No one was there.
I guess even adults have to remind themselves
about their overactive imaginations.

MATT
Did you actually see a person, a shadow…
anything?

WHITNEY
No. No, I couldn't make anything out. I just
woke up, and- I couldn't move. I was frozen.
It was so dark. I could just see the alarm-
2:32AM. Next thing I know, I turn my head, and
it's 5:43AM and it was gone. Maybe it was
sleep paralysis I read about that-

MATT
-Did he say anything?

WHITNEY
He?
     (laughs)
No. No one was there. It must've been one of
those lucid dreams or something. It was crazy-
felt so real. See, I don't need horror movies,
I have my own!

MATT
That sounds terrifying!

WHITNEY
It was! I read that it can happen though. It's
like you're awake but in a dream.

MATT
    Next time, you should keep your phone on the
    stand next to the bed, not all the way across
    the room.

WHITNEY
    Yah, I've been meaning to move the charger-

MATT
    -Never know when you might need it-

WHITNEY
    -True.
            (a bit confused)
    Wait, did I tell you about that…

MATT
            (leans in)
    … and fix the window latch.

WHITNEY
            (realizing)
    What? No, it can't be…

MATT
    Shh.

        He puts his finger up to quiet her.

WHITNEY
    H-how do you know those things- the stand,
    and… and the window- You were there! It was
    you!

MATT
    It took you long enough.

WHITNEY
    No! No, it wasn't- It couldn't have been!?!

        He grabs her, holding her from escaping.
        She frantically bangs on the car door.

WHITNEY
  Let me out! Help! Let me out! HELP!

  As she screams, he grabs her mouth.

MATT
  Maybe you should start believing in the
  boogeyman.

                    END PLAY

Blackberry Fog
By Christina Woods

CHARACTERS
  EIMEAR - *Female, mid 20s*
  BIKER - *Male, any age*
  SCARECROW - *Taller than a man, with claws*

SETTING
  A foggy countryside with blackberry
  bushes, nettles and scarecrows in fields.

A small, unpaved country road. Bumpy and unkempt, flanked by hedges heavy with Autumn bounty, fruits and alive with morning chorus of birdsong.

In the distant fields are scarecrows in various garb. Some with funny hats and noses, others more sinister. The morning is still dark and overcast, heavy with fog and drizzle.

Footsteps. Enter, EIMEAR, a young woman, mid twenties, huddled in modern, autumn attire with a shawl over her shoulders, over her arm, she carries a large wicker basket of blackberries. She is humming a soft folk song to herself as she busies herself with plucking berries.

A rustling in the hedges makes her pause.

EIMEAR
  Hello?

Rolling her eyes, she turns back. More violent rustling.

EIMEAR
  Right, stop messing, you eejits. It's too early.

The birdsong falls silent.

Unbeknownst to Eimear, a soft green glow lights the eyes of a nearby scarecrow.

She narrows her eyes, sighting a pair of fuzzy, yellow lights in the distance.

A roar of engines as a motorcycle flies past, causing her to leap into the nettles, dropping her basket, it gets squashed by the tyres.

She squeals in fright and annoyance as the
pass and sighs sadly, as she sees her
blackberries squashed and ruined.

EIMEAR
  Arseholes… That took me all…

She rises and stiffens at the engine's
quiet, pained grunts.

Curious, Eimear turns following the
sounds; Rending of metal, slashing of
blades and a gurgled, painful moan.

The Biker, face still obscured by his
helmet, crawls into view through the fog.

BIKER
  Please… Help… Something…

He turns his head, green lights looming
over him. Eimear backs up but trips,
laying in frozen fear.

A shadow in the fog, standing taller than
a man, bipedal, with a shaggy mane of
straw, digitigrade in stance and lean,
like an upright wolf but with a horse's
skull, monitors the man's movements.

It raises a hand, well, claws as long as
scythes and ends the biker there and then.

Eimear covers her mouth as the beast leaps
out of sight only to come face to skull,
she scrambles and pushes the squashed bag
towards the beast.

EIMEAR
  Please… I'm sorry… I won't… Please…

The Scarecrow regards her and sniffs.

It tilts its head, looking at the squashed berries.

Eimear holds her leg, now cut and bloody from the fall.

The Scarecrow pets her head softly and gently with its claws.

SCARECROW
  Offering accepted. Fear not, child.

It picks up the bag of squashed berries and backs up so only the green orbs can be viewed before disappearing into the fog.

Eimear faints.

END PLAY

Candlelight
By Evan Baughfman

CHARACTERS
  ALEX - *Robin's childhood friend, any gender*
  ROBIN - *Alex's lifelong pal, any gender*
  DEATH - *No-one's compatriot, any gender*

SETTING
  In a dark attic, at a card table.

*In a dark attic, at a card table, ALEX
sits across from their friend, ROBIN.
Resting between them is a store-bought
cake slathered in frosting. Sticking out
of the cake are five black birthday
candles, arranged in a circle around the
edges of the dessert. The candle flames
are the only sources of light in the
darkness.*

ALEX
  I'm having trouble even thinking of any! What
  about you?

ROBIN
  No. I've got lots of enemies. A plethora.

ALEX
  "Plethora"?

ROBIN
  Thought the English teacher would appreciate
  that. Anyhow, yeah, I know plenty of jerks.

ALEX
  Well, I mean, so do I, but no one is really
  deserving of… of…

ROBIN
  Sure, you do. There's a bunch of them, right
  there with you, every day at work.

ALEX
  Robin, no! That's… That's terrible! I wouldn't
  do this to… to a kid!

ROBIN
  You complain about your students every time I
  see you.

ALEX
  Only some of them.

ROBIN
This is your chance for revenge. Tonight, you
finally strike back against those punks!

ALEX
If I complain about my students…tell you any
"horror stories" about them… It's just to get
some things off my chest. I don't want to hurt
them! Just feels good to vent a little. A
healthy release.

ROBIN
You want to be healthy, get the hell out of
that place. We already survived middle school
once. Still don't understand why you ever
volunteered to jump back into that nightmare.

*Robin leans over and blows out a candle,
making the room a little bit darker. Alex
is stunned, speechless, by this, at first.*

ALEX
You… You… You blew one out! You really did it!

ROBIN
You thought I wouldn't? Your turn now.

ALEX
Thought we were hanging in your mom's attic to
use the Ouija board, like when we were kids!

ROBIN
I stopped doing Ouija years ago. Got boring,
talking to the same old, needy spirits.

ALEX
Since your mom died up here… thought you'd
want to try to speak with her…

ROBIN
Why? She's happier where she is now. And I'm
pretty stoked she's there, too.

ALEX
  Alright… but these candles, Robin… They're…

ROBIN
  Not candles. They're death sticks. Once you
  light these bad boys up, there's no turning
  back. No getting around it. Someone's time has
  come. Guaranteed.

ALEX
  Guaranteed? Really?

ROBIN
  Well, they've got four out of five stars
  online.

ALEX
  It's a lot of responsibility. I don't want to
  choose poorly.

ROBIN
  You won't. You're smart. You'll choose
  whoever's best for you. Now, can you please
  stop being so dramatic, and make your freaking
  death wish already?

ALEX
  This is dark, dark shit! I don't really feel
  comfortable…

ROBIN
  I've already started. You have to continue,
  complete the circle, or It comes for us. Can't
  summon Death unless you intend to use It. Gets
  irritable. Looks for replacement souls.

ALEX
  Robin, what the hell! Why'd you even involve
  me in this?!

ROBIN
  You're like the saddest person I know. Thought
  you'd be full of resentment, like me.

ALEX
  I'm not the saddest person you know!

ROBIN
  Look, I was laid off and had to move back in
  with my mother. That's sad. But you, stuck in
  a job that you hate… Having to work at it year
  -round… Not even taking your summer vacation
  or bothering to make time for yourself… Just
  to make ends-meet… That's sadder.

ALEX
  I don't hate my job!

ROBIN
  Sure, you don't. Now, get on with it!

ALEX
  Who, though? Who?!

ROBIN
  I don't know. But time is ticking here! Whose
  life are you going to snuff out?

ALEX
  I… I can't. If you're so eager, go again.

ROBIN
  I told you how it works! Back-and-forth
  between two parties! Two wishes each! Then,
  together, we make the same wish, before we
  extinguish the final stick! Celebratory cake
  at the end!

ALEX
  This is insane! Worse than anything you've
  ever asked me to do before!

ROBIN
  Make your wish already! Do you want Death to
  come for us? There's no getting around It, so
  why not make It work for you, to your
  advantage? Hurry! Whose absence will improve

ROBIN (Cont.)
  your way of life?

ALEX
  I don't want to cut someone's life short just
  because he's a… a nuisance!

ROBIN
  "He"? "His"? So you do have someone in mind…
  Who is "he"?

ALEX
  He's nobody! I'm using hypothetical pronouns!

ROBIN
  Yeah, right. Focus on whoever he is, and make!
  The! Wish!

ALEX
  You said these things only have a four-star
  rating, right? Which means they don't work
  perfectly every time. They can be defective.
  So I'm going to cross my fingers and hope
  that's the case here.

ROBIN
  You don't honestly—

ALEX
  Bye, Robin. Don't do anything like this to me
  ever again.

        Alex pushes back their chair.
        Stands.
        Notices DEATH, an intimidating figure in a
        black robe and hood, entering the room.
        Death clutches a scythe in a skeletal
        claw.
        Robin sees Death, too.

ROBIN
  Told you.

ALEX

    Oh, God!

ROBIN

    God's not watching you now. But that thing
    definitely is. Sit, and do what you're
    supposed to do! Someone you have some kind of
    personal connection to… Can't be a complete
    stranger…

ALEX

    I know, okay? I know!

        *Alex sits back down as Death stares at
        them from across the attic.*

ALEX

    Shit… Shit! Um… Uh…
        (*to Death*)
    Do I really have to? Can we make some kind of
    deal?

        *Death starts to approach the table. Raises
        the scythe.*

ROBIN

    Come on, Alex! PULL THE FREAKING TRIGGER
    ALREADY!

        *Death is getting closer. Closer. The
        scythe is getting closer. Closer.*

ALEX

    Shit, I hope this works!
        (*shouting to the rafters*)
    DAMN YOU, STANDARDIZED TESTING! PUTTING ALL
    THIS UNNECESSARY PRESSURE ON TEACHERS AND
    KIDS! FORCING CHANGES TO OUR CURRICULUM, EVEN
    THOUGH YOU'RE NOT AN ACCURATE DEPICTOR OF
    STUDENTS' PROGRESS OR ABILITIES! I WISH YOU'D
    JUST DIE ALREADY!

Alex closes their eyes, takes a deep breath, and finally blows out the next candle. The room's a bit darker now. Death halts, nods to Alex. Then, It turns, silently exiting the room.

ALEX
Oh, man! It worked! IT ACTUALLY WORKED!

ROBIN
Jesus Christ! Talk about cutting it close!

ALEX
I… I found a loophole! I personified a thing! The stupid testing process! Made it a "who" instead of a "what"! Hoped I could erase an obstacle from my life, not a person! And it worked!

ROBIN
Knew you'd adapt to this.

ALEX
Want to test it out for yourself? See if it works? Put your next wish on something you hate?

Robin seems to think about this for a few moments.

ROBIN
I think the real-life human turds stinking up my life take precedence.

ALEX
Your mom was right. She called me a couple months ago, all worried that you'd changed.

ROBIN
Mom meddling. What a shocker.

ALEX
Have to admit, I didn't really see what she

ALEX (Cont.)
    was talking about until now. Had my blinders
    on whenever we met for happy hour, I guess.

ROBIN
    You're really not into what we're doing here?
    You don't feel liberated by its power?

ALEX
    Dude, you're like a hitman, taking out people
    who have "wronged" you! Think about what
    you're doing here!

ROBIN
    I've thought about it quite a bit, and all it
    does is put a smile on my face. I know I'm
    making my life easier. Knocking obstacles out
    of my way, just like you said.

ALEX
    Jesus.

ROBIN
    You should be thanking me for choosing to
    include you in this. For giving you this
    opportunity.

ALEX
    I'm not thanking you for dragging me into
    this!

ROBIN
    I'll tell you what I told Mom. This is who I
    am now. This is what I do. If it bothers you…
    worries you… I give you permission to let me
    go. Once we're done here, we can go our
    separate ways.

ALEX
    I care about you, though.

ROBIN
    That was Mom's problem, too.

ALEX

  Christ, Robin… I can't believe how easy this
  is for you!

ROBIN

  Mom… Every wish she made was like torture for
  her. Had her sobbing like a little kid.
  Begging God for forgiveness. She couldn't
  figure out how to mold this opportunity to fit
  her own needs. She wasn't smart like you. No,
  not like you at all.

    Robin blows out their second candle.
    The attic grows darker.

ALEX

  Wow. So, you've done this before? With your
  mom?

ROBIN

  She kept insisting to be involved with what I
  was doing behind closed doors. So, I finally
  gave in.

ALEX

  She died up here. Did that have anything to do
  with these… death sticks?

ROBIN

  You know the answer to that.

ALEX

  Shit… Robin!

ROBIN

  We both agreed that the final wish should be
  directed at her.

ALEX

  God!

ROBIN

  It spared her from living with the guilt of

ROBIN (Cont.)
having such an "evil" child. That look you
have right now… Very similar to the one Mom
had once she realized who I am.

        Alex shakes their head.
        Forces a smile.

ALEX
Think I've got my next wish ready to go, too.

ROBIN
That was a little quicker than before. Making
your world a better place?

ALEX
Not just my world, I hope.

        Alex hesitates for a moment, then blows
        out their second candle. Only one candle
        left! But Death and its scythe have
        returned, approaching through the shadows!

ROBIN
It's back.

ALEX
That was fast. Like almost instantaneous with
my wish.

ROBIN
Because It's coming for you.

ALEX
Me?!

ROBIN
And for me, too, I suspect.

ALEX
You wished for It to come for me?!

ROBIN
  Yes. Before you wished It would take me down.

ALEX
  NO!

      Alex pushes back their chair.
      Stands again.

ROBIN
  I could see where this was heading. How you
  were struggling with everything I've done. I
  knew what you'd eventually have to do. Mom
  didn't have the guts to do it, but deep down...
  you're tough. Work in a freaking middle
  school, for Christ's sake. So, I had to make
  the first move.

ALEX
  I'm sorry, Robin! You're dangerous! But I
  don't deserve this! I didn't do anything
  wrong!

ROBIN
  This way, we can at least both be put out of
  our misery.

      Death is very near now.
      The scythe is ready to strike.

ALEX
  I'M! NOT! MISERABLE!

      Alex tears free a hunk of cake... and
      smashes it right into Death's face!

ALEX
  YEAH! THAT'S RIGHT! IN YOUR FACE!

      Death did not see this coming. It
      frantically wipes frosting from Its eyes.

ROBIN
Really mature! What do you think that's going
to accomplish?

ALEX
Buys me some time! And so! Does! This!

Alex blows out the last candle.
The room is swallowed up by the dark.

LX - Blackout

ROBIN
Hey! Come on! Seriously? You don't think Death
can see in the dark?

The rest of the play takes place in
complete darkness. We hear Alex run across
the room. Pounding on the wall.

ALEX
The door! Where's the door?!

ROBIN
Giving away your position! Nice plan!

More pounding.

ALEX
It was right here! THE DOOR WAS RIGHT HERE,
AND NOW IT'S GONE!

ROBIN
Once It has you in its crosshairs, Death won't
let you go.

ALEX
No, people escape Death all the time! I'm a
good person! Not perfect maybe, but good! And
I still have a lot to offer! So I should get
another chance!

Even more pounding.

ALEX
  WHERE'S THE GODDAMN DOOR?!

ROBIN
  I already told you…

ALEX
  ShitshitshitSHIT!

ROBIN
  Accept it, Alex. It's our time, whether you're
  ready or—

      SHUNK!
      Death's scythe skewers Robin mid-sentence.

  Awwwwww, shiiiiiit… Owwwwwww…

      Robin's body hits the floor. They groan in
      pain. A whimper in the dark.

  No… Alex… Alex is supposed… supposed to be—

      SHUNK! SHUNK! SHUNK!
      We hear the scythe strike Robin again and
      again and again as they gurgle their final
      breaths.

ALEX
  Oh, God. Robin? Robin, are you…?

      Something heavy rolls across the floor.
      Alex shrieks.

ALEX
  What just bounced off my foot?! That… That
  wasn't a soccer ball, was it…?

DEATH
  Not a soccer ball.

ALEX
  Ahhh! Jesus! Robin! Oh, shit! Death… Mr.

ALEX (Cont.)
   Death…? I'm sorry about the cake, okay? Sorry
   that I smashed it in your—

DEATH
   Stop apologizing.

ALEX
   O…Okay.

DEATH
   I like cake.

ALEX
   Oh. Good.

DEATH
   Do you know which bakery this one's from?

ALEX
   Uh, no. No, I don't.

DEATH
   Hmmm… Well, if I find out, I think I'll avoid
   the baker for a few more years.

ALEX
   Good… Good for her. I have to ask… Can… Can
   you not kill me today? Please?

      All is eerily silent, until…

DEATH
   You promise to make a difference out there?
   Help shape the future so I don't have to work
   so damn hard all the time?

ALEX
   Yes! Absolutely! I'll… I'll do whatever I can!

DEATH
   Teachers… Every now and then, someone's got to
   throw you a bone.

A door creaks open.

DEATH
Go on. Live your best life.

ALEX
Thanks! And I'm sorry…"Living my best life"?
Does that mean I have to keep on teaching,
or…?

DEATH
Yes!

ALEX
Okay, just checking. And standardized testing.
Is that really gone? Did I kill it for real?

DEATH
That one might take a while.

ALEX
Of course. Uh, thanks, I guess. Bye.

> *The door closes and Alex runs off to
> safety.*

DEATH
Now, cake. Cake, cake, cakity cake…

> *Moments later, we hear Death bang into
> something. A chair, maybe. Death grumbles.*

My freaking shins! Can hardly see worth a damn
in here…!

END PLAY

Champagne
By Scott Younger

CHARACTERS
  COUNT VLADIMIR STABBENSPINE - *A middle-aged aristocrat with pale skin and strangely sharp teeth*
  DUCHESS MARGUERITE - *An aristocratic woman of forty years*
  IGOR - *The Duchess' hunchbacked servant of indeterminable age*
  EDVIN - *The Duchess' young son, around 10 years old*
  OLGA - *A small waifish woman of indeterminable age (Can be played by the same actor as Edvin)*

SETTING
  Early 19th century.
  A castle in the fictional Eastern European state of Bolgorvia.

PROLOGUE

COUNT STABBENSPINE appears.

STABBENSPINE
  Ladies and gentlemen, tonight in this humble
  theatre you shall witness a tale of terror as
  yet unseen by the human eye. A tale of murder,
  blood-curdling evil, and sparkling white wine.
  Those with nervous dispositions are advised to
  leave the theatre this instant, for the sights
  you see will haunt your nightly dreams and
  chill your very soul. Ladies and Gentlemen,
  behold the horror! Behold the fear! Behold…

  Champagne!

Count Stabbenspine exits.

SCENE ONE

Enter DUCHESS MARGUERITE.

MARGUERITE
  Igor? Igor! Come out this instant!

Enter IGOR, the hunch-backed manservant.

IGOR
  What is your will, mistress?

MARGUERITE
  Sweep the hallways, and put the stuffed bats
  on display in the dining hall. You know how
  the Count is fond of our winged friends.

IGOR
  Right away, mistress!

Igor goes to exit.

MARGUERITE
  And Igor?

IGOR
  Yes, mistress?

MARGUERITE
  We'll have no talk of sledging.

IGOR
  As you wish, mistress.

  Igor leaves.
  Marguerite looks out the window.

MARGUERITE
  Oh, this cursed storm! Will it never cease?

  Igor re-enters swiftly.

IGOR
  Mistress Marguerite! The Count is here! Shall
  Igor show him in?

MARGUERITE
  Be swift about it! Storms are not kind to
  travellers.

  Igor exits.

MARGUERITE
      (*Aside*)
  Oh, dearest Count! Fate and circumstance have
  conspired to keep us apart. Though now,
  perhaps fate will allow us some joy after all?

  Enter Count Stabbenspine.

MARGUERITE
  My dear Count Stabbenspine! You haven't aged a
  day!

STABBENSPINE
  My dear Marguerite! I owe what little youth I
  retain to my pale complexion. Though many
  years have passed, many wars have been fought

STABBENSPINE (Cont.)
and many of my wives have died in mysterious
circumstances…

MARGUERITE
Oh Stabbenspine, you have my eternal
sympathies! I see you take the black of
mourning. How many dearly departed wives is
that now?

STABBENSPINE
Twenty-four. One rather loses count! I mourn
now for my sweet bride Penelope. And what a
woman she was… Such vigour! Such spirit! Such
breasts! What little time we had was sweet.
Until she took an untimely tumble down a well
in the woods…

MARGUERITE
Such misfortune!

STABBENSPINE
I told my dear bride not to wander the woods
searching for water so very late at night. But
what is a man to do with such a spirited
woman?

MARGUERITE
        (*Embracing Stabbenspine*)
All the comforts of my home are at your
disposal. My manservant Igor will bring all
that you desire in these dark times. Now I
pray you drink, I have some of the finest
Champagne in all of Bolgorvia here for your
pleasure.

    She pours champagne into glasses.

STABBENSPINE
I thank you, Duchess. Champagne is a truly
beautiful drink, such aroma!

MARGUERITE
I fear that aroma is rather lost on me. My
nose is not what it was.

STABBENSPINE
How queer, smell tells us of many hidden
dangers in this world… Though please not
another 'Count'! Call me Vlad, like when we
were children!

MARGUERITE
And what glorious times they were, Vlad!
Running amok in the graveyards, digging up
bones and feeding them to wolves… Truly
innocent times…!

STABBENSPINE
Such youthful fun was had!

MARGUERITE
I was utterly relieved that mama never found
out!

STABBENSPINE
She was a mean-spirited woman indeed! With the
most… plump neck…

MARGUERITE
        (Giggles)
You were always too kind to me, dear Vlad…

STABBENSPINE
And how is your husband, the Duke? I have
heard whisperings of a terrible sickness.
Surely this is idle talk?

MARGUERITE
        (Sobs)
Alas, you have heard true. Duke Lastlegs has
been bedridden for some time now. I fear he
may die at any moment.

STABBENSPINE
Oh such tragedy! It weakens my heart to see
you in such distress.
   (Embraces her)
I only ask one thing of you, sweet Marguerite…

MARGUERITE
Anything dear Count, anything!

STABBENSPINE
All my travelling these past days has rather
blunted my knife.
   (Pulls out a knife)
Do you have a whetstone of some kind with
which I could sharpen it?

MARGUERITE
The finest whetstone in all of Bolgorvia lies
in my cellar! It would be an honour to
retrieve it for you, dearest Vlad.

   Exit Duchess Marguerite.

STABBENSPINE
Excellent. Now to pay my respects to the
ailing Duke!

   Exit Count Stabbenspine.

SCENE TWO

   The cellar. Enter Igor, carrying a sledge.

IGOR
   (Sniffing the air)
No mistress…? No master…? No Count…? Yes, yes!
Fun time for Igor!

   *Igor puts the sled on floor and sits in it.
   He sledges around the room, having a whale
   of a time.*

   Enter EDVIN, a young child.

EDVIN
   What are you doing, Igor?

IGOR
   Young master Edvin! You should be in the
   nursery.

EDVIN
   What's that?

IGOR
   This is a sledge, young master. Igor is very
   good at sledging. Igor raced for Bolgorvia in
   1604 Olympic games, and win gold medal. But
   Igor got greedy. Igor take steroids and is
   disqualified for doping!

      *Igor starts to sob. Edvin walks up to Igor
      and hugs him.*

IGOR
   But now, away to the nursery, young master.
   Before your mother sees us-

      Enter Marguerite, holding a stone.

MAGUERITE
   Igor! I gave you clear instructions about
   sledging!

IGOR
   Forgive me mistress!

MAGUERITE
   I have lost patience with you, Igor. Chain
   yourself to the wall!

IGOR
   Right away mistress…

      Exit Igor.

      Edvin hugs Marguerite.

EDVIN
  Sorry, Mama.

MARGUERITE
  Run along back to the nursery, little one.
  Before I have you flogged.

  Exit Edvin, in terror.

SCENE THREE

  *Duchess Marguerite sits on a chair. Enter
  Count Stabbenspine.*

STABBENSPINE
  Murder! Bloody Murder! Oh, the hounds of hell
  have come tonight!

MARGUERITE
  What is the matter, Vlad?

STABBENSPINE
  Your husband, the gallant Duke Lastlegs… has
  been murdered! Killed under our very noses!
  Oh, if only my knife was sharp…

MARGUERITE
  My dear husband, killed? How can this be?

STABBENSPINE
  The fiend came in through the window. In the
  darkness I could see naught but its glowing
  red eyes!

MARGUERITE
  Oh Vlad, protect me from this monster!

STABBENSPINE
  Sweet Marguerite, please forgive me, I must
  confess it all to you…

MARGUERITE
  What is it Vlad?

STABBENSPINE
I believe my dear Penelope did not fall down that wretched well by accident. No! She was pushed to her watery grave! By that self-same creature that murdered your husband! Forgive me, for the monster has followed me here! Oh, why must it torment me?

MARGUERITE
If I am to die, let it be at your side.

STABBENSPINE
Old friends must stay together.

MARGUERITE
Forgive me, but you are far more than an old friend to me.

STABBENSPINE
You don't mean…?

MARGUERITE
Even in our youth my affection went far beyond the love of a friend. I have long envied your wives for their possession of such a gallant man. Now fate, and the untimely and rather unfortunate deaths of our spouses, has brought us together once more. Let us not waste this God given opportunity!
    (Kneels)
Vladimir Stabbenspine, would do me the honour?

STABBENSPINE
I never dreamed that your feelings would match mine-

MARGUERITE
I pray give me an answer! Will you marry me?

STABBENSPINE
Yes, I will proudly make you wife number 25!

MARGUERITE
    Come hell, high water or murderers in the
    night, they'll not take away our happiness!

    Marguerite and Stabbenstein kiss.

STABBENSPINE
    Time is short, the killer may strike again! We
    must consummate our affection while we can.

MARGUERITE
    I've waited an eternity for such words.

    Stabbenspine and Marguerite exit hastily.

                    SCENE FOUR

    *The cellar. Igor sits, chained by the
    wrists. A sledge lies in front of him,
    just out of reach.*

IGOR
    To sledge, or not to sledge? That is the
    question—
    Whether 'tis nobler in the mind to suffer ,
    The slings and arrows of outrageous doping
    allegations,
    Or to take arms against a sea of drugs tests,
    And, by opposing, end them? To retire, to
    sledge—
    No more—and by a retirement to say we end,
    The heartache and the thousand natural shocks,
    That sledging is heir to—'tis a consummation,
    Devoutly to be wished! To retire, to sledge.
    To sledge, perchance to dream…

    OLGA enters.

OLGA
    Sounds familiar… I can free you from your
    chains, Igor.

IGOR
  Who- who are you?

OLGA
  The name's Olga, I live down here.

IGOR
  But how?

    Olga laughs.

OLGA
  All the cellars in Bolgorvia connect in an
  underground complex of tunnels. There's a
  whole community of us down here, all to escape
  Bolgorvia's oppressive feudal society. We
  scavenge what little we can find in the
  cellars, usually excessive amounts of wine and
  mature cheese.

IGOR
  You sound like very sneaky people.

OLGA
  We have to sneak, it's how we survive. But we
  know when to intervene in the affairs of the
  upstairs world.

IGOR
  What do you mean?

OLGA
  You and your mistress are in grave danger.

IGOR
  Stabbenspine protects mistress from danger.
  Igor looks after himself.

OLGA
  How can you be so blind? Count Stabbenspine is
  the danger. It was he who killed the Duke,
  along with all his ex-wives.

IGOR
  How can you know this?

OLGA
  My brother Vulgar spent a summer in
  Stabbenspine's cellar. The Count killed three
  of his wives down there. He saw the Count
  drain his wives of their life-blood.
  Stabbenspine is a vampire, and your mistress
  will be his next victim, unless you stop him.

IGOR
  Mistress, in danger?!
      (Trying to break free of his chains)
  Igor away!

OLGA
  Hold on! Let me help…

  Olga helps Igor free of his chains.

IGOR
  Come Olga! Help Igor slay the monster!

OLGA
  Forgive me, but I cannot. We cellar dwellers
  cannot journey long above ground. But you must
  go now. There is still time to save her!

IGOR
  Very well. Igor, away!

  Igor exits.

SCENE FIVE

  Count Stabbenspine and Duchess Marguerite
  enter.

MARGUERITE
  Well that was rather enjoyable…

STABBENSPINE
Now we've got the physical aspect out of the way, shall we deal with the financial matters of our impending marriage?

MARGUERITE
Always so formal, Vlad! Why such a rush?

STABBENSPINE
I have some gambling arrears to pay down. Cock fights mostly. I've always had a weakness for cocks.

MARGUERITE
As you wish… I'm sure you'll find that I'm more than capable of financing your cock addiction.

STABBENSPINE
I took the liberty of drawing up a pre-nuptial agreement. The documents are in your boudoir for your perusal. Sign it, and we are financially joined.

MARGUERITE
Such a simple gesture to cement our future. I will return momentarily, darling.

STABBENSPINE
Hurry back!

Exit Marguerite.

And now for the final phase of my plan…
(Takes the bottle of Champagne)
To administer dried bloodwort to her favourite Champagne. Bloodwort is an almost perfect poison, with but one fatal flaw, its overpowering stench. But to this foolish wench, blind to all smells, it will be a perfect remedy to my marriage woe, providing yet another sweet tanker of blood to quench my thirst.

74

He flakes the bloodwort into the bottle.
Enter Marguerite.

MARGUERITE
  Your documents bear my signature, darling.

STABBENSPINE
  Excellent, now let us toast to our future
  together.

  He holds up the bottle.

MARGUERITE
  Dawn is breaking outside, the storm seems
  finally to have ceased. Care to bask in our
  new dawn?

  She goes to open the curtains.
  Stabbenspine pulls her swiftly away.

STABBENSPINE
  No! Get away! Dear Marguerite, the light would
  be oppressive to our eyes. Let us drink to our
  happiness!

  Pours a glass of champagne for himself and
  Marguerite. They clink glasses.

MARGUERITE
  To us!

STABBENSPINE
  To us.

  Before they can drink, Edvin enters
  swiftly, and gulps down much of the
  Champagne bottle. He then chokes.

MARGUERITE
  Edvin! Why?

EDVIN
  Poison… Warning… Igor…

Edvin dies.

MARGUERITE
    The wine? Poisoned? But Vlad…

    *Igor enters, wielding his sledge as a
    weapon.*

IGOR
    Step aside, mistress. It's sledging time!

STABBENSPINE
    You swine! I'll teach you to foil my plans!

    Igor and Stabbenspine fight.

IGOR
    The curtains mistress! Quickly! The curtains!

    *Marguerite opens the curtains.
    Count Stabbenspine howls in pain,
    collapsing to the floor, dead.*

MARGUERITE
    Igor! You saved me! How can I ever repay you?

IGOR
    Igor asks mistress only for the chance to
    clear his name to the international sledging
    community.

MARGUERITE
    Your wish is granted, dear servant. Go forth
    and proclaim your sledging purity, you have my
    blessing.

IGOR
    Thank you mistress. Igor away!

    Igor sledges off.

MARGUERITE
As the sun rose above the hills of
Bolgorvia, the terror in the night was
vanquished. At least, for now…

Stabbenspine jerks upright.

END PLAY

Crawl Space
By Lee Lawing

CHARACTERS
  SAMMY - *A person, any gender*
  BLAINE - *A person, any gender*
  DAD - *Off-stage voice, male*

SETTING
  The crawl space below a house.

> *A bare stage representative of the crawl space beneath Sammy's house. There are two chairs on stage in complete darkness.*

DAD
>   *(Off-stage, ferocious)*
>   Sammy!

> *SAMMY turns on a flashlight to light their face with its glow.*

SAMMY
>   You can't find me down here.

DAD
>   *(Off-stage, ferocious)*
>   Sammy!

SAMMY
>   Never, never, never. Not down here.

> *The yelling starts again and then the yelling stops and there is complete silence in which Sammy exhales the breath they were holding.*

BLAINE
>   *(in the darkness)*
>   You're lucky.

> *Sammy is scared by the voice so close and turns off their flashlight.*

SAMMY
>   Who's there?

BLAINE
>   *(in the darkness)*
>   Me.

> *Blaine lights up their own face with a flashlight.*

SAMMY
Who are you?

BLAINE
I'm not really… (sure)

SAMMY
How long have you been down here? Are you
hiding from your dad, too?

BLAINE
No. Just… I'm not sure how long I've been down
here.

SAMMY
I'm staying down here forever.

BLAINE
Can you?

SAMMY
I can try.

    *Sammy turns on their flashlight again and
    Blaine makes their way to the other chair
    and as they do, the lights come up on
    them.*

BLAINE
You can't just hide in here without things.

SAMMY
What things?

BLAINE
Food. Water.

SAMMY
I can always go up and get some.

BLAINE
Isn't he always there?

80

SAMMY
  Who?

BLAINE
  Your dad.

SAMMY
  I don't think so. He doesn't seem to be there
  now.

BLAINE
  Maybe that's the best time to go and find
  food. And water.

    Sammy stands up and starts to exit.

DAD
    (*Off-stage, ferocious*)
  Sammy, where did you go?!

    Sammy hurriedly sits back down.

SAMMY
  He's still here.

BLAINE
  Just like my dad.

SAMMY
  I can go when he falls asleep.

BLAINE
  My dad never fell asleep.

SAMMY
  Everyone has to fall asleep.

BLAINE
  Dads somehow don't. Or it seemed that way when
  I was hiding from mine.

SAMMY
  Down here?

BLAINE
  Yes.

SAMMY
  And you're still down here?

      A beat.

BLAINE
  I guess I am.

      A beat.

SAMMY
  I'm glad. I was getting scared down here
  before you said hello.

BLAINE
  Scared I get.

SAMMY
  You were scared of your dad?

BLAINE
  Yes. The same way you are.

SAMMY
  Just a little. No. You're right. A lot.

      *Blaine gets up and scoots their chair
      closer to Sammy's and sits down and takes
      Sammy's hand.*

BLAINE
  You've got me to help you.

SAMMY
  Thank you.

BLAINE
  And the others?

SAMMY
  Others?

BLAINE
  Yes. Show yourselves.

        *One light appears in the darkness and then
        another one and another one until there
        are ten lights in the dark.*

        Then, they all go off quickly.

SAMMY
  That's a lot of lights.

BLAINE
  Ten to be exact.

SAMMY
  Ten? Really? It seems too small under here to
  even fit one person.

BLAINE
  We are all small for our size.

SAMMY
  I guess so. Small enough to hide from dad.

BLAINE
  In a matter speaking, yes.

DAD
        (*Off-stage, ferocious*)
  Sammy!

        *Sammy is scared and they hold up their
        flashlight as a weapon, but not Blaine.*

SAMMY
  How could you be so calm?

BLAINE
  I've had time to get used to it.

SAMMY
I don't think there could be enough time for
me to ever feel… not scared.

BLAINE
It just happens. The more you forget.

SAMMY
Forget?

BLAINE
Yes. I still remember the most. The others
back there that you saw their lights are
forgetting more and more. It just happens.

SAMMY
He's my dad.

BLAINE
That's what he wants you to believe.

SAMMY
What?

BLAINE
The man upstairs is not your dad.

SAMMY
But he's angry at me like my dad gets.

BLAINE
My real dad never got mad at me.

SAMMY
Never?

BLAINE
Not like this… man.

SAMMY
Who is he?

BLAINE
His name is Tony. You've blocked out
everything except that he is your dad. Or
could be, but no real dad would behave like
this one is behaving. Or would ever behave.

DAD
     (*Off-stage, ferocious, jubilent*)
Sammy! I told you I'd find you Sammy! I told
you.

SAMMY
He found me.

BLAINE
He found all of us.

SAMMY
All of us?

BLAINE
Me and the other lights you saw in the crawl
space and now he's caught you and put you down
here with the rest of us.

SAMMY
That's not my dad?

BLAINE
You just made him into that to help you deal
with the fear and pain and the sadness you
felt for having been caught by him. By having
been killed by him. Turn off your light Sammy.
It's time to settle into your new home.

                    END PLAY

Eisoptrophobia
By Thomas Jancis

CHARACTERS
  ERIN - *Vampire, female, excitable and over-dramatic*
  ADAL - *Vampire, male, teasing and sarcastic*

SETTING
  A lounge, complete with sofa and abandoned shopping bags.

*ERIN and ADAL sit on the floor of a house
next to a sofa, drinking from mugs. There
are shopping bags lying dropped in the
doorway. Adal stirs a spoon in the mugs.*

ERIN
  You're not stirring it right. It's not mixing
  in with the chocolate.

ADAL
  I'm doing my best.

ERIN
  It's going to be all claggy and then-

      Erin *gags*.

ADAL
  You are the most sensitive vampire I have ever
  met. Having to disguise blood in hot drinks.
  Stop pouting. Taste it.

      Erin sips the drink.

ADAL
  Better?

ERIN
      (unsure)
  Yes - ish.

ADAL
  I can throw it away if you're going to be-

ERIN
  No no. I will drink it. Even if it clags.

ADAL
  Such a martyr. You're exhausting.

ERIN
  Okay. Shhh. Right. Um. Never have I ever-

ADAL
  Dare!

ERIN
  No! Stop! We're not playing that!

ADAL
  I dare you to-

ERIN
  Adal, stop.

ADAL
  Go outside.

ERIN
  Adal, no. Be nice.

ADAL
  Scared?

ERIN
  Yes.

ADAL
  Knew it.

ERIN
  I would burn Adal. Into a big pile of ash.
  That's horrible. Shame on you. We only just
  managed to get invited in before it started
  getting light.

ADAL
  I was just joking. This is supposed to be fun.

ERIN
  It was fun and then you went horrible.

ADAL
  I'm sorry. I'll be nice. Promise.

ERIN
  Never have I ever-

ADAL
  Make it a sex thing.

ERIN
  Adal!

ADAL
  Okay fine. Fingers on lips. Being good.

ERIN
  Never have I ever kissed-

ADAL
  Oooo!

ERIN
  Have I kissed a dog.

ADAL
  What? That was it?

ERIN
  I got nervous okay. I didn't wanna do a sexy
  sex thing so-

ADAL
  Have I kissed a dog?

ERIN
  That's the game.

ADAL
  Are we counting werewolves?

ERIN
  Yes?

    ADAL sips.

ERIN
  Oh! Gross, gross, GROSS!

ADAL
  What? He was cute.

ERIN
  But he's a pupper. A big stupid dog. He eats
  his poop.

ADAL
  That's just a rumour. They don't do that.

ERIN
  They might! I have heard it.

ADAL
  Who? Who told you?

ERIN
  Everyone says it.

ADAL
  So it must be true! Duh doy!

ERIN
  Duh doy yourself.

ADAL
  My turn.

ERIN
  Fine.

ADAL
  Never. Have. I Ever. Kissed a-

ERIN
  Dog! Boo! Boo you.

ADAL
  I'll take it back. Nev Have Ev. Got locked in
  a public toilet.

They both drink and sigh.

ERIN
  Those locks!

ADAL
  I know!

ERIN
  They are the worst!

   Erin gets up with a sigh.

ADAL
  And she's off. Where are you going Erin?

ERIN
  I want to do something.

ADAL
  Bored.

ERIN
  Be nice.

ADAL
  I'm going to lie down here while you try and
  find something to fill the long hours until it
  gets dark again.

ERIN
  Right. I'll go first. Get up on the couch.

   Adal pulls himself up onto the sofa.

ADAL
  M'lady. See how I recline. The cock of my leg,
  the curve of my neck. Erin. Erin you're not
  looking at my neck.

   Erin riffles through a drawer.

ERIN
   There has to be something. Ah. A notepad! Also
   a- Ah, come on. Why did she not throw her used
   pens away? Ah! Pencil! Perfection! Ooo! Still
   pointy.

   Now! Stay still. Just going to drag the chair
   over here.

        Erin drags the chair into place.

ADAL
   What's the game?

ERIN
   I'm going to draw you.

ADAL
   Draw me?

ERIN
   I want you to have a picture of yourself. We
   can't look at ourselves in a, you know what.

ADAL
   The old reflective thing. But I have no need.
   I know what I look like.

ERIN
   Do you really?

ADAL
   I have a portrait. It is two hundred years old
   but I don't look a day over five hundred and
   ninety.

ERIN
   Well I want to do my drawing. I get so few
   chances to practise. Please please please!

ADAL
   Fine. But I want a go.

ERIN
  Sorry?

ADAL
  I can draw you. Go on, Erin. Let me.

ERIN
  Fine. Now get into a comfortable pose.

    Adal shifts and poses.

    Erin focuses and scribbles on the pad.

ERIN
  Stay still.

ADAL
  My nose is itchy.

ERIN
  Stay still!

ADAL
  My nose is itchy and I want to scratch it.

ERIN
  I will use my pencil.

    Erin pokes Adal in the nose and scratches.

ADAL
  You're just poking me in the nose.

ERIN
  I need to work on my art! You keep wriggling
  about like a worm!

ADAL
  Art. More like still life. You could draw her
  still, warm body in the hall.

    A pause.

ERIN
I don't find that very funny.

ADAL
I'm sorry.
    (Pause)
My nose doesn't itch anymore. Thank you.

        More scribbling. Adal shifts.

ERIN
Stop wriggling. Adal, I'm trying to blend.

ADAL
My turn.

ERIN
But I need-
    (she pauses)
-to catch the-
    (pause)
-ambambamlance.

ADAL
Hush. Now strike a pose. My turn to sketch.

ERIN
I couldn't possibly. No. I need to be made up.

ADAL
Let's see what is in the shopping bags.

        Adal raids the shopping bags.

ERIN
I guess she didn't get round to unpacking
before we-

ADAL
Got invited in and then made quote 'pre bed
time hot chocolate' unquote.

Adal sits on the sofa and plays with something from the bag.

ERIN
  Thank goodness we got into this house before
  it got light.

  *Erin opens a makeup kit and begins to work
  on her face.*

ERIN
  I will start with the little brush for my
  eyes. Now if I open them real wide and- Ow.
  It's just poking me.

ADAL
  Gimmie. You don't know what you're doing. Plus
  there is no looking in the You-Know-What. Come
  on. Sit down next to me.

  *Erin sits next to Adal. He turns her head
  and begins applying the makeup.*

ADAL
  Turn your head. Let's start with some lovely
  lipstick. Reddest lips.

ERIN
  My lips are plenty red.

ADAL
  Hush.

ERIN
  You haven't done this before, have you?

ADAL
  I am trying my best.

  He hums to himself as he works.

ERIN
  Can we go to the zoo when it gets dark?

ADAL
  Why?

ERIN
  I remember seeing an elephant about two
  hundred years ago.

ADAL
  Want to see if they've changed? Been upgraded?
  Stand up.

    Erin stands.

  Do a twirl. Now look over your shoulder.
  Growl.

ERIN
  Rar!

    Adal laughs.

ERIN
  How is it?

ADAL
  You look alive.

ERIN
    (small)
  Oh.

ADAL
  You can wash it off.

ERIN
  No, I'll leave it.

    Pause. Adal lifts the pad.

ADAL
  Why! I look here at your drawing and it shocks
  me! A large worm appears to have crawled on my
  face.

ERIN
  That is a nose you jerk. I will push you down!

ADAL
     (*laughs*)
  Come on. Come have a hug.

ERIN
  I only stay with you because you have soft
  shoulders for me to lay my head on.

     They quietly snuggle.
     A contented moment.

ERIN
  I miss the sun.

ADAL
  Overrated. One star.

     She snorts.

ERIN
  I'm just going to shut my eyes.

ADAL
  Day Day, Sleep Okay!

ERIN
  Day Day, Sleep Okay to you too, Adal.

     Erin yawns and smacks her lips as she goes
     to sleep.

                    END PLAY

Flesh and Blood
By Peter Briffa

CHARACTERS
  DORRIE - *Female*
  CLIFF - *Male*

SETTING
  The bottom of a ravine.

CLIFF and DORRIE are stuck at the bottom of a ravine. They are injured and dirty. There is a child car seat nearby.

DORRIE
  Don't say it.

CLIFF
  Say what? You don't know what I want to say.

DORRIE
  Yes I do.

CLIFF
  We have no choice.

DORRIE
  We always have a choice.

CLIFF
  We'll die soon. I've had enough woodlice.

DORRIE
  Eat a spider then. He's your own son.

CLIFF
  I'm hungry. You're hungry. We're starving.

DORRIE
  We cannot eat our own son.

CLIFF
  We can. We must. We'll die otherwise. Soon.
  You're injured. You can't walk. I'm running
  out of energy to look after you. Can't watch
  you die.

DORRIE
  He's our son.

CLIFF
  But he's dead. He's been dead for days. If we
  don't eat him now he'll be too dangerous to

CLIFF (Cont.)
eat tomorrow when we're really desperate.
He'll be rancid. And we probably won't be
able, anyway. Physically. I don't want to eat
him.

DORRIE
He's your son, Cliff.

CLIFF
You keep saying that. But actually he isn't
now. Not any more. He's dead. He's flesh.
That's all he is. Dead flesh. Whatever was
there, whatever was Timmy has long gone.
Dorrie, you're the atheist here-

DORRIE
-What has that got to do with it?

CLIFF
I'm the religious one. Aren't I? Remember? You
don't believe in any of it. When you die, you
die. That's it. That's the one thing you
believe. Well, Timmy's dead. That's it. He,
his body, is no use to anyone, except us, as
food. If we don't eat him the bugs will.
Someone will. Dorrie, we survived the crash.
You and I survived this. There must be a
reason for it.

DORRIE
There is no reason-

CLIFF
-In which case, why not just eat him?

DORRIE
You want to live that much?

CLIFF
Yes, actually I do

DORRIE
So much that you'd be happy to eat your own
son?

CLIFF
Yes. We are here for a reason. We survived for
a reason. The car ended up here in this
ravine. Timmy's dead. You and I survived.
There has to be a reason for this.

DORRIE
Then what? You eat him. You survive a few
days. Weeks maybe. Then what? Nobody's come
for us. If they haven't come now, they never
will. Nobody knows we're here. We crashed, you
crashed. We left no trace, clearly. The car
just went off the road, and somehow, you and I
survived. Timmy survived, a while. They'll
wonder where we've gone if they ever even
wonder, and they'll think we've driven
somewhere. There won't be search parties. If
they were going to come they already would
have been here.

CLIFF
I know.

DORRIE
So you eat Timmy. And in a day or two, I die
too. I go into a coma. And you either watch me
die, or put me out of my misery. Smash me over
the head with a tree branch. And then you eat
me too. So you survive down here for maybe a
fortnight. Couple of weeks. Drinking my blood.
Eating my body. And then you too starve to
death. All alone, and lonely. Full of regret.
Full of fear. Am I missing something?

CLIFF
We survived for a reason, Dorrie. Someone will
come and get us. We can't give up. You know
the Andes survivors? The Uruguayan rugby
players who crashed into the snow? They were

CLIFF (Cont.)
 all Catholics. Half of them survived, half of
 them died. And the ones who died? Their bodies
 were frozen in the snow. Eventually the
 survivors decided they should eat them. They
 didn't want to do it. They were their friends.
 But they did it, and it gave them enough
 energy to go walking through the snow, and
 they found help. Afterwards, when people
 discovered what they did, a lot of them were
 repulsed. Disgusted. But the Pope? He told
 them they did the right thing.

DORRIE
 Lucky old pope.

     *Cliff starts to rifle through a backpack
     he has and finds a knife.*

CLIFF
 I think, if I tear him into tiny strips, they
 can dry out just a little and maybe I can chew
 them.

DORRIE
 You're actually going to do this?

CLIFF
 Yes.

DORRIE
 I won't forgive you. What do you think people
 will say, if you survive, when they know you
 ate your own son?

CLIFF
 I'm hungry. And he isn't my son.

DORRIE
 No?

CLIFF
 I know. I've always known. These things

CLIFF (Cont.)
  happen. I wasn't a perfect husband. I worked a
  lot. I neglected you. I'm sorry about that.

DORRIE
  You knew?

CLIFF
  I knew. I just didn't think it mattered. Timmy
  was a lovely kid. But he wasn't mine.

    *Cliff plunges the knife into the child
    seat and pulls out a bloody piece of
    flesh. He bites it and starts to chew.*

DORRIE
  That's why you crashed the car, isn't it? You
  wanted to kill us. And now, because we
  survived you think there must be a reason?

CLIFF
  Just like sushi. You want some?

DORRIE
  Never.

    *Cliff plunges the knife into Dorrie. She
    starts to bleed. He cups his hands to the
    knife wound, then drinks the blood.*

CLIFF
Everything happens for a reason, Dorrie.

                    END PLAY

Gluttony on the High Seas
By Steve Duprey

CHARACTERS
  SKIP - *Male, mid-20s, an American country bumpkin, skinny and gaunt*
  HARRY - *Male, mid-40s, a British socialite, almost portly*

SETTING
  On a lifeboat, stranded at sea.

SCENE ONE

Lights up on a lifeboat. Two men are in tattered clothes and both sport beards that look to be about four weeks old. SKIP is awake and HARRY is asleep.

Skip spends a bit of time gazing hungrily at Harry. He looks around... what an absurd thing to do in the middle of the ocean... to make sure no one is looking.

He moves to Harry, careful not to wake him. He lifts Harry's hand up towards his mouth, focusing on the pinky finger... He won't miss that.

As he opens his mouth to bite Harry's finger off, we hear the loud screech of an albatross. Harry wakes to see Skip's mouth wrapped around his little finger.

HARRY
  Can I help you?

SKIP
    (Around a mouthful of little finger)
  No, thanks. I'm okay.

HARRY
  Then, may I have my finger back?

SKIP
    (Still holding it in his mouth)
  Oh yeah... Sure.

HARRY
  Now?

SKIP
    *(Slowly pulling back and letting the pinky
    finger slide out of his mouth)*
  Oh. Yeah. Okay. Sorry.

105

HARRY
How in the world am I supposed to get any rest
at all?

SKIP
You can sleep if you want.

HARRY
And wake up missing a digit? Every time! You
do this every time I so much as doze off for a
few minutes. Do you honestly think I won't
feel it if you bite my finger off?

SKIP
Well, I figured if I bite real gentle…

HARRY
And do you honestly think that I won't wring
your skinny little neck if I wake up as nine
fingered Willy?

SKIP
        (Chuckling)
Nine-fingered Willy… That's funny, Harry.

HARRY
And do you really think that you will EVER see
the shore again if you so much as nibble on a
fingernail?

SKIP
Fingernails got no meat on 'em. Besides, I got
my own fingernails to chew on. Ain't much left
of 'em though.

HARRY
How many times do I have to tell you? One
fingernail a day. Don't be a glutton.

SKIP
Yeah, but it's been thirty-three days and my
fingernails ain't growing fast enough. Say, do
you suppose they ain't growin' because I ain't

SKIP (Cont.)
  feedin' 'em enough?

HARRY
  How in the world do you think you can feed
  your fingernails?

SKIP
  They made outta minerals, right? Calcium and
  such? I read once in a…

HARRY
  You? Read something? I hardly think that the
  chemical make-up of fingernails is covered in
  Archie comics, or whatever passes for juvenile
  literature in America these days.

SKIP
  I ain't read Archie comics since I was twenty-
  two. Why you gotta get all uppity all the
  time, anyway?

HARRY
  Listen, Skip…
      (To himself)
  …Skip, what a ridiculous name.
      (To Skip)
  Listen, Skip. I understand that fate has
  thrown us together in this incredibly
  untenable situation and I understand that you
  are who you are and I am who I am. You asking
  me why I have to be so "uppity" all the time
  is like me asking you why you have to be such
  an idiot all the time. And I haven't done that
  now, have I. I'm simply being who I am and so
  are you. Why can't you simply accept that? I'm
  not going to be your friend. It's simply out
  of the question. And I'm not going to be your
  lunch either, so you can just forget about
  that. I expect to get out of this situation
  with my fingers fully intact.

SKIP
  You expect to get out of this?

HARRY
  Of course, I do.

SKIP
  But if they ain't found us after thirty-three
  days, what makes you think they're even still
  looking?

HARRY
  Young man, you are extremely lucky to have
  been stranded with me. They may have stopped
  looking for you after a week but they
  certainly haven't stopped looking for me and
  won't until they find me… us… Well, you know
  what I mean.

SKIP
  What makes you so special?

HARRY
  We've been over this. I am English and I'm
  rich. That's all you need to know.

SKIP
  Seems to me rich and poor don't matter a whole
  lot out here in the middle of the Pacific.

HARRY
  Atlantic.

SKIP
  Right… Atlantic. Seems to me that we're just
  two men in a boat. Hell, I've seen you tear
  into a raw fish with your bare hands. Now go
  ahead and tell that's how you eat 'em at home.

HARRY
  Well, I certainly haven't…

SKIP
  I've seen you scratch so hard at them bites
  that you've almost cried.

HARRY
  Yes, well…

SKIP
  Hell, I've seen you poop in the ocean. Seems
  to me that's the great equalizer, wouldn't you
  say?

HARRY
  I suppose you might have a point there. The
  only blessing of having so little food is that
  I don't have to do that too often.

SKIP
  It was no picnic for me either.

HARRY
  So, Skip…
    (Rolling his eyes at the name again)
  What do you propose?

SKIP
  I ain't proposin' nothin'! I ain't that
  desperate.

HARRY
  No, you idiot…
    (Catching himself)
  …Sorry. I mean, how would you like to move
  forward with this… relationship?

SKIP
  Again, Harry, I got nothing against you, but I
  don't swing that way. Nobody from Texas does.

HARRY
    (Frustrated, taking Skip's face in hand)
  Listen closely. I am not proposing any type of
  romantic or sexual relationship. I would

HARRY (Cont.)
    simply like you to tell me how you imagine we
    should proceed… treat each other… behave
    towards one another from this point forward.

        After a long moment of the two of them
        looking at each other, Skip's face
        squished in Harry's hands…

SKIP
    Harry.

HARRY
    Yes, Skip?

SKIP
    I don't like it when people touch my face.

HARRY
        (*Pulling his hands away quickly*)
    Terribly sorry. Yes, I can understand that.

SKIP
    Thanks.

HARRY
    Certainly. Now… do you understand my question?

SKIP
    I think so.

HARRY
    Excellent!

SKIP
    You wanna know what I wanna do next.

HARRY
    Essentially, yes.

SKIP
        (*Considers, then finally*)
    I think we gotta eat each other.

HARRY
  What?!?

SKIP
  Now don't go blowin' up on me. Hear me out.

HARRY
  I will not hear you out. That's the most
  ridiculous thing I've ever heard.

SKIP
      (*Finally standing up for himself*)
  Now, I said hear me out!

HARRY
      (*Shocked, listens reluctantly*)
  All right young man. The floor, such as it is,
  is yours.

SKIP
  Huh?

HARRY
  Speak.

SKIP
  Right. The way I figure it, we ain't got much
  time left out here before we kill each other
  outta sheer frustration. Am I right?

HARRY
  You are correct.

SKIP
  We ain't got no water, even though we're
  surrounded by the damn stuff, and strainin'
  your piss through my skivvies didn't work for
  either of us. Am I right?

HARRY
  A very astute and accurate observation.

SKIP
  Huh?

HARRY
  Right.

SKIP
  Right. And catching a fish out here is near
  impossible without some kind line. We've only
  done it twice, and you can't rely on that. Am
  I right?

HARRY
  I suppose you are.

SKIP
  Finally, if we don't get something to eat
  soon, we're going to die anyway. Right?

HARRY
  It is seeming to be more and more inevitable.

SKIP
  So, what I propose… propose? Is that the right
  word?

HARRY
  Yes.

SKIP
  What I propose is that we start with the
  fingers and work our way up to the…

HARRY
  See, now you've lost me again. I'm not eating
  you and I'm not letting you eat me!

SKIP
  Well, if you won't even consider it then I may
  just have to take matters into my own hands.

HARRY
  Meaning?

SKIP
  That ain't none of your concern.
    (Pause)
  Why don't you take a little nap? I'll be right
  here when you wake up and we can talk more
  about it.

HARRY
  Why don't you take a little nap? You're
  looking particular tired after all the
  "thinking" you just did.

    They stare at each other from opposite
    ends of the raft, each trying to keep his
    eyes open longer than the other.

                    SCENE TWO

    A sign/projection: "2 WEEKS LATER"

                          SD - Ships horn

    Lights up on Skip standing alone in the
    lifeboat and looking up at the ship that
    has pulled up alongside of the lifeboat.
    The ship can be represented offstage…
    we'll get it. He's looking hale and
    healthy… even a little fatter. He should
    have a "fat suit" in the bottom of the
    boat that he can slip on in the blackout.

VOICEOVER
  Ahoy there. Are you alone?

SKIP
  All by myself for six weeks. Thank God, you
  found me!

    Lights fade, but not before we see Skip
    pick up a shin bone, nibble a bit of
    something off of it, and toss it over the
    edge of the boat.

                    113

His Face
By Gerardo Rodriguez

CHARACTERS
  DR. STRAUSSBERG - *A Therapist*
  MIGUEL - *A Patient, Male*

SETTING
  A Therapist's Office.

DR. STRAUSSBERG
Your wife made you come in here.

MIGUEL
I'm fine man, she's just tripping. I just let
that slip out.

DR. STRAUSSBERG
Why do you think she made you come in?

MIGUEL
She didn't make me do anything.

DR. STRAUSSBERG
Well, what brought you in today? Anything
happen recently happen that's on your mind?
Maybe it brings up certain things that you
don't like thinking about?

MIGUEL
Nothing man, it's just we moved into a new
house, it's nothing.

   Miguel starts to rub his hands together,
   then clings onto a pillow.

DR. STRAUSSBERG
That seems like good news, but it seems to
cause you stress.
   (Miguel lets go of the pillow)
It's ok man, let it out.
   (beat)
Really Miguel, it helps to talk about it. That
way it won't get in between those you love.

MIGUEL
I was a kid when this happened, honestly don't
know if I remember it right. I woke up in the
middle of the night, I heard some rustling in
the trees outside of my window. I pull the
curtain back and look to see what it is.
There's something perched in the branches. I
can't make out what it is, I can tell it's got

MIGUEL (Cont.)
feathers, white feathers. It's huge, like
something out of Jurassic Park and from what I
can remember, it's staring right at me. It
didn't move an inch, I felt like I was frozen.
I wasn't scared, I was just frozen. I heard a
twig snap and it snapped me out of it. I close
the curtain and go to my dads room. I tell him
that I saw something outside, he grudgingly
gets up and heads towards the front door. I
follow him. He opens the door, steps out and
he freezes.

I'll never forget that look on his face. It
was like he just saw someone die. He stood
there with this face, just staring back at
this thing, finally he snapped out of it. He
grabbed me and we slept in the same bed that
night and for the rest of the week. That
happened the first night we spent in this new
house.

Before this place, we lived in a projects
called Los Campitos. We shared the same bed
for 7 years because that was all he could
afford. I didn't know what to make of what
just happened, he saw something that scared
him so much that he didn't let me out of his
sight for weeks, especially at night.

After all his hard work, he still couldn't
enjoy his own bed. My dad has seen life, he
crossed into the country illegally, spent a
week in a barn with nothing to eat, but peanut
butter. He knew people that didn't make the
journey. He's not someone that's easily
shaken. I never asked my dad about that night,
his face on that front porch was burned into
my memory. Now, I'm about the same age he was
that night and I have my own kids. Finally got
our own house when we moved into our new
house, I made sure to chop down every tree on
the property, just like my dad did. I wonder

MIGUEL (Cont.)
    if my kids will see that face on me.
        (clings to a pillow again)
    I wonder if I'll lose what he was afraid to
    lose.

DR. STRAUSSBERG
    Your father sounds like a brave man. How is
    he?

MIGUEL
    He passed a while back, miss him. I wish he
    could see the house we got.

DR. STRAUSSBERG
    Do you think he would've liked it?

MIGUEL
    He'd probably start gardening in the backyard.
    I really do miss him.

DR. STRAUSSBERG
    It sounds like he loved you alot. It also
    sounds like he was afraid to lose you, just
    like you're afraid to lose what you've got.

MIGUEL
    Yea, I love my family and I worked hard to get
    what we have now.

DR. STRAUSSBERG
    Everyone is afraid to lose things they care
    about, but it's a natural part of life. You
    had to say goodbye to your dad.

MIGUEL
    Yea, you're right I guess.
        (Lets go of the pillow)
    It doesn't make it any easier though.

DR. STRAUSSBERG
    You got me on that one. So, do you want to
    schedule another appointment for next week.

A loud twig snap can be heard off stage with the wind blowing. A faint owl hooting can be heard. Miguel snaps his head towards it and stares off stage, he begins to cling to the pillow even tighter.

MIGUEL
 (Still staring offstage)
 Nah doc, I umm—
 (Clears throat)
I need to—umm do some work around the house.

END PLAY

Hold All Devils In My Heart
By Thomas Jancis

CHARACTERS
  TIG - *Female, demon. Full name: Tig'dranur Seven Claws, Bane of Travellers and Vexer of Pilgrims*
  HENRY - *Male, human*

SETTING
  A living room with a circle on the floor.

*A living room with a circle on the floor.
Tig'dranur Seven Claws, Bane of Travellers
and Vexer of Pilgrims (or TIG) sits in the
circle, her arms tightly crossed and her
cheeks puffed with a held breath.*

Eventually, she puffs it out.

TIG

So that must have been about a week? Maybe
two.
(Nods)
Yep. Two weeks and three days. I'm very good
at this game. Okay. Round two. Now how long
can I hum for?

She begins going "MMMM". She stops.

TIG

Oh no. That makes my lips feel funny.

*The sound of movement off stage. Tig makes
herself look small and scared.*

TIG

Oh my! Right.
(voice wavering)
Hello. Who's there? You have got to help me!
This mad man. He, he kidnapped me. He put me
in this circle and said I had to do the most
terrible things. You-

*Enter HENRY carrying a mug of tea. He
moves slowly. Tig's demonor changes
completely, back to the way she was
before.*

TIG

Oh, it's just you.

*She turns away with a pout and sticks her
nose in the air.
Henry sits down in his chair. He pulls out
his notebook and a pen. He sips the tea*

and begins to read through the notebook,
making small notes and ignoring Tig.
Tig glances back.
When Henry looks up, she goes back to
looking away with a grumpy snort. He
returns to the notebook.
Tig glances back.
Henry doesn't look up.
She turns to face towards him.
Henry doesn't look up.
She tries to look at what he is doing.
Henry doesn't look up.

TIG
  I did something with my hair.
      (Waiting)
      (Nothing)
  It wasn't like this last time.
      (Waiting)
      (Nothing)
  I can do that you know. Make it any colour or
  style I want. I'm very good at that.
      (Waiting)
      (Nothing)
  Are you cross with me?

  Henry looks up!

HENRY
  Hello.

TIG
  Hello. Are you cross?

HENRY
  You were sulking.

TIG
  I had many reasons to be sulky. You left me
  here.

HENRY
  During the day.

TIG
  Three weeks.

HENRY
  Lie.

TIG
  It felt like three weeks.

HENRY
  How were you today?

TIG
  Bored. Bored, bored, bored. You don't give me
  anything to do all day. Like could you give me
  a pen and paper? To do some poetry?

HENRY
  I can't trust you. You'd write a way out.

TIG
  Oh, I don't know how to do that.

HENRY
  Lie.

TIG
  You going to keep doing that?

HENRY
  Everytime you lie.

TIG
  Well, that's rude.

HENRY
  You are a demon. It's what you do.

TIG
  Yes, well! You wouldn't point out someone's
  nose would you? That would be very rude
  indeed.

HENRY
     (Points)
  Look. A nose.

TIG
  Rudeness beyond reckoning. I don't deserve
  this. To be trapped in a circle and be pointed
  at like, like, like a rhino! I am Tig'dranur
  Seven Claws, Bane of Travellers and Vexer of
  Pilgrims. You will fear and love me.

HENRY
  Oh, Tig.

TIG
  You shorten my name! You remove my honorifics!
  When I escape I shall, I shall, I shall bite
  your fingers off.

HENRY
  Don't want that!

TIG
  And put them in your mouth. Yeah! Your grubby
  little fingers! Show you.

     She nods. He laughs.

TIG
  It's not funny. It's a really big threat. You
  should be shaking.

HENRY
  I'm not scared of you Tig.

TIG
  Maybe if you don't fear me, then maybe I have
  other skills.
     (Hesitant)
  Big Boy?

     She begins winking. Shaking her chest.
     Making kisses. It isn't that seductive.

TIG

  Are you seduced? Are you driven mad with lust?

HENRY

  You're not a succubus are you?

TIG

  BE SEDUCED.

HENRY

  Oh no. It is very attractive. What ever shall
  I do?

TIG

  I WILL SHOUT YOU INTO ONANISM!

      He laughs.

TIG

  I'm being bullied.
      (She sulks)
  All those centuries sitting alone in the pit
  and then when I do get summoned it is to
  someone who bullies me.

HENRY

  I'm teasing. You're very sexual. It was very
  hard not to kiss you.

TIG

  Ha. Knew it.
      (small fist pump of celebration)
  I am very well known for making mortals lose
  their minds because of my schemes, my plots
  and my big eyes.

HENRY

  And for vexing travellers.

TIG

  NO! I am the BANE of travellers. I vex
  pilgrims. You don't listen, mortal.

HENRY

How do you have seven claws?

TIG

Why should I have more?

HENRY

Did you break one off?

TIG

No. Stupid.
(Mumbling)
I lost three in a game of wits and wagers. But
they cheated. Now my claws are used as part of
a throne.

HENRY

Oh crumbs.

TIG

I will not be pitied! I could get them back. I
am very capable with seven. More than you
would ever be. Can you rend? I see zero amount
of rending on your side, magician! And when I
get out of this pitiful circle I shall cut you
into seven pieces and then eat them, one a
day.

He smiles sadly.

TIG

Why are you smiling? Are you smiling because
you think that will make me like you again? It
won't.
(Pause)
I can smile better than you.

She gives a very friendly smile.

HENRY

I'm sad.

TIG
  Because I threatened you? I didn't mean it.
  Yes I did. I am very dangerous. Fear me.

HENRY
  I'm dying.

    A long pause.

TIG
  No.

HENRY
  No?

TIG
  No, I won't allow that.

HENRY
  I don't think that you have much of a choice
  in the matter.

TIG
  Of course I do. I can do anything.

HENRY
  How do you mean to save me then?

TIG
  Let me out.

HENRY
  Sneaky.

TIG
  Let me out and we can make a deal. You can
  sign a contract. I can give you fifty years.

HENRY
  Tig.

TIG
  One hundred years.

HENRY
  Tig.

TIG
  Until California crumbles into the sea. You
  can live that long. Just let me out.

HENRY
  I'm going to let you go. It's not fair that
  you'll be stuck here.

TIG
  Yes. Exactly. Then we need some paper. Your
  book will do. I can write something about
  making you better and then we both sign. Easy
  as breaking cups and hearts.

HENRY
  I don't want to make a deal.

TIG
  Of course you do. Maybe not for fifty years
  but I can help fix you.

HENRY
  I have taken too much from you. I'm going to
  let you go.

TIG
  It's a trap. Right? You're going to make me-
    (A considered pause)
  This is a trap?

    He lights a match.
    He holds it near his book.

HENRY
  I wanted you to see this. To see me destroy
  all my notes. All the ways that I found to
  conjure. How I made your circle. The
  information you gave me of the true names of
  stones and the way to command the animals.
  I'll banish you back to your home.

TIG

Stop. Don't. Just let us talk. You don't need
to do that right now. He puts the match out.

HENRY

Maybe I deserved this. Messing around with
cosmic powers. Keeping you trapped here for
months. It's been nearly a year with you stuck
in my front room. You must have been
miserable. Wanting to get home.

She looks away.

HENRY

You don't want to go?

TIG

It's not that nice, 'home'. The rings of Hell.
It's all spikes and fire and people who have
trumpets put up their bottoms. You ask someone
why they are there. There are murderers of
course, but then someone is all "Oh I ate
fruit from a tree I planted before four years
were up." How does that make sense? After a
while you just stop asking.

People don't really want to talk to you when
they're being punished for eating fruit. Or
for having a haircut.

What is happening to you? Is it a curse?

HENRY

My heart. I talked to the doctor. It is just a
matter of time. Could be a few months. Could
be a year. But my time is running out.

TIG

I can get you a heart.

HENRY

Just go and rip someone's heart out and, what,
have me eat it?

HENRY (Cont.)
     (He sees her look)
  That's not how these things work.

TIG
  Do you want one of mine?

HENRY
  Do you have spares?

TIG
  I have many things.
     (Looks annoyed)
  You were going to say "But she doesn't have
  all ten claws"! I can tell. You started
  breathing like you were amused.

HENRY
  You said it, not me. Now hold on. I will just
  need to break the circle. Then you can go
  home.

TIG
  I don't want to.

HENRY
  I need to do it now. I don't want to collapse
  and then have someone come into my house and
  see I have a woman sitting in my living room
  in a circle.

TIG
  Please. I'm begging you.

     *He sighs. He slowly begins moving his hand
     back and forth, scything through the air.
     He stops.*

HENRY
  The circle.

TIG
  Stop.

HENRY
The circle is broken.

They stare at each other.
She looks away first.

HENRY
When? When did I get so careless?

TIG
About two weeks.

HENRY
TWO WEEKS!?

TIG
YOUR HEART! YOU MUST BE CALM!

HENRY
How did I get so stupid? If I hadn't-

TIG
You were drinking that leaf water of yours and
I had given a very pithy bon-mot.

HENRY
You were talking about how that Necromancer
lost his genitals to an infection because he
was wearing necro-pants.

TIG
He thought he would have cash in his hand with
trousers made from a man. It was very silly.
Anyway, you had the giggles and spilt the
water.

HENRY
And broke the circle?

TIG
Yes.

HENRY
  Wow. So you've been free to go for that long.
  Well, cross that off the list. Now I just need
  to cancel Netflix and try and use those cinema
  vouchers.

TIG
  Well, maybe…
      (She gets shy)

HENRY
  Go on.

TIG
  Well, if they are going to go to waste, maybe
  I can
      (Talking quickly)
  come to the cinema with you and we can eat
  popcorn?

      He grins.

HENRY
  You like me.

TIG
  No! NO! I said nothing of the sort. I don't
  like being here. I was trying to lull you into
  a false sense of security. Now I will work my
  new plan to see you destroyed.

HENRY
  Lies.

TIG
  The plan involves seeing films. And getting a
  pizza after. Then seeing you flayed.

HENRY
  You know, the whole "You will suffer, mortal"
  performance worked better before you offered
  me one of your hearts.

TIG

   One of them. Not like it would be much of a
   loss.

HENRY

   Fine. Now, come on. You get out of that
   circle. We go to the cinema. Then you can rend
   or flay or whatever. I don't care.

TIG

   Lies.

   *They smile. Both a bit shy, both a bit
   nervous.*

END PLAY

In-terror-gation
By Kerri Duntley

CHARACTERS
  IVAN - *Male, Boris' brother, kidnapper*
  BORIS - *Male, Ivan's brother, kidnapper*
  ERIC THOMPSON - *Male, down-to-Earth, a*
  "regular guy"
  ANNOUNCER - *Costume contest announcer, any*
  gender

SETTING
  A shadowy room.
  A stage.

SCENE ONE

Lights up on ERIC tied to a chair center stage and blindfolded. His arms are tied behind his back. He appears to be sleeping (or perhaps even dead?) with his head hanging down.

It is dark on the stage, except for a spotlight on the hostage in the chair. There are 2 shadowy figures, IVAN and BORIS, pacing in the background. We hear footsteps walking ominously and rhythmically around the hostage.

IVAN
    (Monotone voice)
We have him just where we want him, Boris.

BORIS
    (Monotone voice)
Yes, yes, Ivan. He is ours. We will finally get exactly what we've always wanted.

Eric wakes up and coughs a little bit, still blindfolded and moving his head in different directions trying to figure out where he is.

ERIC
Huh? Where am I?

Ivan and Boris continue pacing in rhythm very slowly circling Eric always on opposite sides. Finally...

LX - Lights up

IVAN
    (Leans in close to Eric)
Wakey- wakey sleepy baby... Wouldn't you like to know where you are?! Stay calm!!

ERIC
Wait… what? Wh… what's going on?

BORIS
    (Mocking nasally voice)
Wait, what? What's going on? I want to know
what's going on? Where am I? Poor me, I'm so
confused. I have no idea what could possibly
be…

    Ivan shakes his head no along with a hand
    gesture to stop and Boris stops.

ERIC
You won't get away with this! And, I really
don't understand what this is all about!

    Ivan and Boris finally stop circling him.
    Boris walks behind Eric and removes the
    blindfold while Ivan is standing where he
    can see and speak to him.

IVAN
We might not, but does… Ahem… The Pleasant
Valley Halloween Costume Contest ring a bell?

ERIC
    (relaxed tone)
Oh, man! That's right! The contest is tonight,
isn't it?!

BORIS
Uh-huh… DON'T play dumb with us, Eric
Thompson! It isn't lost on us that you've been
winning the contest consistently each year for
the past SEVEN seasons!

    Ivan begins counting on his fingers.

ERIC
No kidding! Has it really been 7 years in a
row now?!

IVAN
A costume contest is NOT some kind of fun
thing to be taken lightly!

ERIC
No, no… I mean of course not!

BORIS
This is serious business.

> *Boris gives a definitive head nod with a
> very stern serious look. Ivan makes the
> same gesture. Followed by Boris again.*

IVAN
So serious, in fact, that you will provide us
with all of your best tips on costume design
right now. And you will not be released until
you do so. We will win this contest tonight.

BORIS
Or, you see, at the very least you will not
win because you will not enter the contest.
You will be here… where you will remain… until
we win!

> *Both brothers laugh evilly.*

IVAN
Our Dearest, Eric Thompson, allow me to
explain. Year after year we watch YOU win the
title of Best Costume while we don't even get
so much as an honorable mention.

BORIS
NOT EVEN an honorable mention.

IVAN
Take for example last year… We dressed up
together as a majestic Arabian horse!

BORIS
I was the horse's ass!

IVAN
 Not even an honorable mention! So… Start
 talking! What is the secret to costume contest
 success?

ERIC
 I mean, I don't even know what to say… I …
 just… ahh…

BORIS
 Oh, what's the matter? Cat got your tongue,
 huh? You don't want to give away your secret
 of winning, do you, Eric Thompson? Well, we'll
 see if you talk…

    *Ivan starts fanning Eric with a small
    accordian fan.*

ERIC
 Uhhh, thanks? I guess it is a bit hot in here…

IVAN
 This is not some spa day or some kind of joke!
 This is serious, remember?!

    *Ivan throws the fan away and makes the
    serious head nod gesture again. Followed
    by Boris and Eric as they speak.*

BORIS
 Serious!

ERIC
 Serious!

IVAN
 We need you to start spilling the tea.

    *Boris brandishes a rubber chicken that
    squeaks or something similar.*

BORIS
 Or face the wrath of the squawking chicken!!

> *Boris squeaks the chicken in Eric's face as he holds it up to his neck as if he were holding a knife.*

ERIC
I mean, I don't know… I really don't give it that much thought…

IVAN
I guess this is going to have to get nasty before you start talking. I didn't want to have to pull out the big guns, but….

> *Ivan squirts him with a water gun or sprays him with a water bottle.*

ERIC
Look guys, I must just get lucky I guess… Okay?

> *Ivan and Boris begin to wield feathers as if they are swords in a threatening posture.*

BORIS
We warned you, Eric! This is the last straw… Be prepared to be tickled until you speak!

> *Eric is now visibly nervous, shaking, restless, eyes wide.*

ERIC
No, not the feathers! You wouldn't!! Please NO! Anything but the feathers! I'm deathly ticklish!

IVAN
You are forcing our hands and leaving us no choice, Eric Thompson!

> *Ivan and Boris both begin tickling Eric with the feathers.*

ERIC
    (Laughing hysterically)
  Alright-
    (laughs)
  Alright, I'll-
    (laughs)
  Talk… Just PLEASE stop tickling me!

    *Ivan and Boris both stop tickling, throw
    the feathers and look at each other
    smirking.*

IVAN
  I had a feeling you'd see it our way!

ERIC
  I mean, I don't know… I guess if I had to
  figure out my best advice for choosing a
  costume to enter in the contest, I'd have to
  say keeping it realistic. Show what you know.
  You know, just be something that represents
  your life and who you are.

BORIS
  I mean of course! So simple, yet so complex!
  This makes total sense! Brother, let's create
  the perfect costume for the contest tonight!

IVAN
  Eric Thompson, you may go… but only on one
  condition!

ERIC
  Sure! What is it?

IVAN
  You must attend the contest as a spectator
  tonight so that you have to watch us be
  crowned the winners of this year's
  competition!

ERIC
  Absolutely! I'll be there front and center!

ERIC (Cont.)
  Good luck!

> *Ivan and Boris run off stage to prepare for the contest.*

LX - Blackout

SCENE TWO

The Costume Contest.

ANNOUNCER
  It is my pleasure to welcome everybody to the 8th Annual Pleasant Valley Halloween Costume Contest!

  This year's winner is…

  Drumroll, please……

> *Boris and Ivan are dressed in clown costumes and start giving each other high fives and chest bumps sure that they have it in the bag.*

ANNOUNCER
  …Eric Thompson for his costume: Hostage Victim!

> *Eric stands up on stage with the chair still attached to him, his arms still behind his back, blindfold around his neck and the rubber chicken in his hand as he bows… confused. He then shrugs to Ivan and Boris.*

END PLAY

Kuchisake-onna
By Marilyn Ollett

CHARACTERS
  YUREI - *The Protagonist*
  CHILD 1 - *Played by an Adult*
  CHILD 2 - *Played by an Adult*
  FATHER

SETTING
  A Noh-style Play.

NOTES
  There are numerous versions of the legend
  of Kuchisake-onna, the most common being
  that she was the adulterous wife of a
  Samurai. As punishment for her infidelity,
  her husband sliced the corners of her
  mouth from ear to ear. Upon her death, she
  returned as an onryõ - a vengeful spirit.

  Yurei is Japanese for Ghost.

*There is a bench at the back of the stage
on which sit FATHER, CHILD 1 and CHILD 2.
The musicians sit down stage right.*

                              SD - Eerie

*YUREI enters dressed in Geisha attire. She
wears a golden mask of great beauty and
walks as if gliding.
She stops mid-stage.*

                      SD - Happy and gentle

*Yurei mimes looking at herself in the
mirror and brushing her hair and nods. She
circles to the side of the stage and
observes from the shadows.*

                              SD - Eerie

Child 1 and 2 come forward.

                           SD - Playful

*Child 1 and 2 mime happily skipping and
playing hopscotch.*

Yurei steps out of the shadows.

                           SD - Silence

YUREI
  Children, how happily you play. Your smiles
  light the sky. May I play with you today?

        *Yurei kneels and motions for the children
        to come closer.*

                        SD - Harsh, urgent

        *Father comes forward, coming between
        Yurei and the children.*

                    142

FATHER
  Away, Yurei. You will not spread your sorrow
  today.

      Father draws a sword and advances on
      Yurei.

YUREI
  I mean no harm to these beautiful children.

FATHER
  Then be gone.

      Yurei slides out of sight.
                              SD - Eerie

      Father gathers the children and herds them
      back to the bench at the rear of the
      stage.

      Yurei returns, now angry and moving with
      less elegance. She picks up a cloak with a
      hood and mimes looking at herself in the
      mirror. She nods (it is an adequate
      disguise) and moves back to the shadows.

      Child 1 comes forward.

                              SD - Happy dance

      Child 1 performs a simple dance.

      Yurei approaches Child 1 at the same time
      Father comes forward. They bow to each
      other (the disguise works). Yurei
      continues walking past Child 1, then stops
      back in the shadows.

      Father looks all around, then nods
      satisfied. He pats Child 1 on the head and
      steps to the side of the stage.

      Yurei walks back to Child 1.

YUREI
  How nicely you dance. May I dance with you a
  while, child?

    Child 1 bow politely.

                SD - Subtly heavier, more sombre

  They both dance.

YUREI
  Do you not think I dance beautifully?

CHILD 1
  Indeed. You dance with great grace.

YUREI
  And do you not think my mask is beautiful?

CHILD 1
  Indeed, your mask is very beautiful

    *Yurei turns her back and removes the gold
    mask.*

YUREI
  And do you think I am beautiful?

    *Yurei turns to reveal a grey mask with a
    grotesque slash where the mouth should be.*

                                    SD - Harsh

    *Child 1 recoils in horrror, trying hard to
    compose himself. He shakily bows.*

CHILD 1
  You look - fine.

YUREI
  In that case, I must leave you to your dance.

*Yurei replaces the gold mask and moves
back into the shadows. Child 1 leaves to
stand next to Father.*

                          SD – Happy, light

*Child 2 comes forward, skipping. He looks
around for Child 1, but finding himself
alone sits, miming reading.*

Yurei approaches, miming holding a book.

                                SD – Eerie
YUREI
  How cleverly you read. May I read with you a
  while, child?

      Child 2 stands and bows politely.

      *Yurei mimes opening a book which she shows
      to Child 2.*

YUREI
  Look. Is this not a beautiful illustration?

CHILD
  Indeed, it is very beautiful.

YUREI
  And do you not think my mask is beautiful?

CHILD 2
  Indeed, your mask is very beautiful.

      *Yurei removes the gold mask to reveal the
      hideous grey mask.*

YUREI
  And do you think that I am beautiful?

                                SD – Harsh

Child 2 recoils in horror.
But then controls himself and bows
politely.

CHILD 2
  Indeed, I think that you are beautiful.

                    SD - Crashing, loud, chaotic

YUREI
  Liar. You shall pay for your untruthfulness.

  Yurei reveals a small knife and slashes at
  the face of Child 2 who falls to the
  floor.

  She places a grey mask, identical to hers
  on his face.

  Yurei glides back into the shadows.

  Father enters and throws himself over
  Child 2 sobbing. He lifts his head and
  looks around but sees nothing.

                              SD - Silence

                    END PLAY

Lenore
By Christine Emmert

CHARACTERS
  LENORE - *Young woman*
  EDGAR - *Young man*
  ANNABEL - *A girl*
  RAVEN - *Plays the violin, does not speak*

SETTING
  A half-crumbled tower of an old castle.

A half-crumbled tower of an old castle. It is growing dark. A young woman enters in a ball gown holding a candle. Her name is LENORE.

After a long moment, a figure emerges from the shadow. He is a handsome and not so-well-dressed young man by the name of EDGAR.

LENORE
Oh thank goodness, you've come. I thought you would not keep your promise.

EDGAR
Why would I leave so beautiful maiden alone here in this haunted ruin.

LENORE
(looks about)
It is a tad depressing. Who did you say lived here?

EDGAR
A maiden who died suddenly during a thunderstorm. She was my first love.

LENORE
Not a happy beginning to our assignation.

EDGAR
She had a weak heart.

LENORE
Is this supposed to be seductive…

                    SD - Roll of thunder

EDGAR
(grasping Lenore)
My love, don't leave me alone in this kingdom by the sea.

LENORE
The ocean is at least fifty miles away.
Have you been drinking again?

EDGAR
...

LENORE
That horrid absinthe! I knew it. You promised...

EDGAR
It is my oxygen. I cannot lie. It inspires me.

LENORE
You told me I inspired you.

EDGAR
Ah yes, you do.

He goes to embrace her again.

SD - Roll of thunder

LENORE
Does this tower leak?

EDGAR
Just a little. Enough to create the dampness
that taxed her lungs and killed her.

LENORE
And who is this 'Her'? Don't tell me there was
a second lady.

EDGAR
Well, yes... after a suitable period of
mourning.

LENORE
How many?

EDGAR
There were five or six...

LENORE
Good lord, Edgar. You are cursed.
(sudden realisation)
I am cursed. In loving you.

EDGAR
Funny. That's what the last one said.

LENORE
No wonder you drink and smoke the pipe…

EDGAR
Ah yes, my pipe of dreams.

LENORE
Opium.

EDGAR
Don't say it with such disdain. It has yielded
many a stanza…

LENORE
But quoth the Raven 'Nevermore.'
Remember that's what that bird said the last
time you had a vision.

EDGAR
And then I wrote a poem about your name. And
then I met you. From out of a vision.

LENORE
I picked you out of the gutter in front of my
door. Literally. Then I found out you were the
famous writer…

EDGAR
That your father forbade you to read.

LENORE
And still does. He wouldn't be happy I'm here.

> *They sit down on pieces of the ruined
> tower.*

LENORE
He thinks I'm at a concert. Improving my mind.
Not ravishing my body.

EDGAR
Ah yes, the ravishment.

LENORE
But where? These stones aren't very appealing.

EDGAR
The place is a bit run down.

LENORE
Nevermore, to quote the Raven. Next time we go
to a proper house with a proper bedroom.

EDGAR
    (aside)
Should there be a next time.

LENORE
What? What did you say?

EDGAR
You mentioned I was cursed.

                    SD - Roll of thunder

EDGAR
There is never a second time.

LENORE
That doesn't seem… very fair.

EDGAR
I would agree. It comes from an old family
legend that I should never be happy.

LENORE
You personally?

EDGAR
  Any of the males.

LENORE
  It can't make the women very happy either. And
  also how do you keep the line going?

EDGAR
  I don't see…

LENORE
  If the women are to die after a night with
  you, where do all the babies come from?

EDGAR
  I never thought about that.

LENORE
  We live in an age of science.

EDGAR
  Well, I…

LENORE
  Did you not have a mother?

EDGAR
  I had a raven from the time I was born. He's
  rather elderly now. But a mother?

LENORE
  What am I doing here with you?

EDGAR
  Not much. Unfortunately.

LENORE
  Do you want to kill me?

EDGAR
  I want to kiss you.

LENORE
  Both end in the same state from what you say –
  death.

EDGAR
  Blame it on the Conquering Worm! It was He who
  made the curse!

LENORE
  I'll remember you all my life, but I think I
  must go.

EDGAR
  On such a night as this?

                              SD - Rolls of thunder

LENORE
  Better a wet virgin than a dead wife.

EDGAR
  I don't like the way this conversation is
  going.

LENORE
  Nor do I. On that we agree.

EDGAR
  But… but…

LENORE
  I wish you luck and happiness. Goodbye!

     She races off.

EDGAR
  Where did I go wrong?

     *A small figure of a girl, ANNABEL, steps
     from behind a pillar. She too is wearing a
     ballgown.*

     Edgar turns.

EDGAR
  Annabel Lee! Where did you come from?

ANNABEL
  Did you think a simple thing like death would
  keep me from you?

EDGAR
  It always has before.

ANNABEL
  Such a night! The sky is moaning under the
  weight of stars. My Edgar needs me once again.

    She claps her hands.

    *A RAVEN with a violin comes and begins to
    play.*

EDGAR
  Oh Annabel, shall we dance?

      *They waltz as the thunder builds and the
      lightning flashes.*

                    END PLAY

Let The Dead Bury The Dead
By Mike Brannon

CHARACTERS
  CLINT BAZEMORE - *A grizzled veteran zombie survivalist*
  EVAN TURNER - *A younger, more desperate man trying to survive the zombie apocalypse*
  KARIN SOMMERS - *Evan's part-time girlfriend*

SETTING
  An old abandoned building, somewhere in what used to be considered "civilization" in the near future or alternate present day.

The stage is briefly quiet, empty, the lights low. Lightning crashes, thunder booms, rain falls in sheets from the black sky. From off in the distance, we hear the low, gravelly murmur of the undead as they get closer, and closer…

Suddenly, we hear shouting and cursing.

CLINT bangs open the upstage door, holding a shotgun in one hand and dragging EVAN with the other. He glances around, throws Evan into the room – then turns and securely latches the door.

EVAN
        (panicking)
  Jesus. Jesus, they're everywhere. Did they follow us here? Did they follow us? Christ, I've never seen a zombie swarm that large. I thought we'd be okay in the RV. I thought we'd be OK. Jesus Christ, they were everywhere.

CLINT
  Keep it down.

EVAN
  What? Oh, right. Sorry. I'm just a little freaked out. Jesus. I've never seen so many… Jesus. Wait. Hold on. Karin. Where's Karin? What happened to Karin?

CLINT
  Who?

EVAN
  Karin. My girlfriend Karin. She was in the RV with me. Did she get out? Is she OK?

  Evan runs up to the door at the back of the room, unlatches it, swings it open, and begins shouting into the storm.

EVAN
     (screaming)
   Karin! Karin!!!

     *Clint marches back and grabs Evan by the
     shoulder, shoving him to the side; Evan
     stumbles, falls as Clint bolts the door.*

CLINT
   Are you out of your goddamn mind?!?

EVAN
   I'm sorry… I'm sorry… It's just that… Well, I
   mean, Karin and I… We've only been together
   for a few months… but I still can't… I can't
   believe…

     *Clint sighs and pulls a metal flask out of
     his pocket.*

CLINT
   It's okay. I understand. Here. Drink this.

     *Clint hands the flask to Evan, who takes
     it somewhat reluctantly.*

     *Evan sits down in the chair,
     contemplating.*

CLINT
   If it makes you feel any better… it was too
   late for her. The swarm was overpowering.
   There's no way she survived.

EVAN
   Sure, but… I mean, if somehow there was a way…

CLINT
   There wasn't. Trust me. Drink.

     *Evan sags somewhat in his seat, then kicks
     back a shot and chokes.*

EVAN

What the hell?!? What is that- paint
thinner?!?

CLINT

Everclear 151. Close enough, I suppose.

EVAN

Holy shit. That's almost pure grain alcohol.
That stuff is strong enough to eat a hole
through your stomach lining.

CLINT
      (squinting)
You got some kind of plan to live forever?

      Evan looks down at the flask, considering.

EVAN

I guess not. I guess none of us do.

      He sips gingerly from the flask and
      winces.

EVAN

I suppose I should feel lucky to be alive.

A few months ago, I was a pharmaceutical rep
with a nice cushy office. Now look at me -
dirty, bleeding, scared all to shit. And I
can't stop shaking. Look, here… I can't stop
shaking.

Man, when those hulking things lunged through
my windows… I thought I was done for. And then
you shot that big bald guy with the yellow
eyes… and dragged me off to safety…

CLINT

Don't mention it.
      (Pause)
How are you feeling?

EVAN

How am I feeling? I'm feeling good. Well, I'm feeling okay. To be honest with you, I'm think I'm feeling…

Evan glances down at the flask and then back at Clint, then down at the flask again. He throws the flask down and leaps from his seat.

EVAN

Wait a minute- What the hell- Did you just poison me?!? Is that your plan? Drug me, torture me, perform some sort of sadistic Edgar Allen Poe, Pit and the Pendulum type shit on me? Is that your plan, you sick son of a bitch? Answer me. Answer me!

Clint just stares at Evan, who eventually calms down.

EVAN

You're right, you're right- I'm sorry- that's crazy talk. I know you didn't poison me. Sorry. Everything that's happened… I guess we all go a little bit crazy sometimes.

CLINT

It's all right. I understand. Times like these… seems like every B-movie horror cliché suddenly applies…

Suddenly, KARIN, bangs on the door.

KARIN

Hello? Hello? Is anybody in there?

EVAN

Karin???

Evan leaps to his feet; Clint catches him by the shoulder and spins him around. Karin continues to beat on the door.

KARIN
   Evan? Evan, is that you? Help me, Evan. I'm
   bleeding… I don't… I don't know what's
   happening to me…

EVAN
   Let me go! Let me go! She's-

CLINT
   She's already gone, son. She's bit, and she'll
   turn. She's already dead. You have to let her
   go.

EVAN
      (still struggling)
   What are you talking about? I hear her. She's
   alive. She's right there.

CLINT
      (angrily)
   You want proof? You want to see? Here.

   *Clint tosses Evan to the side, reaches for
   his shotgun and marches to the back door.
   Clint slams back the latch, yanks the door
   open and grabs Karin, throwing her into
   the room.*

   *Evan starts to dart towards Karin, but
   freezes when Clint points the shotgun at
   him.*

EVAN
   What do you think you're doing?

   In the middle of the room, Karin retches.

KARIN
      (shivering)
   Evan… Evan, I don't… I don't think I can…

   *Karin looks down and touches the red blood
   that is oozing from her stomach.*

She takes a step toward Evan, and then falls to the ground.

EVAN
  Karin!!! My God, we have to help her-

CLINT
  Don't you dare move a goddamn muscle. You wanted to watch? Fine. Watch. You need to see what happens.

KARIN
  Oh, God, I'm bleeding – I'm bleeding – those things, they bit me, I… I think I'm going to be sick.

  Karin retches again, then looks up.

KARIN
  Evan? Oh, Evan, you're here. Thank God you're here. Thank God you're all right. Help me, Evan. Please. I'm bleeding… I don't feel…

  Karin collapses. Evan takes a quick step forward, but is stopped by Clint's gun.

  There is a beat as they stare at her.

EVAN
  Oh my God… is she dead? I think she's dead.

CLINT
  Not exactly. Watch. Watch what happens next.

  On the floor, Karin twitches.

  After a moment, she coughs, then stumbles to her feet, staring at Evan incomprehensively.

KARIN (as HISPANIC WOMAN)
  ¿Que esta pasando? ¿Por qué estoy aquí?

EVAN
     (confused)
  What? I don't understand.

KARIN (as HISPANIC WOMAN)
  ¿Que esta pasando? ¡Tú no eres mi marido! ¿Qué
  le pasó a mi familia?

EVAN
  I don't speak Spanish. Karin didn't… Neither
  of us spoke Spanish…

     Karin clutches her gut again, spasming.
     Clint readies his shotgun.

CLINT
  The herd probably fed upon some Hispanic
  family somewhere. But just watch. Watch what's
  happening.

     Karin lurches up again, taking on the
     voice of an Elderly Southern Woman. She
     turns on Evan reproachfully.

KARIN (as ELDERLY SOUTHERN WOMAN)
  You shouldn't have gone after them. You should
  have stayed with us. Let the dead bury the
  dead, Pa. Let the dead bury the dead…

EVAN
     (bewildered)
  What?

KARIN (as ELDERLY SOUTHERN WOMAN)
     (shrieking)
  Let the dead bury the dead!

     Karin shivers, jerks again, and then
     screams monstrously.
     Clint cocks his shotgun; Karin turns
     towards the sound, and he fires, knocking
     her back into a heap at the other side of
     the stage.

EVAN
    (screaming)
  Karin!!!

    Evan sinks down to his knees and weeps;
    Clint breaks open the shotgun and begins
    reloading.

EVAN
  I don't understand. I don't understand what's
  going on.

CLINT
  It took me a while to figure it out. Most
  people don't get to see what really happens.
  People get grabbed, people get eaten. Nobody
  sees a thing. But if you're patient, and
  quiet, and you sit and you watch…

EVAN
  Jesus. I can't stop shaking. I need a drink.
  Jesus.

    Evan picks the flask up from off the
    ground, uncaps it, sits down in the chair
    and takes a long pull.

CLINT
  At the end, when the disease takes hold… all
  of the memories of the victims come bubbling
  up to the surface. Maybe these zombies don't
  have thoughts and feelings of their own…
  maybe… maybe they eat other people to somehow
  capture their essence, their emotions… so they
  can feel something again.

EVAN
  I don't… God, I don't feel good. My stomach is
  twisted… tied up in knots…

    From behind Evan, Clint puts the shotgun
    on the ground, and pulls a pair of shiny
    handcuffs from his pocket.

CLINT
I understand, son. I know exactly what you're going through.

Evan sits down and Clint springs into action. He grabs Evan's wrist, slaps the handcuff on it, then twists it back and grabs for Evan's other arm.
Evan fights to get free.

CLINT
Hold still. Hold still, you stupid son of a bitch.

EVAN
What the - what the hell do you think -

Clint wrenches Evan's other arm back and locks on the other handcuff through the back of the chair. Evan continues to struggle, futilely.

CLINT
Just sit still…

EVAN
    (screaming)
Help!!! Help!!! Somebody, help me! Help me!

CLINT
Bah, quit your yapping, you zombie-infested fuck. You think anybody cares enough to help you? There's nobody in this whole goddamn world that gives two shit about you. So shut the fuck up.

EVAN
Please, man, please. Don't do this. Don't do this. Whatever you think of me, please, don't do this. Look, I'm not one of them! I'm not! I'm a human being, just like you!

CLINT
  You're a human right now. That won't last
  long.

EVAN
  What do you mean?

      *Clint bends down, picks the metal flask up
      off the ground, and takes a chug.*

CLINT
  You've been bit.

EVAN
  What? No- no, I haven't. That's ridiculous.

CLINT
  See that blood coming from your arm?

EVAN
  That's… I probably caught it against the metal
  siding of the RV when you dragged me out…

CLINT
  Nah. You remember that bald fucker with the
  yellow eyes who came through the window of the
  RV? I was watching him through binoculars, saw
  him take a big old juicy bite out of your arm.
  Last thing he did before I put a bullet in his
  head.

EVAN
  Wait… you… you were watching me? You were
  watching me, and you let that thing… you let
  that thing bite me???

CLINT
  Of course, I did. I've been waiting on a
  moment like this for weeks now, waiting for
  the same zombie to grab ahold of someone.
  Almost got my chance at the Piggly Wiggly in
  Gastonia, but the lady bled out before I could
  get to her. I almost lost hope… and then I saw

CLINT (Cont.)
you getting out of your rust-colored Coachman in the woods… and I knew I'd found my mark.

Evan sputters, then chokes a bit, and vomits on the floor beside him. Clint ignores him and continues talking.

Eight minutes. First the tremors, then the nausea. Right on schedule. Anyway, in the end, it was pretty easy. All I had to do was lead the zombie pack over to your little clearing and wait for them to do their thing. It was simple… Not like you were smart enough to properly barricade your home or put the lights out at night.

EVAN
(beginning to slur his words)
You're crazy. Nobody would do that. You led them to me? You wanted them to bite me? Why? Why would you…?

Clint crosses to the other side of the stage, finds a folding chair and drags it over so he can sit next to Evan. He glances at his watch, then at the puddle of vomit on the floor.

CLINT
I'd managed to protect my family, to keep my wife and my daughter safe, since the very first hordes started invading our towns. We kept on the move. I scrounged for supplies, and my wife Marsha kept an eye on Matilda. That was my daughter's name. Matilda. Eight years old, never lost that childlike innocence, even when… even in the worst…

Evan slumps in his seat, gurgling. Clint gets up from his seat and starts pacing back and forth as Evan gasps for air.

CLINT
I was coming back from a Chevron station in
Athens when I saw the zombie mob breaking
through the steel shutters on the house. I
ran, and I ran, and by the time I'd gotten
there… My wife was gone. My daughter was gone.
That goddamn bald bastard was staring at me
with those unholy yellow eyes, and I knew- I
knew, if it was the last thing I'd ever do…

I'd get my chance to say goodbye.

> *Evan takes one last deep breath and then*
> *dies with a long sigh.*

> *Clint sits down in his own chair, waiting.*

CLINT
I'm sorry, kid. I'm sorry you had to go out
this way. If there was… if there was only some
other way…

> *Evan stirs in his chair.*
> *Clint stands up and then kneels in front*
> *of Evan, peering eagerly.*

CLINT
Marsha? Marsha? Can you hear me? Are you in
there?

EVAN (as MARSHA)
Clint? Clint, is that you?

CLINT
       (taking Evan's hand)
I'm here, baby. I'm here.

EVAN (as MARSHA)
You weren't there… You were gone when -

CLINT
I know, Marsha. I know. I'm so sorry. I'm so
sorry.

EVAN (as MARSHA)
  It's all right. It's all right, my darling.

    Evan (as Marsha) *struggles against the handcuffs.*

EVAN (as MARSHA)
  My hands… Why can't I…?

CLINT
  Oh, my love, I'm so sorry. Here. Let me help
  you with that…

    Clint reaches back and unlocks the handcuffs. Then, he moves back around in front of Evan (as Marsha) *who puts his arms around Clint's shoulders as he weeps.*

EVAN (as MARSHA)
  Sssh, sssh, it's all right. It's all right.
  It's not your fault. It's not your fault. You
  were always there for us…

    Evan (as Marsha) begins fading.

    Clint reaches over and holds the hands of his wife, gazing into her face.

CLINT
  I love you, Marsha. I always have. Ever since
  we were in grade school together. When we
  moved into that tiny apartment in Anderson.
  When Matilda came along. When we had that
  miscarriage, when we fought, and when we would
  make up. I've always loved you. I always will.

EVAN (As MARSHA)
  I love you… I love you, too…

    Evan slumps over again as Marsha dies. Clint remains holding her hands as, slowly, the glimmer of his child, Matilda, lights up Evan's face.

EVAN (as MATILDA)
  Daddy?

CLINT
  Oh, my Matilda. Oh, my sweet baby girl.

    Clint grabs Evan (as Matilda) and hugs him
    tightly, sobbing as he does.

EVAN (as MATILDA)
  I miss you, Daddy.

CLINT
  I miss you, too. It's okay, baby. You don't
  have to be afraid. I'll be with you soon. It's
  okay. Daddy will be with you soon…

    Evan (as Matilda) shudders, slumps over,
    and then Matilda dies. Clint staggers back
    a bit, and collapses in a heap.
    After a pause, Evan begins reanimating,
    reaching out for Clint, who remains on the
    floor, looking up at him.
    Simultaneously, Karin begins crawling over
    from where she had fallen onto the floor,
    groaning and hissing.

CLINT
  All right, you zombie sons of bitches. All
  right. Come and get me. Come and get me. You
  bite me, I blast your fucking head off, and
  then my wife and my child get one more chance
  to live. It's all right. It's all right. Come
  and get me.

    Karin cackles. Evan lunges at Clint and
    begins feasting on him.
    Clint screams.

                              LX - Fade to Black
                              SD - Gun shot
            END PLAY

Memento Mori
By Donna Latham

CHARACTERS
  ANNABELLE — *Female, a ghost*
  LUCRETIA — *Female, a daguerreotype photographer*
  CAPTAIN RUNDLE — *Male, a British firefighter*
  LOUISE — *Female, Captain Rundle's widow*

SETTING
  Nineteenth Century.
  A Memento Mori Shoppe specialising in Daguerreotype photography. The veil between life and death is flimsy.

SCENE ONE

Lights on LUCRETIA, who hangs a newly developed daguerreotype among other images.

ANNABELLE
        (Offstage)
    Lucretia, help!

Lights on ANNABELLE, who's trying to position slumped CAPTAIN RUNDLE on a chair.

LUCRETIA
    Corpus bones! Who the devil—?

Lucretia helps Annabelle position Captain Rundle. Though she does not see or hear Annabelle, they interact.

ANNABELLE
    Wretched scoundrel dumped this poor soul at our doorstep. Like a busted sack of gravel.

LUCRETIA
    Holy Mother Mary...

ANNABELLE
    There's blood clotted round his neck—

LUCRETIA
    Blood crusted at his mouth—

ANNABELLE
    Stomped and battered as an old boot.

LUCRETIA
    Poor soul's met a terrible end. His face wears the very image of torment.

Lucretia crosses herself.

ANNABELLE
  Despicable!

        Annabelle uses a handkerchief to wipe away
        blood from Captain Rundle's face.

LUCRETIA
  Is he a corpse for a Memento?

ANNABELLE
  I reckon so. But whose dang corpse?

LUCRETIA
  Who so inhumanly deposited this broken,
  desecrated body? Has he no loved ones?

        Lucretia searches Captain Rundle's
        clothes. She turn faces from the stench.

ANNABELLE
  Gawd, what a stench. Reckon he done drowned
  hisself in a vat of moonshine mash.

LUCRETIA
  There's no note. No name, no address. Who—?

ANNABELLE
  Search the feller's britches and waistcoat.

        Lucretia turns out his pockets.

LUCRETIA
  Nor pocketwatch.

ANNABELLE
  Not even a calling card. A big ole heap of
  nothin'. Blast furnace in hell.

LUCRETIA
  Not one clue to the poor soul's identity.

ANNABELLE
  Well, I'm rendered thoroughly kumfumbled.

ANNABELLE (Cont.)
  (To Captain Rundle)
  I'm awful sorry for the terrible treatment
  befell ya'll, Mister.

      Captain Rundle sits up straight, adjusts
      clothing, combs hair and smooths mustache.
      Lucretia doesn't respond to him, although
      Annabelle does.

CAPTAIN RUNDLE
  Quite kind of you, my dear. And it's Captain.

LUCRETIA
  Shroud Monsieur for now. And wash him later.

ANNABELLE
  And then—?

LUCRETIA
  Someone's sure to come for their dearly
  departed.

CAPTAIN RUNDLE
  I hope…

ANNABELLE
  From your sweet lips to the eager ears of God.

CAPTAIN RUNDLE
  I'm afraid Mrs. Rundle will be terribly
  distressed.

ANNABELLE
  Mrs—?

CAPTAIN RUNDLE
  My wife, Louise Rundle. We live in the white
  cottage. 'Round the corner. Well, she does.

LUCRETIA
  After five years in this city? I'm still
  unaccustomed to its rough ways.

CAPTAIN RUNDLE
  Louise doesn't like when I tipple at the
  tavern.

LUCRETIA
  We never should have left—

ANNABELLE
  Hush, Lucretia! It's not so! We fashioned a
  righteous life here.

LUCRETIA
  If we hadn't journeyed here to start our
  business?

CAPTAIN RUNDLE
  Insists nothing good comes of carousing.

LUCRETIA
  The calamitous event wouldn't have—

CAPTAIN RUNDLE
  Indeed.

LUCRETIA
  The fire that— No, no, stop. Mustn't think
  about it.

ANNABELLE
  Ain't that the truth, Dearheart?

LUCRETIA
  What's done is done.

ANNABELLE
  Got that right. Now this here feller? Deader
  than a crawdaddy in dry dirt.

CAPTAIN RUNDLE
  Tut-tut, no need to be crass.

LUCRETIA
  Mercy. Where are we to store you, Monsieur?

ANNABELLE
Got us a right full house tonight.

LUCRETIA
Forgive me, Monsieur. I mean no disrespect.
But I've no time to dilly-dally. The
thunderstorm rustled up a hellish heat, and
many souls beckon.

ANNABELLE
Reckon it's hotter than blazes. Gonna have to
shroud the poor devil right here.

CAPTAIN RUNDLE
Must you? It's terribly humid. Dear…?

ANNABELLE
It's Annabelle.

CAPTAIN RUNDLE
Annabelle, won't you get a message to Louise?

SCENE TWO

Lucretia is escorting LOUISE offstage.

LOUISE
I—I can't thank you enough, Lucretia. For
tending to the Captain.

LUCRETIA
My pleasure. I now the comfort these images
provide. If only—

LOUISE
Must be so hard for you. All by your lonesome
here.

LUCRETIA
Well…

ANNABELLE
Plenty of company here, Ma'am.

Annabelle pats Lousie's arm.

LUCRETIA
  I'll send for you when the daguerreotypes are
  ready.

LOUISE
  Bless you.

  Louise Exits.
  Lucretia struggles to attach Captain
  Rundle to the photography stand. Annabelle
  assists her.

CAPTAIN RUNDLE
  My dear, Annabelle. You're strong as a
  quarryman.

LUCRETIA
  Dapper again, eh? He hails from the peninsula
  of Cornwall and will sail back to his people
  for burial. Mrs. Rundle wishes a lifelike pose
  to remember her husband.

ANNABELLE
  She don't much care for the repose of eternal
  slumber? Can't say as I blame her. It's final.

LUCRETIA
  I fashioned a portrait of the Rundles earlier.

ANNABELLE
  Dang, I missed it. How'd you pose them?

LUCRETIA
  Nestled together on the sofa like lovebirds.
  With a halo of roses above them. A private
  keepsake for the grieving widow.

  Image of woman nestled with man, eyes
  closed and clearly deceased, on a sofa. A
  rose wreath is behind their heads.

ANNABELLE
I will ever adore your tender heart.

LUCRETIA
A Memento works wonders. It soothes the
mournful soul. If I could shift Time's sands,
I'd— No! No, Lucretia! Smother that thought.

ANNABELLE
You conjure magic with daguerreotypes.

> *Annabelle* kisses *Lucretia*'s hand who holds
> the kissed hand to her own cheek for a
> beat.

LUCRETIA
Death is an inevitable part of life. So I tell
myself. Don't I, Captain Rundle?

ANNABELLE
Guess he's plum tuckered with the heat
prostration.

> *Lucretia continues to attach Captain*
> *Rundle to the photography stand.*

LUCRETIA
So I tell myself in these unending, sleepless
nights. But I find no Balm of Gilead.

ANNABELLE
Death is ever nippin' at our heels.

LUCRETIA
It's inevitable. Perhaps if I claim so often
enough? I'll believe it.

ANNABELLE
Well, heck. That ravenous beast can kiss my
big round bum.

LUCRETIA
Ouch!

ANNABELLE
  Careful, Lucretia.

LUCRETIA
  Pinched my fingers in the crank.

ANNABELLE
  Those delicate hands are an artist's tools.
  And that knowing eye…

LUCRETIA
  I wish to capture the deceased's essence.
  Transform a bereaved lover's melancholy ache.
  Create joy in remembrance. Wish I'd created an
  image of my own beloved— Oh, why must my mind
  ever stray to what I forbid it to?

ANNABELLE
  Drawn to it. Like a tongue. Yep. On one of
  them grievous canker sores. Jest leave it be.

LUCRETIA
  What's done is done.

ANNABELLE
  Ain't never gonna be undone.

LUCRETIA
  I've not a moment for self-pity! Humidity is
  having its way with him.

ANNABELLE
  Rub the peppermint oil under your nostrils
  right quick. It's the only Balm we got round
  here.

      *Lucretia rubs oil from a little vial under
      her nose.*

LUCRETIA
  Let's affix his neck first.

ANNABELLE
Now suck in that breath real, real hard,
Dearheart. Poor feller's ripe as a rotten
goose egg.

    Lucretia struggles to speak through held
    breath. She twists the crank.

LUCRETIA
Hurry!

    Annabelle places her hands over Lucretia's
    and helps to twist the crank.

ANNABELLE
A few more twists of the crank.

LUCRETIA
    (*Still struggling. Twists crank.*)
Quickly!

ANNABELLE
Attached! Like a cocklebur on a billy goat's
fur. No disrespect meant, Cap'n.

    Lucretia exhales a great gasp of air.

ANNABELLE
Ready for the shoulders?

    Annabelle pauses to blot her brow and wipe
    peppermint oil under nose.

LUCRETIA
    (*Feeling Captain Rundle's midsection*)
Belly's swelling. Soon his uniform won't fit
round his middle.

ANNABELLE
Crankin' lickety-split.

LUCRETIA
About to burst his buttons!

ANNABELLE
  Dang-diggity crank jammed.

LUCRETIA
  Hold tight, Sir.

        Lucretia dashes to get oil can from table.
        Then oils the crank.

ANNABELLE
  Brilliant, Dearheart! Quick as greased
  lightning. Tell you what. Fixin' to get things
  done? Takes a good Southern woman.

LUCRETIA
  Perfect! He's proud and tall.

ANNABELLE
  You fixin' to make a standing portrait? For
  Cap'n's comrades?

LUCRETIA
  He was a man of vitality and action.

ANNABELLE
  Chopped down like a pawpaw tree by unknown
  ruffians.

LUCRETIA
  His widow hankers for a portrait in his fire
  brigade uniform.

        Lucretia pins a badge to Captain Rundle's
        shirt and places a hat on his head. She
        fusses to get it just right.

ANNABELLE
  Dignified as all get-out. Ready to hop the
  last train to glory.

LUCRETIA
  May his dear soul rest in peace.

Lucretia crosses herself. Annabelle fusses with Captain Rundle's face.

ANNABELLE
  More dapper with the eyes propped open. Don't ya think?

LUCRETIA
  Rouge his cheeks…

ANNABELLE
  He's gray about the gills. No disrespect intended, Sir. Just the nature of the beast.

LUCRETIA
  And his mouth…
        (Rouges Captain Rundle)
  I'll add a rosy tint to the image later.

ANNABELLE
  Cap'n, ya'll pure elegant as ever. Just a tad blue round the gullet.

LUCRETIA
  A spray of lavender beneath his collar sweetens him right up.

    Annabelle makes a spray of lavender while Lucretia arranges her equipment.

    Captain Rundle shifts weight.
    The women scream.

    After a few beats, they laugh at their alarm. Lucretia pushes the arm down with great effort and attaches it to the stand.

ANNABELLE
  Reckon I'm a silly goose.

LUCRETIA
  Mercy!

ANNABELLE
  Nearly tinkled in my knickers. Cap'n popped
  loose from the cuff. Death chill stiffened him
  up but good.

LUCRETIA
  I thought he had risen from the—

ANNABELLE
  My heart like to burst through my bazooms.

LUCRETIA
  My teeth are chattering loud enough to rouse
  the dead.

ANNABELLE
  Got enough to rouse in these parts. Law!
  Mouth's dry enough to spin cotton.

    They laugh again for a few beats.

LUCRETIA
    (*Growing serious*)
  Some days these ghastly duties wind me a bit
  tight.

ANNABELLE
  And carcasses piled like bricks around us.

LUCRETIA
  I'll tackle the stench straight off. I don't
  much wish to add myself to the body count.

ANNABELLE
  I'll fancy up Mrs. Brant, yes? Iron her
  Sunday-go-t'meetin clothes so's we can deck
  her out nice and purty. While ya'll make
  Cap'n's portrait.

LUCRETIA
  Clip some fragrant rosemary from the kitchen
  garden…

ANNABELLE
  Lily of the valley too.

LUCRETIA
  A bit of sage…

ANNABELLE
  All's beastly with the stank round here. Foul
  enough to knock a dawg off a gut wagon.

LUCRETIA
  Once I ensure a just death for my charges? I
  fancy a walkabout. Straight into the storm.

ANNABELLE
  We'll stroll arm in arm, Dearheart.

LUCRETIA
  Yes, in the cool, fresh air.

ANNABELLE
  I must get my lady outside in the daylight.
  Y'all spend entirely too much time hunkered in
  darkness.

    Lucretia takes images of Captain Rundle.

                            SD - Howling wind

    She pauses and listens.

LUCRETIA
  Oh, it's just the wind. Almost as if I hear
  your voice, Captain.

CAPTAIN RUNDLE
  Kind Lucretia, let me breathe a message in
  your ear. The missing love you spoke of?

LUCRETIA
  Yes?

CAPTAIN RUNDLE
  Self-same whom cruel fates devoured in the
  shipyard flames?

LUCRETIA
  What of her?

CAPTAIN RUNDLE
  She came home to you.

LUCRETIA
  No, she—

CAPTAIN RUNDLE
  The love for whom you have not wept—

LUCRETIA
  My love perished in the inferno. Death denied
  me a daguerreotype.

CAPTAIN RUNDLE
  She is with you always.

LUCRETIA
  My love is gone. I must accept that finality.

CAPTAIN RUNDLE
  She is ever at your side.

LUCRETIA
  Would that she were. Now, hold that pose, sir.
  And… hold it…

ANNABELLE
  Kind Lucretia—

LUCRETIA
  Splendid!

ANNABELLE
  I will always adore your tender heart.

LUCRETIA
  Your face is tranquil as moonlight, Captain.

ANNABELLE
  How could I ever leave you?

LUCRETIA
  And… another!

      Annabelle stands behind Captain Rundle.

LUCRETIA
  One more!

      *Annabelle poses for photograph with
      Captain Rundle.*

ANNABELLE
  A Memento works wonders.

      *Image of Captain Rundle with Annabelle
      posed behind him.*

LUCRETIA
      (Gasps, crosses herself)
  Annabelle! My love!

ANNABELLE
  A Memento soothes the mournful soul.

LUCRETIA
  You—

ANNABELLE
  I walked through fire.

LUCRETIA
  You came home—

ANNABELLE
  Fierce as a squall.

LUCRETIA
  Came home.

ANNABELLE
  Strong as a quarryman.

LUCRETIA
  Came home to me.

ANNABELLE
  With no earthly need of a body. Evermore.

LUCRETIA
  Evermore, my love.

                    END PLAY

Olly Olly Oxen Free
By Jacquelyn Priskorn

CHARACTERS
  JESSY - *Not safe*
  MARTY - *Looking for safety*
  OFFSTAGE VOICE - *A menacing voice*

SETTING
  A circle made of stones.

JESSY runs on stage and straight to the center of the stone circle.

JESSY
  Olly olly oxen free! You can't get me!

MARTY runs on to the stage, out of breath.

MARTY
  Aw, c'mon!

JESSY
  Ha! Ha!

MARTY
  Fine. You win. Come on out.

JESSY
  No way! I come out, you'll get me!

MARTY
  No I won't. It's over. You won.

JESSY
  Yeah, right. It's never over. You'll start
  everything over the second I come out. You'll
  get me.

MARTY
  I promise. I won't.

JESSY
  Nope. Not coming out.

MARTY
  Like, ever?

JESSY
  Maybe.

MARTY
  That's dumb.

JESSY
  Nuh-uh. Dumb would be leaving safety and
  letting you get me.

MARTY
  I'm not gonna!

JESSY
  I don't believe you.

MARTY
  You have to!

JESSY
  No I don't.

MARTY
  So, what? You're gonna just stay there
  forever, then?

JESSY
  Maybe.

MARTY
  You're being stupid.

JESSY
  You're being stupid. I'm being smart.

MARTY
  If you don't leave, we can't play any new
  games.

JESSY
  You'd like that, wouldn't you?

MARTY
  Um, yeah.

JESSY
  Of course. So YOU can win.

MARTY
    You might win, too.

JESSY
    But I for sure won't lose if I stay right here.

MARTY
    What if I came in there, too?

JESSY
    You can't come in here! This is safety!

MARTY
    I want to be safe, too.

JESSY
    I'm trying to be safe from you.

MARTY
    I'm not gonna do anything.

JESSY
    Well, you can't do anything in here anyway.
    Because if you do, it doesn't count.

MARTY
    Okay then, I'm coming in.

JESSY
    Um, okay then.

        *Jessy tenses up as Marty enters the
        circle.*

MARTY
    Olly olly oxen free?

JESSY
    Why did you say it?

MARTY
    I dunno. It's not really safe unless you say
    it, right?

JESSY
I guess not. But if you're "it" you're
technically not supposed to be in here anyway.

MARTY
Unless the game has changed.

JESSY
Well, no one told me the game was changing.

MARTY
Sometimes it just changes.

JESSY
I don't like that. That's why I think I should
just stay here.

MARTY
Maybe I should stay here, too.

JESSY
I don't think that's a good idea.

MARTY
Why not? I don't want to be alone out there.
That's no fun.

JESSY
I don't think you're alone out there.

OFFSTAGE VOICE
Come out, come out wherever you are!

MARTY
Oh yeah. I forgot about that game.

OFFSTAGE VOICE
You can't hide forever!

MARTY
I don't have to hide at all! We're in olly
olly oxen free!

JESSY
  I don't think they're playing by the same
  rules as you.

MARTY
  What do you mean?

JESSY
  This feels very familiar.

MARTY
  Wait. How long have we been playing?

JESSY
  It feels like always.

MARTY
  Yeah.

JESSY
  But you just got here.

MARTY
  I did?

JESSY
  This wasn't always a game.

OFFSTAGE VOICE
  Just wait until I find you!

MARTY
  I don't think I like the sound of that. Maybe
  we should call time out?

JESSY
  That won't work.

MARTY
  But those are the rules. If I call time out,
  the game stops. You'll be safe, too.

JESSY
  I don't think so.

OFFSTAGE VOICE
  Marty! Where are you?!

JESSY
  Don't answer.

MARTY
  I'm just going to call time out.

JESSY
  Even if you call time out, your time will
  still run out.

MARTY
  That's not fair. If they can't play right,
  then we should just quit.

JESSY
  I don't get to play anymore.

MARTY
  Well, I don't want to play anymore.

JESSY
  I remember. I remember I said that, too. It
  didn't matter. My time still ran out.

MARTY
  I don't get it. No one got you. You're in olly
  olly oxen free.

JESSY
  They didn't play by the rules.

MARTY
  Didn't?

JESSY
  I was never safe. And neither are you.

MARTY
   I said olly olly oxen free. It counts.

JESSY
   It doesn't.

MARTY
   Those are the rules.

JESSY
   There are no rules.

MARTY
   Then there is no game.

OFFSTAGE VOICE
   I'm not playing with you, Marty! You better
   come out! Now!

JESSY
   They make you think it's a game at first. You
   think it will be fun. But there's no way to
   win-

MARTY
   -There is no game.

JESSY
   Not for you.

MARTY
   Olly olly oxen free?

JESSY
   Was never real. I remember now.

MARTY
   I don't want to lose. I'm scared.

JESSY
   It's very scary to lose. But once you lose,
   you never have to play again.

MARTY
I want to play a different game. Let's play a
different game.

JESSY
I told you, I don't get to play anymore.

MARTY
Then why are you here?

JESSY
This is where they left me when their game was
done.

MARTY
Left you? You should go home!

JESSY
You should go home.

MARTY
So should you!

JESSY
I wanted the game to be over. I let myself be
found. I said, "I give up. You win." But they
tagged me anyway.

MARTY
You gave up?

JESSY
I was in olly olly oxen free. I said, "Time
out! I quit!" It didn't matter. They kept
tagging me.

MARTY
Tagging?

JESSY
Over and over. Harder and harder. They tagged
me until my words fell wet and sticky from my
mouth.

MARTY
  What?

JESSY
  The game is only over when they're the only
  player left.

MARTY
  I don't understand. Who are you?

JESSY
  I lost.

OFFSTAGE VOICE
  That's it! Game over, Marty!

MARTY
  I'm scared.

JESSY
  You can't win. But you don't have to lose.

MARTY
  How?

    *Jessy suddenly has blood in their mouth
    and on their hands.*

JESSY
  Run.

    *Marty is terrified, stumbling backwards
    out of the stone circle.*

JESSY
  Run!

OFFSTAGE VOICE
  MARTY!!!

JESSY
  OLLY OLLY OXEN FREE!

                                    LX - Blackout

Playwrights Versus Zombies!
By Christopher Plumridge

CHARACTERS
  STEVE/SARAH - *Playwright, calm, assured*
  NICK/NICOLA - *Playwright, stressed, working to a deadline*
  ZOMBIE MR/MRS HARRIS - *Formally a friendly neighbour from across the hall of Nick's apartment*
  SANDRA/SIMON - *Nick's agent*

  ALL - *Gender irrelevant, any age*

SETTING
  Two playwright's offices/studios.

*Steve's office/studio can be furnished as
seen fit, but must include a desk and
computer/laptop. He should have a TV
remote, but the TV will be 'in the
audience'. STEVE is stood to one side of
his desk/table, he is watching the news on
an unseen TV. He's concerned but not
overly worried.*

*Nick's side is similar, including desk and
laptop, upstage needs to be some balcony
doors leading to a shallow balcony. The
Front door is offstage. NICK is stressed,
typing quickly at his laptop, he curses,
deletes, types again.*

NICK
No no no, this is all trash, complete garbage.
Sandra can't be in Los Angeles. Not while her
mother is there, it just won't tie in!

STEVE
Oh no, really? They're getting everywhere.

NICK
But Sandra has to be in Los Angeles to get the
money. So where on Earth should her mother be?
Her Dad's in New York, so she could be with
her Dad, but no… no no NO!

STEVE
It's about time the army is drafted in,
they're getting out of control.

NICK
Oh but what the hell, no one will notice. Who
am I kidding? Everyone will! Nothing for it,
I'll have to redraft act one! Damn it!

STEVE
And who's going to tidy them all up now that
the… Oh… New season of Top Gear, cool.

NICK
   Steve will know what to do.

   Nick taps away and waits.

                    SD - Video Call Ringing

STEVE
   I need to tell Nick there's a new season.
      (taps ringing laptop)
   Speak of the devil! Yo, Nick, what's up buddy?

NICK
      (Urgent, almost panicky)
   Sandra's in Los Angeles but she can't be
   because her mother Elaine is there too, only
   Elaine can't be there because her husband's in
   New York, where Elaine should be! So to get
   Elaine back in New York I have to make sure
   Sandra has got all the money because otherwise
   Jeff won't be able to see Elaine!

STEVE
   So are you saying Jeff and Elaine are in New
   York?

NICK
   No, only Jeff. But Elaine needs to be there,
   or-

STEVE
   -Are they safe?

NICK
   Yes of course, eh? Why do you ask?

STEVE
   New York isn't that safe at the moment. Too
   many. Who's Jeff?

NICK
   Jeff is Elaine's husband, Sandra's dad. Keep
   up.

STEVE
  Ah, OK. There's a new season of Top Gear
  coming on.

NICK
  Cool.

STEVE
  New hosts apparently.

NICK
  Not cool.

STEVE
  Agreed.

NICK
  So, how do I get Elaine back to New York?

STEVE
  I don't know. Train? Greyhound?

NICK
  You're missing the point.

STEVE
  Am I? Anyway who's Jeff and Elaine? Friends of
  yours? Relatives? Either way they shouldn't be
  here. Not safe.

NICK
  Jeff and Elaine are Sandra's parents!

STEVE
  Yes, we've established that. So…?

NICK
  So I need to get, well, if I don't, well… if I
  don't I will have to completely rewrite act
  one.

STEVE
  Oh, right. Your play.

NICK
  Yes, what did you think I meant?

STEVE
  Have you eaten?

NICK
  No. Why? Does it matter?

STEVE
  To me it does. I'm your friend, I worry. You
  sound hangry.

NICK
  I'm fine. Just a bit touchy. I need to get
  this finished by Thursday noon, otherwise
  Sandra will pull the plug!

STEVE
  Ah yes, Sandra.

  So, tell me why you've named the heroine of
  your latest play after your agent?

NICK
  Because she insisted, said she'll prom… Wait,
  did you say New York is not safe?

STEVE
  When is it ever? But it's worse right now.

NICK
  How so?

STEVE
  They're everywhere.

NICK
  Who's everywhere?

STEVE
  Them!

NICK
  I don't follow.

STEVE
  You know!

NICK
  No.

STEVE
  Really?

NICK
  No. No idea.

STEVE
  Have you had your head in the clouds?

NICK
  I've been too busy writing, as I told you I
  only have until Thursday at lunchtime.

STEVE
  But they must be with you too, I've heard
  they're everywhere now.

NICK
  Mexicans?

STEVE
  No!

NICK
  Then who do you mean? Who are everywhere?

STEVE
  Zombies.

NICK
      (pause)
  Have you eaten?

STEVE
   No, not yet. I have a pizza in the freezer I
   think. Why?

NICK
   I'm your friend, I worry. You sound hangry.

STEVE
   Ah, touché!

NICK
   Seriously man, what, or who are you on about?
   Zombies?

STEVE
   Has Sandra been working you that hard? Have
   you not been watching the news for the last
   three weeks?

NICK
   No. You know I'm busy. This is a big deal. If
   I don't get this written they'll drop it. All
   the actors and crew will be out of work.
   They've already started rehearsals, run starts
   next month.

STEVE
   If they're still alive.

NICK
   What?!

STEVE
   They're everywhere buddy. In every city and
   town, this is already making Covid look like a
   kitten!

NICK
   Wow, really? Even here in L.A?

STEVE
   I expect so.

NICK
  Wait a minute! Haha well done!

STEVE
  What?

NICK
  You totally had me there!

STEVE
  No, listen Nic-

NICK
  Hook, line and sinker, nice one! Catch me
  while I'm tired and stressed. Revenge will be
  sweet my friend, watch your back haha!

STEVE
  Nick!

NICK
  Haha, brilliant!

STEVE
  NICK!

NICK
  What?

STEVE
  I'm not joking, not this time, put the news
  on, any news. It's everywhere, they are
  EVERYWHERE!

NICK
  Now you want me to Google 'Zombie Apocalypse'
  I guess- Oh OK, I'll humor you.
      (taps at his laptop)
  Oh… but… No! Damn, you're not joking!

STEVE
  I told you. So I wouldn't worry about your
  script for a while. Maybe call Sandra, see if

STEVE (Cont.)
  the cast are still alive or have joined the
  walking dead.

NICK
  That's not funny.

STEVE
  I wasn't trying to be.

      *There is a knocking from Nick's side of
      the stage.*

NICK
  Hold up man, there's someone at the door.

STEVE
  Don't answer it! It might be one of them!

NICK
  I doubt it. I'm on the twenty-seventh floor.

STEVE
  How many times do I have to tell you, they're
  everywhere Nick!

      Another knock on the door.

NICK
  Let me just go check.

STEVE
  No!

NICK
  Relax, I have one of those eye hole peeking
  things in the door, what do they call them?

STEVE
  Squinty holes I think. Just don't open it!

      *Nick goes to his door, holds his face up
      to the door, he recoils.*

NICK
  Yikes!

STEVE
  What's up Shaggy?

NICK
  There's one in the corridor!

STEVE
  Don't let it in.

NICK
  I wasn't planning to!
      (has another look)
  Hold up, I think it's Mr Harris from across
  the hall.

STEVE
  Don't let it in.

NICK
  Him.

STEVE
  It. He's definitely an it now. Sorry buddy.

      Another loud knocking, this time frantic.
      A shout is heard.

NICK
  What do I do? Steve, what do I do? I've never
  met a Zombie before!

STEVE
  Calm down, come to the screen so I can see you
  properly.

      Nick crosses over to the camera.

  That's better, man you look like you've seen a
  ghost!

NICK
  Haha.

STEVE
  Sorry, just sit down for a minute, you've had
  a shock. It's a shocking state of affairs I
  can tell you. Does it smell?

NICK
  Does what smell?

STEVE
  The Zombie that is, I mean was, Mr Harris?

NICK
  I can't smell him through the door.

STEVE
  He can smell you though. That's why he's there
  probably.

NICK
  Why? Why does he want me?

STEVE
  Because he's HANGRY!

NICK
  Honestly man, there's a zombie at my door and
  still you make jokes?

STEVE
  Has he asked for your brain yet?

NICK
  No, he just said 'rain' which is odd because
  he's indoors. Oh… Maybe he did say brain? Do
  they really say "Brains!"?

STEVE
  Not sure to be fair, no one whose got that
  close to one has lived to tell.

Another loud, frantic knocking.

ZOMBIE MR HARRIS
    (Offstage)
  Brains!

NICK
  He's going to break the door down, what do I
  do?

STEVE
  Have you got an escape route? Outdoor steps?

NICK
  No, just a balcony.

STEVE
  Oh, bummer.

NICK
  What are you saying?

STEVE
  So, your only way is through that door and
  past Zombie Mr Harris?

NICK
  …Yes, I guess so.

STEVE
  Then, you'll have to sit it out, hope it gets
  bored, or its head falls off.

NICK
  Is that what happens?

STEVE
  In some cases, apparently. I haven't seen one
  yet, well not up close. When I look down onto
  the streets I see loads of them, and loads of
  bits of them, arms, legs, heads, pairs of legs
  still walking, well staggering. It's quite
  funny really!

ZOMBIE MR HARRIS
    (Offstage, garbled whilst knocking)
  Brains! Brains!

NICK
  You've got to help me Steve, what do I do?

STEVE
  Not much you can do I'm afraid.

NICK
    (Starting to panic)
  Is that it? Is that all you can say?

STEVE
  Calm down buddy, breathe.

NICK
  I can't, I can't! It's going to break the door
  down!

STEVE
  That's good.

NICK
  What? How is this good?

STEVE
  You're using the past tense to describe Mr
  Harris, that's good. It shows you have
  accepted the situation.

NICK
    (starting to hyperventilate)
  This isn't a script!

STEVE
  It would make a great script, are you
  recording this?

NICK
  Steve!
    (heavy breaths)

NICK (Cont.)
  Help me!

STEVE
  OK, OK… Nick, sit down at your screen so I can
  see you properly.

  Good, now big, deep breaths, in through your
  mouth, out through your nose. That's it, good.

  Now, remember what we did the last time? When
  you had the panic attack about where the
  intermission should go.

  Remember what to think about, where to take
  your mind?

NICK
  Empty desert. Empty desert. Empty desert…

STEVE
        (Casually opening a chocolate dessert
        treat and taking a bite)
  That's it, calm, quiet, empty dessert, just
  you and chocolate… I mean just you and the
  sand.

NICK
  Empty desert, just me and-

                    SD - Wood splintering

  -STEVE!! IT'S GETTING IN!! Help me!

STEVE
  Calm, ignore it, sit still.

NICK
  What, but how, how am I supposed to do that?!

                    SD - Door breaking

  -It's getting in, it's getting in!

STEVE
  Nick, Nick, NICK! Stay with me buddy. Do some
  writing.

NICK
  WHAT!?

STEVE
  Write some of the script you're working on,
  just write anything that comes to mind!

NICK
  I really can't see how that's going to help!

STEVE
  Trust me, do as I say. Sit!

NICK
    (shaking)
  What shall I write?

STEVE
  Anything, write anything! Write what Sandra is
  doing, give her some extra lines.

    The door completely breaks up and ZOMBIE
    MR HARRIS enters behind Nick, it's a total
    mess, scruffy hair, rotting face, dirty
    torn clothes – a typical Zombie.

NICK
  IT'S IN! Help me Steve!

STEVE
  Write!

NICK
  OK I'm trying! I get that the pen is mightier
  than the sword but this is stretching it!

STEVE
  Let me help you, screen share quickly and I'll
  help you write the lines.

*Zombie Mr Harris is staggering around,
confused.*

NICK
  OK… you're in, can you see it?

STEVE
  Yes, I've got it.

NICK
  Then help! What do I write?

STEVE
  I don't know, what is Sandra up to right now?

NICK
  Er, she's just arrived in her apartment in LA.

STEVE
  Ok, good. Is she tired? Does she make a phone
  call?

NICK
  Well she's supposed to call her mom, but I
  don't know where her mom is!

  *Zombie Mr Harris finally realises Nick is
  there, so he starts to walk towards Nick,
  slowly, awkwardly.*

NICK
  It's coming for me Steve!!

STEVE
  Yes, it will.
    (beat)
  Maybe Sandra's hungry… Open brackets, stage
  directions - she goes to the fridge, close
  brackets.

  *Nick types as fast as he can, mouthing
  Steve's last words.*

NICK
  Got it.

ZOMBIE MR HARRIS
  Brains!

NICK
  Help me!

STEVE
  Write with me,
      (starting to sing)
  Write with me our strange duet!

NICK
  No time to be quoting Phantom at me!

STEVE
      (singing)
  Write once again with me, our strange duet!

NICK
  STEVE!!

STEVE
      (singing)
  The Zom......bie of Mr Harris is there... inside
  your flat!

  Steve laughs at his own joke.

NICK
  Not helping! It's coming for me, albeit very
  slowly. Shouldn't I just smash it with a chair
  or something?

STEVE
  Write this...:
  Sandra goes up stage left to the fridge and
  finds a slice of left over pizza.

  Nick starts typing frantically.

NICK
  OK, if you think that will help, but just know
  that as soon as I'm a zombie I'm coming for
  you, buddy!

ZOMBIE MR HARRIS
  PIZ-ZA!

NICK
  What?

STEVE
  Did it just say pizza?

NICK
  I think so.

STEVE
  Weird, maybe it's even more confused than we
  thought?

ZOMBIE MR HARRIS
  PIZ-ZA!

NICK
  It said it again.

STEVE
  Interesting turn of events.

NICK
  Maybe it's listening to us?
    (To Zombie Mr Harris)
  There's pizza in the fridge if you're hungry!

STEVE
  Does it still have ears?

NICK
  I can't really tell, er yes, one at least is
  intact.

ZOMBIE MR HARRIS
  BRAINS!

STEVE
  Oh, back to brains.

NICK
  It's going to kill me Steve! Help me man, help
  me!

STEVE
  Write this! Sandra takes a bite of pizza and
  notices a bottle of wine in the fridge door,
  it's open, she takes a swig.

NICK
  Right.

ZOMBIE MR HARRIS
  WINE!

NICK
  What?

STEVE
  Now that is odd.

NICK
  Yes Mr Harris, have some wine, it's in the
  fridge!

ZOMBIE MR HARRIS
  BRAINS!

NICK
  No, not BRAINS! WINE! Much nicer than brains!

ZOMBIE MR HARRIS
  BRAINS!

STEVE
  BRAINS!

NICK
  Steve!

STEVE
  Sorry. Write some more, anything!

NICK
  My mind's gone blank, what?

STEVE
  OK, let me think. Sandra finishes the slice of
  pizza, takes the bottle of wine and walks down
  stage centre, sits on the couch.

      *Nick types the above very quickly, then
      looks round.*

ZOMBIE MR HARRIS
  WINE!
      (turns and sits)
  WINE!

STEVE
  Well, I never!

NICK
  What's it doing? Shall I make a run for it?

STEVE
  I wouldn't advise it. They're everywhere. If
  you do, take the stairs not the elevator.
  Zombies hate stairs.

ZOMBIE MR HARRIS
      (starts to stand up)
  BRAINS.

NICK
  Oh no, back to brains.   ·

STEVE
  Write this:
  Sandra drinks some more wine, lays back on the

STEVE (Cont.)
  couch and takes out her phone. She calls her
  mother.

NICK
      (he types quickly)
  OK, I'm writing it.

ZOMBIE MR HARRIS
  WINE!
      (collapses onto the couch)
  PHONE! ...MOTHER!

STEVE
  This is getting really odd.

NICK
  Agreed.

STEVE
  I've got an idea. Write this: There's no
  answer from her mother so Sandra stands up and
  begins to tap dance.

NICK
  What the hell, Steve, you're really enjoying
  this aren't you?

STEVE
  Just type it quick, it's getting up again.

ZOMBIE MR HARRIS
      (trying to stand)
  BRAINS!

STEVE
  Type it quick!

      Nick types quickly. Zombie Mr Harris
      starts tap dancing badly.

ZOMBIE MR HARRIS
  TAP!

NICK
  What the… It's doing just what we say.

STEVE
  Close. It's doing just what you… type!

NICK
  Really?

STEVE
  Seems to be the case. Write, erm write… Sandra
  raises her arms up and dances the Riverdance,
  her legs kick up.

NICK
  Ok.

    *Nick types quickly. Zombie Mr Harris
    stands awkwardly, raises his arms and
    starts to dance, kicking his legs out.*

ZOMBIE MR HARRIS
  De de de deee de!

STEVE
  Hahaha I love it! Write Sandra scratches her
  butt!

ZOMBIE MR HARRIS
      (scratches his butt)
  BUTT!

STEVE
  Brilliant! Write Sandra sits on the couch and
  eats a cushion.

NICK
  How will that help?

STEVE
  It will buy you some time.

ZOMBIE MR HARRIS
     (stops dancing)
  BRAINS!

STEVE
  Write it quickly!

NICK
     (types quickly)
  There!

     *Zombie Mr Harris sits back down, picks
     up a cushion and starts to eat it.*

ZOMBIE MR HARRIS
  CUSHION!

NICK
  OK, it seems to be working.

STEVE
  You need to get out of there, but don't use
  the elevator.

NICK
  Right, I'm going to check the hall first and
  then come back to the screen.

STEVE
  Go for it.

     *Nick goes to the broken down door. He is
     off stage for a moment, then returns in a
     rush.*

NICK
  The hall is empty, but I can hear screams all
  round.

STEVE
  Yep, it's getting pretty messy.

NICK
  How come you're so calm? Aren't there any in
  your block?

STEVE
  No, not yet. I don't think they can get in,
  this place has great security. Fingerprint
  entry, you need a pulse.

NICK
  What shall I do now, it's nearly eaten the
  whole cushion!

STEVE
  Go to your balcony, keep clear of Zombie Mr
  Harris, whatever you do, then open the doors.

NICK
  Am I writing this or actually doing this?

STEVE
  Best to actually do it this time, its hand
  might fall off in the door mechanism.

NICK
  OK, I'm going. Don't go anywhere man, stay
  with me I need you!

      *He carefully skirts around Zombie Mr
      Harris.*

STEVE
  Be brave young man, I have your back!

      *Nick opens the glass doors upstage, he
      carefully returns giving Zombie Mr Harris
      a wide birth.*

ZOMBIE MR HARRIS
  BRAINS!

NICK
  Oh no!

STEVE
  Quickly, Nick, write this Sandra stands up,
  walks up stage and onto the balcony.

NICK
    (Typing quickly)
  Right!

ZOMBIE MR HARRIS
  BALCONY!

    Zombie Mr Harris stands and staggers his
    way upstage to the balcony.

STEVE
  Excellent, it's working. Type Sandra screams
  "SAUSAGES" and throws herself off the balcony.

NICK
  Why would she say that?

STEVE
  I just thought it would be funny!

ZOMBIE MR HARRIS
  SAUSAGES!

    Zombie Mr Harris disappears off the
    balcony and out of sight.

NICK
  It worked! It worked!

STEVE
  It did. I've absolutely no idea how!

NICK
  Thanks buddy!

STEVE
  No worries. Now, if you don't mind I have a
  screenplay to finish. You going to be alright
  now buddy?

NICK
  Yes. No. I don't know. I can hear more
  screaming from down the corridor.

STEVE
  Ah yes. Annoying isn't it? Don't use the
  elevator.

NICK
  I won't.

STEVE
  Get some supplies, quickly, as much as you can
  grab, then lock yourself in the bathroom, wait
  for all this to blow over. That's kind of what
  I'm doing.

NICK
  Thanks man, I will. You're the best!

STEVE
  No, you are!

NICK
  No, you are!

STEVE
  Just get your stuff together!

NICK
  I'm on it!

      *Nick is about to close the call on his
      laptop.*

STEVE
  Oh, and Nick?

NICK
  What's up?

STEVE
  Nothing… Take care buddy.

NICK
  You too.

> *He closes the laptop, looks around. Then*
> *rushes to the fridge, finds some pizza and*
> *an open bottle of white wine. He scoffs*
> *some pizza and swigs from the wine bottle.*

NICK
 Nice!

> *There is a loud knock coming from the*
> *broken door. Nick rushes to the door to be*
> *faced with his agent, SANDRA. Sandra looks*
> *fairly well, if only a little dishevelled.*
> *He shows her in.*

NICK
  Ah, Sandra, thank God you're here! How did you
  get past the zombies? Anyway, you'll be
  pleased, I've nearly finished the script, I'll
  have it on your desk in two days I promise,
  just one little bit to tie up. Have a seat,
  do. Would you like some wine?

Sandra
    (Walking towards Nick)
  BRAINS!

                                    LX - Blackout

                    END PLAY

Possessed by the Ex
By Clinton Festa

CHARACTERS
  DWAYNE - *A middle-aged man, Gina's husband and Emma's father*
  GINA - *Dwayne's wife and Emma's mother*
   ~as NAOMI - *Dwayne's ex-fiancée*
  EMMA - *Dwayne and Gina's high school or college-aged daughter*
   ~as GRANDMA - *Dwayne's mother, has a thick country accent*

SETTING
  Inside the family's home. Somewhere in North Carolina.

GINA, possessed by NAOMI, sits in a chair,
bed, or some large piece of furniture. She
is tied up, struggling to move. EMMA
monitors her closely, ready with a rolling
pin.
DWAYNE comes rushing in.

EMMA
　Dad, thank God you're home!

DWAYNE
　I got here as fast as I could. What's wrong
　with your mother?

EMMA
　She's acting really strange. She must have
　snapped or something; she won't respond.

DWAYNE
　Gina? Gina, honey, are you okay?

GINA (as NAOMI)
　　(*Snarling demonically*)
　No Gina. No Gina here anymore.

DWAYNE
　Oh my goodness; you weren't kidding. How did
　this happen? Did she try to attack you?

EMMA
　No! Everything was fine! She was just cleaning
　out some old photo albums in the attic, and
　just- lost it. She started cursing like I've
　never heard before.

DWAYNE
　　(*Confused*)
　Photo albums?

EMMA
　Old stuff, from before you met. All of the
　sudden she started saying, "Dammit, I thought
　he threw these out."

DWAYNE
    That's weird. Did she say anything else?

EMMA
    She kept cursing the name "Naomi" like she was
    shouting at the devil.

GINA (as NAOMI)
        (Snarling)
    Gina is gone. GOOONE! Only Naomi now!

DWAYNE
    Oh boy. This is bad.

EMMA
    Dad, I'm scared. Do you think Mom's possessed?

DWAYNE
    Hold on. Naomi? Naomi Munson?

GINA (as NAOMI)
        (No longer snarling)
    Dwayne? Dwayne Carlson, is that you?

DWAYNE
        (Guarded)
    Gosh, how long has it been? Thirty years?

EMMA
    Wait- Dad, you know her?

DWAYNE
        (Scoffs)
    Know her? I almost married her.

GINA (as NAOMI)
    It's nice to see you again, Dwayne. You're
    looking well.

DWAYNE
    Thanks. So, you're dead. What happened?

EMMA
Dad! Who cares! You never listen to the spirit during a possession! We need to get rid of her and bring Mom back!

GINA (as NAOMI)
Fine by me. My death is a little embarrassing anyway, and I'd rather not discuss it. Now if you'll kindly untie me, I'll depossess your wife and be on my way.

EMMA
Great idea.

DWAYNE
Oh no you don't. It may have been thirty years ago, but I haven't forgotten a thing. You've got a lot of explaining to do, Naomi.

EMMA
Dad. Mom is possessed by a demon that wants out. Let her go.

GINA (as NAOMI)
Demon? Excuse me, young lady. I am no demon.

DWAYNE
After what you did to me? You're the devil herself.

EMMA
     (Beat)
Okay, this I gotta hear.

DWAYNE
First tell me how you died, then tell me how you wound up in my wife's body.

GINA (as NAOMI)
If I must, but it's completely humiliating.

DWAYNE
Good.

GINA (as NAOMI)
  Okay, well, you know those women's one a day
  multi-vitamins?

DWAYNE
  Ha. What happened, you took two?

GINA (as NAOMI)
  No. I didn't take two. I took one.
    (Beat)
  And I choked on it.

DWAYNE
  Ha. Not the healthiest things when you choke
  and die on 'em.

GINA (as NAOMI)
  Yes, I am fully aware of the irony.

EMMA
  So how'd you wind up possessing my mom? She
  had to allow you in somehow, right?

GINA (as NAOMI)
  As for that, all I can say is one minute I'm
  wandering through the afterlife, minding my
  own business, and the next I'm being summoned
  by your mother's curses, getting sucked into
  her body. I never meant to intrude, so I'll be
  on my way now, if you'll just untie me.

EMMA
  Wait! I have so many questions. What's the
  meaning of our existence? What's the afterlife
  like?
    (Beat)
  Actually, never mind that stuff. What happened
  between you and my dad?

DWAYNE   GINA (as NAOMI)
  She dumped me.   It was mutual.

GINA (as NAOMI)
  (Sighs)
  We were young. I was a city girl from San
  Diego, and your father was a handsome country
  boy from North Carolina. We were both back-
  packing across Europe when we met in Rome. We
  immediately fell in love and promised
  ourselves we'd find a way to get married once
  we got back to the States.

DWAYNE
  Except she didn't live up to her end of the
  bargain.

GINA (as NAOMI)
  It's true.

DWAYNE
  I saved every penny I could to move out and be
  with her.

GINA (as NAOMI)
  But I wasn't honest with you, Dwayne. I… still
  had my old boyfriend back in San Diego.

DWAYNE
  Finally, I had enough money to come out and
  surprise her, and… surprise.

GINA (as NAOMI)
  I went from having two boyfriends to having
  none. I'm sorry, Dwayne. I should have broken
  up with Mike as soon as I got back from
  Europe.

DWAYNE
  I've been waiting thirty years to hear that.
  Thank you.

GINA (as NAOMI)
  We'll always have Rome.

DWAYNE
    (*Wistful*)
  Ha. Yeah.

EMMA
  So, wait… My Mom is possessed by my Dad's "one
  who got away?"

DWAYNE
  Yeah, it's perfect, isn't it?

EMMA
  No, it's weird.

DWAYNE
    (*As he exits*)
  Hang on; I'll be right back.

GINA (as NAOMI)
  Life is… complicated, Sweetheart. And I
  wouldn't say I have the afterlife figured out,
  either.

    Emma releases Naomi from her restraints.

EMMA
  Well, thank you for the story, Ms. Munson.
  But, I think I'm ready to have my mom back
  now.

    Dwayne returns with photo album.

DWAYNE
  Hey, Naomi, check it out.

GINA (as NAOMI)
    (*Looking at album*)
  Oh, look at how young we were.

DWAYNE
  Remember our kiss by that fountain?

GINA (as NAOMI)
   I sure do. It might have been a Roman
   fountain, but it was definitely a French kiss.

EMMA
      (Cringing)
   EWWWWWWWWWWWWWWWW!!!!

DWAYNE
   How 'bout this one of you posing with the
   Vespa scooter? Wow, you were something.

      Gina (as Naomi) giggles, putting her arm
      around Dwayne.

GINA (as NAOMI)
   Oh, Dwayne.

EMMA
   Uh, creepy. Leave my dad alone, please.

DWAYNE
   Relax, Sweetie. It's your mom's arm.

EMMA
   Yeah, possessed by your ex-girlfriend!

GINA (as NAOMI)
   Fiancée, dear.
      (Noticing her hand)
   Goodness, I'm going to have to do something
   about these nails. Dwayne, did you ever get
   that motorcycle you always wanted?

DWAYNE
   The Harley? Gosh, you remember that?

GINA (as NAOMI)
   Of course! It was very important to you.

DWAYNE
   Nah, Gina says we can't afford it. She would
   never let me buy a motorcycle.

EMMA
  Right. So I can go to college. And learn
  stuff.

GINA (as NAOMI)
    (Laughing)
  Oh, and I'm the demon.

EMMA
  Uh, Naomi? Could you please not talk about my
  mother that way?

GINA (as NAOMI)
  Quiet, dear. Dwayne, I have an idea. We should
  rent a brand new Mustang and see who can drive
  it faster.

DWAYNE
  Man, that sounds like a good time.

EMMA
  What? Dad, she's using you, and Mom! You could
  both get killed!

GINA (as NAOMI)
  Listen, Emma… is it? Take it from me. You
  gotta live a little while you can.

EMMA
  Or die trying, apparently. Look, I'm onto your
  game. Have a little fun, and if your host body
  can't handle it, just jump to another, right?
  Give me my mom back. Now.

GINA (as NAOMI)
  Maybe later. You know what I miss most about
  the material world? The food. I could really
  go for a double bacon cheeseburger right now.

DWAYNE
  Oh, man, I would love that. With some onion
  rings. But Gina's got me on this diet.

EMMA
  Dad! You're pre-diabetic!

GINA (as NAOMI)
    (Flirty)
  Come on, fella. Let's go get that burger.

DWAYNE
  Great idea.

EMMA
  Dad, seriously? You're going on a date with
  your ex?

DWAYNE
  No, Sweetie, it's still your mom. Look same
  hair, same clothes, same shoes.

GINA (as NAOMI)
  Well, until I can find a Neiman Marcus.

DWAYNE
  This is your Momma, just with a few…
  improvements.

EMMA
  IMPROVEMENTS!?

  Being possessed by a dead woman is NOT an
  improvement!

GINA (as NAOMI)
  Dwayne?

DWAYNE
  Emma, don't talk to your mother that way.

EMMA
  This is not my mother! Okay, look. You're
  obviously having a mid-life crisis. And you-
  well, you're having some kind of after-life
  crisis.

DWAYNE

  Listen, Sweetie. You know you're always going
  to be number one in my life.

EMMA

  Would you stop it? You're acting like Mom's
  dead! She's not, and she still loves you!
  Naomi over here? She's dead. And she's using
  you. Time to move on.

DWAYNE

  Emma, this is normal in any marriage. We all
  change over time. Look, we're gonna go out for
  a burger and a beer.

GINA (as NAOMI)

  Yes. Then some drag racing, and maybe some
  shopping. I wouldn't be caught dead in a dress
  like this.
      (Beat)
  I was buried in Versace.

DWAYNE

  We'll see you when we get back, Sweetie.

  Dwayne and Naomi exit.

EMMA

      (Sitting)
  Unbelievable. I'm losing both my parents at
  once.

  Emma picks up and looks at photo album.

EMMA

  Oh, Grandma, I wish you were alive right now.
  Dammit, Grandma, why can't you be here right
  now? Dammit, dammit, dammit!!!

                                    LX - Flashes

  *EMMA (as GRANDMA) rises, picking up a
  rolling pin.*

EMMA (as GRANDMA)
    (yelling loudly)
  BOY! GIT YER BUTT BACK HERE RIGHT NOW AND
  BRING THAT NO GOOD WOMAN WITH YOU!

    Dwayne and Naomi return.

DWAYNE
  Momma? Momma, is that you?

EMMA (As GRANDMA)
  Hell yeah, it's your mother! What on Earth has
  gotten into your silly head, boy?

DWAYNE
  Momma…

GINA (as NAOMI)
  Is this your mother, Dwayne?

EMMA (As GRANDMA)
  YOU. I know you. Yer the two-timin' tramp who
  broke my son's heart. You ain't half the woman
  Gina is. When she was givin' birth to little
  Emma, the doctors said she was comin' out feet
  first. Gina stood up between contractions, did
  a backflip, sat back down and pushed out my
  granddaughter, head first. You ain't go no
  right to take over that body.

GINA (as NAOMI)
  That… sounds a little exaggerated.

DWAYNE
  It is. But Gina did take care of my mom the
  whole time she was dying. Handled all the
  funeral arrangements and everything. Gina's
  somethin' else.

EMMA (As GRANDMA)
  Damn right she is. As for you, boy… What do I
  always tell you?

DWAYNE
  Uh… Don't be stupid?

EMMA
  On your weddin' day, boy! Gosh, don't be
  stupid.

DWAYNE
  My weddin' day? Oh… you said, 'Remember, boy.
  You ain't marryin' the person. You're marryin'
  the whole family.'

      Emma (as Grandma) waves the rolling pin
      near Gina (as Naomi)'s face.

EMMA (as GRANDMA)
  That's right. Well, guess what, Naomi? Welcome
  to the family. I'm yer mother-in-law now, and
  I'm gonna make yer life miserable 'til you
  give us our Gina back.

GINA (as NAOMI)
  Hmmm. Dwayne, Gina sounds like pretty stiff
  competition. I guess I was lucky I met you
  first.

EMMA (as GRANDMA)
      (Quickly)
  Oh, hell yeah. You shoulda seen the birthday
  parties she'd put together for Emma. And
  little Dwayne, here. She's a good wife, a damn
  good mother, and the best player on her
  bowling team.

GINA (as NAOMI)
  Mrs. Carlson, thirty years ago I broke your
  son's heart and changed the course of his
  life. I lived with that guilt until the day I
  died, and I'm not going to live with it
  anymore. I… I want to fix all of my mistakes.
  All of them, right now.

DWAYNE
What are you saying, Naomi?

GINA (as NAOMI)
You'll see. Dwayne, come over here and kiss me like we're back in Rome.

EMMA (as GRANDMA)
Don't be stupid, boy.

Dwayne contemplates, hesitates, then goes in to kiss Gina (as Naomi). Naomi escapes Gina's body. GINA slaps Dwayne before he kisses her.

DWAYNE
Hey, what did you do that for?

GINA
(Deliberately)
Dwayne? Do you mind telling me why you still have pictures of your ex-girlfriend Naomi?

DWAYNE
Uh-oh. Gina? Gina darlin', is that you?

Gina grabs the photo album.

EMMA (as GRANDMA)
Haha! You get 'em, Gina! Okay, I gotta get back to hell before they realize I'm missin'. Bye now!

Gina grabs Dwayne.

GINA
(Deliberately)
Come with me, Dwayne. You have some pictures to throw away.

Gina leaves, dragging Dwayne with her.

DWAYNE
  Gina, baby, I swear I didn't even know I still
  had those!

EMMA
      (Looking up, smiling)
  Thanks, Grandma.

                                    LX - Blackout

                    END PLAY

Severance
By j. Snodgrass

CHARACTERS
  WENDY - *18,* Female , *a bookish Christian high school senior*
  LUCY - *18,* Female, *a high school senior with a bad reputation*
  MAN - *25,* Male, *the dead body of a murderous psychopath*

SETTING
  A haunted church.

A haunted church. Altar at center, we can see that a MAN is lying unconscious behind it, his pant-legs and black boots are showing.

LUCY and WENDY stand on either side of the altar, out of breath. Their clothes are totally shredded and bloody. Lucy holds a bloody shovel. They stand, gasping for breath a minute, staring in terror at the dead man and at each other.

WENDY
  We… We killed him…

LUCY
  Damned right we did!

WENDY
  We killed him…

LUCY
  Yeah. After he killed Blitz. And Stoner! And Barbie. And yeah, he sort of did the world a favor with that one 'cause she was always a jerk to me, but-

  Lucy experiences a surge of anger and kicks the Man. His legs twitch.

LUCY
  You killed Blitz!

WENDY
  But now Hallelujah he's dead! Rejoice!

LUCY
    (kicking him again)
  I am rejoicing. We're alive!

WENDY
  And stop kicking him! He's dead, I think it's a sin.

LUCY
  …What? This psycho maniac has been stalking us
  all night, butchering our friends, trying to
  murder us and I'm a sinner for kicking his
  dead stiff?

WENDY
  He's already condemned. To awaken on judgment
  day and be cast into a giant blender and
  pureed to pulp and blood. But if you mangle
  his corpse how will they even recognize him?

LUCY
  I don't know. I mean how are they gonna
  recognize our mangled friends after what this
  psycho did to them? And if they've been
  rotting in the ground for years? How will they
  recognize anyone?

WENDY
  Well, some of us who've remained untainted
  will-

LUCY
  On second thought? Before we get into that. Go
  get an axe.

WENDY
  For what?

LUCY
  To chop his head off, silly.

WENDY
  What?

LUCY
      (with slow pantomime gestures)
  You go. Get axe. Chop. Off his head.

WENDY
  But he's dead!

LUCY
So he won't mind at all! But in case you've
forgotten, he's already been "dead" four times
tonight! Till we turn our backs and start
talking about something else and he pops up
slashing again! So get the axe and chop his
psycho head off!

WENDY
We killed him, it's done.

LUCY
The exact words you said when we ran him over
with the car. When we shoved him off the
steeple. When we drowned him in the baptismal
font. Listen, we can discuss this whole thing
after you've severed his head.

WENDY
No, no way am I touching a- You know. A body.

LUCY
I'm not telling you to touch his junk, I mean
his head, this one, cut it off-

WENDY
You know so much about male anatomy - you do
it.

LUCY
I'm the one who got us this far.

WENDY
So? Your hands are already bloody.

LUCY
Yeah. And he was trying to kill both of us. So
now it's your turn.

WENDY
But look at these palms, lily-white,
blameless. Yours have already- You know.

LUCY
  Already what?

WENDY
  Already performed wifely duties. Without a
  bless-ed ring to sanctify-

LUCY
  Whoa! Are you telling me- While we stand over
  this mass murderer? Who we just killed? Except
  he's probably not even dead? And you're on my
  case 'cause of premarital hand-jobs?

WENDY
  I'm just saying if someone's hands were gonna
  defile this body, yours would be the logical
  obvious choice. But what I'm really saying -
  why make things worse? Let God sort it out.
  He's dead, we're safe.

LUCY
  But that's what he wants. Us calm and la-dee-
  da, babbling on, giving each other a foot
  massage and-

WENDY
  Who's calm? I'm freaked out!

LUCY
  Then chop his head off! You'll feel so much
  better, and I'll massage your-

WENDY
  And where do we find an axe? This is a church!

LUCY
  So use this shovel.

WENDY
  I'm not touching that!

LUCY
  Do it!

WENDY
  No! You do it. I'll make you a deal.

LUCY
  I'm listening.

WENDY
  You hack off his head, if it's what you so
  deeply desire, and then I'll take the shovel
  and, real gentle, I'll remove that hand for
  you.

LUCY
  ...What?

WENDY
  Real gentle, I'll even sing some calming hymns
  while-

LUCY
  You want to cut off my hand?

WENDY
  No, I don't want to. But I will. For you, for
  your soul. Jesus himself said if your hand
  causes you to sin, 'tis better to cut it off
  and cast it in the fire-

LUCY
  No, and shut up about it! And where was Jesus
  when this monster killed our friends?

WENDY
  He's been right here with us. Protecting us!
  This is his house, you know.

LUCY
  What about them? Blitz and Stoner? And Barbie?

WENDY
  I don't know. He works in mysterious ways. And
  when the seventh trumpet sounds he will raise
  up the righteous, so I think at least some of

WENDY (Cont.)
  them might be alright.

LUCY
  And this mysterious wacko here? I don't think
  he's waiting for any trumpet — he's been
  resurrecting himself all night. And he's right
  here, fooling us again into thinking his
  murder spree is over. And you won't finish him
  off. Just do it!

WENDY
  No! This is a crime scene — we've gotta call
  the police. And they'll have a zillion
  questions. Barbie's parents will have to come
  here and see her on the stairs. And how many
  times we tripped over her running away…
  Stoner's folks will see his body wrapped
  around the steeple. And Blitz's parents…

LUCY
  No one ever imagines they'll see their
  linebacker son… beaten to death with a Bible…

WENDY
  And then my parents will show up and chop my
  head off for sneaking in here with you guys.
  And your Mom will find out you lied to her…
  Wow. And I thought this was a nightmare.
  Tomorrow's gonna be Old Testament.

LUCY
  Not to mention the news crews, photographers —
  I can't let them see me like this. This might
  be the only time in my life I make the news,
  and my perm is… dead…

WENDY
  You're lucky to be alive.

LUCY
  You look terrible.

WENDY
  I've been fighting this maniac all night!

LUCY
  And the TV cameras will add ten pounds to the
  bags under your eyes - they'll go from carry-
  ons to luggage. Also your muffin-top there.

WENDY
  It's not a modelling audition!

LUCY
  That's what some people say. When tragedy
  strikes? Local newsworthy tragedy? But you and
  me? Tomorrow's a screen-test for talk-shows,
  and I think we can nail it. Go national. Look,
  look.
      (Innocent, tearful)
  "My friends and I gathered in this old church
  for Bible-study, and we were deep into the
  Gospel of Thomas when this wacko attacked us-"

WENDY
  Nobody's gonna believe that. And there is no
  Gospel of Thomas.

LUCY
  That's your opinion. Anyway. "My friends and I
  were cramming for an algebra exam and this
  homicidal whack-job attacked us. I don't know
  how it started-"

WENDY
  Yeah, because Blitz was doing an exam in your
  algebra.

LUCY
  Well do you think we should say we broke into
  a church to play Truth or Dare?

WENDY
  I don't-

LUCY
   Oh! And by the way - when the game stopped? It
   was your turn.
      (Pulls out a one-minute hourlass)
   So, I dare you to finish him off!

WENDY
   This is not a game! And-

LUCY
   Time's running out. You know the penalty.

WENDY
   I'm not playing! Now cool down!

LUCY
   Yup. Just what he wants - we get all relaxed
   and give each other a foot massage and SLASH!
   GUSH! BLOOD!

WENDY
   QUIT IT, you're freaking me out!

LUCY
   So chop his head off!

WENDY
   I meant stop looking at my feet!

LUCY
   I would, but your big toe is really big.

WENDY
   Can you not? Fine, it's big. Why do you think
   I never wear sandals? It makes me- But that
   has nothing to do with-

LUCY
   See that? He moved.

WENDY
   What?

LUCY
  He moved. When you distracted me with your
  toes. Like he was gonna RARR!

WENDY
  STOP IT.

LUCY
  Look at you! You're a mess! And now you're
  shouting at me. Just hack off his head so we
  can relax. I'll give you a massage.

WENDY
  What is up with you? I can't relax. Three of
  my friends were slaughtered tonight and you've
  been possessed with some weirdo kind of foot-
  fetish.

LUCY
  Or maybe you have a dirty mind.

WENDY
  Look who's talking. Slut.

LUCY
  Nerd.

WENDY
  Hey, wait a minute…

LUCY
  No, I know it's true, I remember the assembly
  when you got your perfect attendance
  certificate.

WENDY
  No, it's not that. I am a nerd. Blitz was a
  quarterback, Stoner was a pot-head, that's why
  he was alone in the yard.

LUCY
  Actually marijuana was just a gateway drug, he
  was a chronic masturbator.

LUCY (Cont.)
    (Laughs)
  You get it? Chronic masturbator? I thought of
  that years ago but I never had a chance to say
  it and now there'll be no joking about him
  after this.

WENDY
  And Barbie was going to be this year's prom
  queen. You know, popular?

LUCY
  Well. "Most Likely to Succeed" at pissing me
  off. But what's your point?

WENDY
  I've seen slasher movies before, and the slut
  always dies. Like first.

LUCY
  Well, yeah. 'Cause losers who shoot movies
  about violence against women couldn't get
  their high school slut's attention. Which is
  not to say I agree with your labeling. And
  those are just movies, not real life. And, if
  you're so concerned about slasher movie
  patterns, you should already know this dude's
  about to pop up and kill one of us.

WENDY
  Well, it won't be me. 'Cause I still have my
  maidenhead. Everybody knows it's the best
  protection against Hollywood slashers.
  Also this.

    Wendy holds up a toy Jesus.

LUCY
  A toy? Is that Jesus the action figure?

WENDY
  Well, I'm alive, aren't I?

LUCY
So? You're protected! Get down there and hack his head off!

WENDY
Wait a minute… You…

LUCY
What?

WENDY
Of course! You would have died first, except that you're the killer. You did this to get on the news. And this guy, he just showed up, maybe in response to all the screaming from the house. And now you're trying to get me to kill him so I'll be in on it too. And have to protect your alibi, and get blackmailed into fulfilling your foot-fetishistic perversion! And for having defiled this innocent man I'll have to join you in eternal perdition!

LUCY
That's insane!

WENDY
        (flips the hourglass)
Your turn. Truth - Confess!

LUCY
Alright. You want to know so bad? Fine!
        (Deep breath)
I do… have a thing about feet, more a fixation than a fetish. Any time I've been honest about it, I get called names like some freak weirdo. And I'm so starved for positive attention, sometimes I'll give a guy what he wants, to get it… Can you at least understand…?

WENDY
        (shocked)
…You're a monster…

LUCY
    Well maybe I am. But that doesn't mean I-

MAN
        (pops up from the floor)
    SHIVER ME TIMBERS!

        *Man stabs Lucy, who collapses to the
        floor, and turns to Wendy.*

WENDY
        (polite swearing)
    CHEESE AND CRACKERS!

        *Wendy grapples with Man, wrestles the
        knife away and stabs him. He falls to the
        floor behind the altar.*

        *Wendy stands over him, out of breath like
        she was at the start of the play.*

        Pause.

WENDY
    Oh, to Hell with it. This head is definitely
    coming off.

        *She kneels down behind the altar and
        begins. We see his legs twitch.*

                                    LX - Blackout

                    END PLAY

Silence in the Library
By Benjamin Peel

CHARACTERS
  PAT – *Council worker, mid-40s professional, any gender (Can also provide the ghost voice from offstage)*
  FREYA – *Photographer, mid-30s, Female. Quite serious and also a bit sad*
  JOSH – *Photographer, late 20's-early 30's, Male. Enthusiastic, bubbly but also a bit insensitive*

SETTING
  An abandoned library somewhere in the UK.

Music plays. FREYA and PAT enter.

FREYA
  So it's finally going to be demolished?

PAT
  Yes. It's become too structurally unsafe and
  there's been some trespassing and vandalism.
  The whole area is going to be redeveloped.

FREYA
  I'm sorry I never returned any of your
  messages. I went away for quite a while and
  tried to process what happened here.

PAT
  What happened to Josh if you don't mind my
  asking?

FREYA
  I tried to help him but I couldn't so I left.

PAT
  I'm sorry to hear that.

FREYA
  He takes photographs of landscapes now.

PAT
  It was the anniversary of the lady's death
  last week.

FREYA
  I know.

PAT
  A couple of paranormal investigators spent the
  night here.
      (beat)
  They recorded nothing.

FREYA

So you don't believe what I told you happened?

PAT

I believe you experienced something. There's a
reason I tried to get in contact with you.

FREYA

Oh, what's that?

PAT

I got in touch with one of the librarians who
worked here. She said the lady was a down and
out. They thought she was very strange, she'd
had a very tragic life I gather. The library
was the only place where she was treated with
compassion and kindness even though on
occasion she had to be asked to leave.
Apparently because in the winter she wore so
many layers all the time no one knew she had
become pregnant.

FREYA

Poor woman.

PAT

Anyway, thirty-five years ago she gave birth
to a baby girl but then died from
complications.

FREYA

What happened to the baby?

PAT

She survived and was adopted. On the day she
gave birth, she was in the children's section.
She wasn't allowed to keep the baby though and
with nowhere else to go she kept going back to
the library and the children's area but was
found dead there one day.

Afterwards, this librarian I spoke to said she
could feel something sometimes when she was in

PAT (Cont.)
there but that it was a benign presence. Your
visit coincided with the anniversary of her
death.   .

    Pat produces an A4 envelope.

Anyway, I hope you don't mind but this retired
librarian and myself, between us, did some
digging, well as much as we could without your
consent.

FREYA
And?

PAT
I think this might answer some of your
questions.

    Pat offers the envelope to Freya which
    she takes whilst wiping away a tear.
    They exit as the music plays.

                    LX - Fade to Black

        SCENE TWO - FLASHBACK

    Pat, Freya and JOSH enter with various
    camera equipment. Freya no longer has
    the envelope.

PAT
I'm Pat from the Council. We spoke on the
phone. In you go.

FREYA
I'm Freya and this is Josh. Thanks for letting
us do this.

PAT
Rather you than me. I've always found
abandoned buildings pretty weird.

JOSH
  We just love documenting them. We were at a
  disused hospital recently.

FREYA
  The most poignant part of that was the
  children's ward as the wallpaper was still
  there along with some toys.

PAT
  Poignant. Sounds downright creepy to me.

JOSH
  How come this library was closed?

PAT
  It just became unfit for purpose and a new
  bigger one was built. It needs demolishing
  really.

JOSH
  Well, I can't wait to get started.

FREYA
  There's lots of large windows for natural
  light.

PAT
  And you also want to take photos at night?

FREYA
  Well as it falls as we prefer not to use
  artificial light.

PAT
  That's just as well as there's no electricity
  any more as you can imagine.

JOSH
  Buildings like this always come across as much
  creepier as it starts to get dark.

PAT
    You should have a few hours daylight before it
    starts to get dark. I'll swing by after I
    finish work about 6.30 to lock up. Here's the
    spare key for the front door so you don't get
    anyone wandering in.

FREYA
    OK, thanks.

PAT
    Hope you get what you want and I look forward
    to seeing your photos. You've got my number in
    case you need me or finish early.

FREYA
    Yes I have.

PAT
    Right, I'll see you later then. Just be
    careful though as it's starting to crumble in
    places.

FREYA
    We will.

        Pat exits.

        *Josh and Freya begin to unpack their
        cameras as well as a video camera and
        tripod.*

FREYA
    Can you set the video up here in the
    children's section whilst I take a few shots?

JOSH
    You don't want it in the main area whilst we
    have the light?

FREYA
    No, I think this part is more interesting. You
    can still tell that this was the kid's area.

*Freya starts taking shots. Josh places the
camera on the tripod and connects a
battery pack to it.*

JOSH
　How come you wanted to come here on your
　birthday?

FREYA
　Have you never felt anything in the places
　we've been into?

JOSH
　No. I can't say I have. Sure, they can feel
　creepy at times but that's just because they
　are empty.

FREYA
　You have absolutely no imagination at times.
　Think of all the places we have been into. All
　the people who have passed through these
　places with their hopes and fears. That
　children's ward especially where life ended
　for some of them.

JOSH
　What's got into you?

FREYA
　Nothing. I just think we are doing more than
　taking photographs and your flippancy about it
　all annoys me.

JOSH
　No, there's something else. You haven't been
　yourself at all recently.

FREYA
　Sorry. You're right. It's just that since my
　Mom died I've felt lost and before she went we
　had a long heart-to-heart about…

JOSH
   Yes, you were very close despite you being
   adopted. I could see that. But she wouldn't
   have wanted you to be like this.

FREYA
   Like what?

JOSH
   I've never met anyone with as much intensity
   and passion as you but you are so serious all
   the time.

FREYA
   Maybe.

JOSH
   I'll go and take some shots in the main
   library.

      Josh exits.
      Freya looks at the viewfinder of the video
      camera and slowly pans the camera around.
      She brings it back to a downstage corner
      so the audience can't see the viewfinder.
      She looks up puzzled then back down at the
      viewfinder. She walks into the corner then
      back to the camera. She radios Josh on a
      walkie-talkie.

FREYA
   Hey, Josh, come down here a minute.

      Freya looks through the viewfinder again.
      She radios Josh again.

FREYA
   Did you hear me Josh?

      Josh leaps onto the stage.

JOSH
   Boo!

FREYA
  Bloody hell, Josh. Do you not get tired of
  doing that? I'm really not in the mood for it
  today.

JOSH
  Sorry. What is it?

FREYA
  Just look through the viewfinder into that
  corner.

     Josh does so.

FREYA
  Can you see a fuzzy outline of something?

     Josh looks again through the viewfinder
     then stands up and looks into the corner.

JOSH
  I'm not sure.

FREYA
  Take a few shots with your camera.

     Josh does so.
     They both look at the screen.

FREYA
  There's something fuzzy in the same corner on
  those.

JOSH
  I'm still not sure if I can see anything.
  Maybe it's the pattern in the wallpaper
  causing it?

FREYA
  Could be.

JOSH
  It's been abandoned for five years hasn't it?

FREYA
  Yes. No one seems to want to take
  responsibility for knocking it down.

JOSH
  I've been trying to imagine what it was like
  when it was in use.

FREYA
  I used to spend ages in my local library. It
  was a sanctuary for me.

JOSH
  I'm going back upstairs to take some more
  shots whilst it's still light. I've found some
  old local history index cards. They should
  make for a good photo.

FREYA
  I'll take some more down here.

        Josh exits.
        Freya takes some photos, all the while
        avoiding the corner where the video camera
        is pointing.

        The lighting state darkens noticeably.
        The video camera emits some static noise.
        She goes back to the video camera and
        looks through the viewfinder. She jumps
        up.

FREYA
  What the hell?
        (She radios Josh)
  Josh, get down here.

JOSH
        (On Radio)
  OK. I'm coming back down.

        Freya goes back to looking through the
        viewfinder until Josh enters.

JOSH
  What's going on?

FREYA
  Look. Look through it again.

        Josh looks through the viewfinder.

FREYA
  Now do you see something?

JOSH
  Yes but it looks like a chair.
        (standing up)
  I can't see anything with just the naked
  eye though.

FREYA
  No, you're right.

JOSH
  Perhaps we should leave.

FREYA
  You can if you want. I'm staying.

        *The video camera emits an even louder
        static noise, as do the walkie talkies.*

JOSH
  What's wrong with the equipment?

        *Freya looks through the viewfinder again
        and flinches.*

JOSH
  What is it now?

FREYA
  Look for yourself.

JOSH
  I'm not sure that I want to.

*Josh looks at the viewfinder and leaps
back.*

JOSH
  What the…

  That looks like a figure sitting on the chair.
  There must be some interference from
  somewhere.

                              LX - Darkens

FREYA
  It seems to be getting dark quickly.

  They both switch on torches.

  *Freya forces herself to look at the
  viewfinder.*

FREYA
  It's too dark to see anything properly now.

  *There is another burst of static from the
  walkie talkies.*

EERIE GHOST VOICE
      (distorted, from the camera)
  Freya.

JOSH
  That's coming from the camera.

EERIE GHOST VOICE
      (at increasing volume and clarity)
  Freya. Freya. Freya! Freya!

  *Their torches snap out as does the video
  camera and it is pitch black.*

JOSH
  I can't see a thing.

EERIE GHOST VOICE
    (distorted, from the walkie-talkies)
  Freya! Freya!

EERIE GHOST VOICE
    (from the figure's corner)
  Freya!

JOSH
  It sounds like it's coming from that corner
  now.
    (beat)
  It's saying your name. Why's it doing that?

EERIE GHOST VOICE
    (clearly, from the figure's corner)
  FREYA!

    Josh screams.

FREYA
    (shouting)
  Mum. Mum it's me.

    Silence.

                                    LX - Blackout

                    END PLAY

Spa-mageddon
By Scott Younger

CHARACTERS
  SALLY DENTON - *Female, 30s, First-time
  visitor to Detox Spa and Leisure*
  TABITHA JILLMAN - *Female, 40s, Meditation
  and relaxation specialist*
  COLIN JONES - Male, 50, *Undead zombie*

SETTING
  The relaxation suite of Detox Spa and
  Leisure. The present day, but that just so
  happens to be the end of days.

*The relaxation suite of Detox Spa and
Leisure. There is a small gym mat centre-
stage. The fourth-wall downstage is a
large window to the characters.*

*SALLY enters, wheeling on a small
suitcase.*

SALLY
  Hello?
      (A beat)
  Is anyone there?

  *Sally looks around, growing increasingly
  frantic.*
  TABITHA enters.

TABITHA
  Here for the guided meditation?

SALLY
      (Startled)
  Hello! Yes… but didn't think it was 'til half
  1?

TABITHA
  We'll move it forward. I'm Tabitha, I run the
  mediation sessions.

SALLY
  I'm Sally. Sally Denton. I was just trying to
  check in, where's reception?

TABITHA
  I'll sign you. None of the reception team have
  made it in.

SALLY
  Because of the fog?

TABITHA
  Lucky I live near enough to walk in. The rest
  of our staff aren't so lucky.

SALLY
  It's terrible, everywhere's just jammed! It
  took me over an hour to get here… and I'm only
  the next village over!

TABITHA
  Well, you're here now, no harm done. Time to
  relax and detox.

SALLY
  It's so thick, and red…
  Do you think it's true what they've been
  saying?

TABITHA
  Oh, I wouldn't worry about that.

SALLY
  That it's the end of the world. They said that
  on the news. Red fog, all the dogs running
  away, that four-day long eclipse last week…
  The end of everything! I really hope not,
  because I like being alive and it's all a bit
  scary really…!

TABITHA
  Sally, you're here to relax, remember? Put all
  your worries, troubles and apocalyptic fears
  to one side. You're at Detox Spa now.

SALLY
  Sorry, it doesn't take much to set me off.
  Even driving through that graveyard next-door
  gave me the heebie-jeebies!

TABITHA
  There's nothing to worry about. We're a little
  Kingdom of Calm here.

SALLY
  'Kingdom of Calm'? That sounds nice!

TABITHA
  Are you ready to start? I think I'll make your
  session a bit longer…

SALLY
      (Gesturing to her case)
  Is there anywhere I can put my things?

TABITHA
  Just put them to the side for now.

      Sally puts her case to the side.

TABITHA
  Have you done any meditation before?

SALLY
  I tried once, in the bath. But my mind kept
  wondering. I got all worried that I'd fall
  asleep and end up drowning… So, I stopped.

TABITHA
  Well, you certainly won't drown in here. Now
  if you'd like to make yourself comfortable on
  the mat, we'll begin.

      Sally sits on the mat.

TABITHA
  Close your eyes.

      Sally closes her eyes.

TABITHA
  Now picture a lake, with the calmest, stillest
  water you've ever seen. It's a warm summer's
  day, not a cloud in the sky and you're sitting
  by this lake. As you breathe in…

      Tabitha inhales dramatically.
      Sally follows.

TABITHA
You breathe in its peaceful, shimmering
stillness. Its aura fills you with a deep
contentment- a sense of wholeness, imagine
this aura is a white light. Running from the
lake to its banks, absorbed by soles of your
feet, travelling upwards into your body, your
neck and finally your head… Imbued by this
healing energy you step into the water-

SALLY
          (Opening her eyes suddenly)
Are there snakes!?

TABITHA
What?

SALLY
Are there any snakes in the lake? Please- tell
me!

TABITHA
No, there's only…

SALLY
I swam in this lake once in India, and I felt
a little pinch on my foot. Turns out there
were hundreds of water snakes, all trying to
eat me! I nearly died!

TABITHA
Okay, let's try something different…

          Sally closes her eyes.

TABITHA
Imagine that you're a sapling in the middle of
a huge sprawling forest. As you grow you draw
energy from the earth. You shoot roots down
from your feet, into the ground, through the
warm, welcoming soil…

SALLY
     (Opening one eye)
  Are there any ants?! I once nearly-

TABITHA
  No, no ants. Just mother earth welcoming you
  as your roots sink down gently, deep below the
  forest floor…

     A loud groaning noise.

SALLY
     (Opening her eyes)
  What's that?

TABITHA
  That's just… a snoring squirrel!

SALLY
  Oh?
     (closes her eyes)
  Squirrels are lovely…

TABITHA
  Your soft green stem grows taller, reaching
  out as you grow your branches. As you stretch-
  leaves burst out from you, filling the forest
  with life! You grow rapidly now, until you're
  taller than all the other trees in the forest,
  shooting high above the forest's canopy, up
  into the sky…

     A loud bang followed by groaning.

SALLY
     (Eyes closed)
  What was that? Thunder?

TABITHA
  No, there are blue skies above the forest…

     More groaning, closer now.

SALLY
  All I can see is… a red fog…

> *Enter COLIN, a zombie. Tabitha doesn't
> notice him, instead focusing on Sally.*

TABITHA
  Just focus on your leaves, absorbing the
  sunlight…

> *Colin growls and shuffles slowly towards
> Sally. Sally opens her eyes, spots Colin
> and leaps back in fright. Tabitha notices
> Colin and watches him intently.*

SALLY
  Oh my god! Help! Help! Somebody help!

TABITHA
  Sally, stay calm.

SALLY
  But there's a…!

TABITHA
  It can't move very fast.

SALLY
  Neither can I!

> *Colin shambles closer to Sally.*

SALLY
  Ah!

TABITHA
  Walk in a circle.

SALLY
  But… I…

TABITHA
  Trust me!

> *Colin lunges at Sally, who evades and*
> *walks around the stage in a circle.*
> *Colin follows, slowly.*

TABITHA
  Zombie! I want you to close your eyes and
  visualise a very still lake…

SALLY
  That won't work!

TABITHA
  The calming aura of the lake fills you with a
  deep contentment…

SALLY
  You can't make a zombie meditate!

> *Colin's eyelids droop slightly.*
> *Sally picks up her case and continues to*
> *flee from Colin.*

SALLY
  Stay back!

TABITHA
  Feel the aura of the lake as it moves through
  your body…

> *Sally stops and holds her case up in front*
> *of her like a shield.*

TABITHA
  …like a white cleansing light!

> *Colin claws at Sally's suitcase.*

SALLY
  Help me!

TABITHA
  The light fills deep inside you, you no longer
  need to… er… eat brains!

Colin's eyes close and he stops.

COLIN
  Brains…

SALLY
  Holy shit!

TABITHA
  Shh!
      (To Colin)
  Now, zombie…

COLIN
      (Awakes)
  Actually, it's Colin.

SALLY
  Ahh!

TABITHA
  Hello… Colin. Do you know where you are?

COLIN
  I was in my car… On my way to work, now I'm
  here…

SALLY
  I think you died.

TABITHA
  Sally!

COLIN
  Typical. Is this heaven?

TABITHA
  No, this is Detox Spa and Leisure.

COLIN
  Really? I used to drive past here! Everyday!
  Back when I was alive…

SALLY
  You're not going to… eat me?

COLIN
  Is that what I was doing? Sorry. I just feel…
  really hungry…!

      Sally leaps back.

SALLY
  Ahh! Put him in a trance again, Tabitha! He's
  not safe!

TABITHA
  It's okay, Colin. We all have cravings.

SALLY
  Not for human bloody flesh!

TABITHA
  Colin is just as much of a guest here as you,
  Sally. Is there anything else troubling you,
  Colin?

COLIN
  I've got aches and pains all over. My arm
  feels like it could fall off any second…

TABITHA
  Your posture could do with a bit of work…
  See how straight you can stand before we begin
  our group meditation.

      *Colin attempts to straighten his hunched
      posture.*

SALLY
  Tabitha, can I have a word?

TABITHA
  Of course…

      Sally takes Tabitha aside.

SALLY
  I don't mean to be rude… but Colin shouldn't
  be allowed in the session.

TABITHA
  Why not?

SALLY
  He's a zombie! If he was faster, he'd have
  eaten me by now.

TABITHA
  You've seen the effect the meditation's had on
  him. He's different now.

SALLY
  How can I relax when he could sneak up and eat
  me while I'm meditating?

TABITHA
  I won't let that happen. Trust me.

SALLY
  It's not you I don't trust…

TABITHA
  We just need to get to know him. Who knows?
  You two might have something in common…

    Tabitha approaches Colin who is still
    struggling to straighten his posture.

TABITHA
  Well done, Colin. Much better.

COLIN
  I've still got it!

TABITHA
  Before we start, why don't you both tell me a
  bit about yourselves?

COLIN
Well, I used to be a salesman… before, well…
you know.

SALLY
What did you sell?

COLIN
Cleaning supplies. Carpet cleaner, mops… You
name it I sold it.

TABITHA
Did you enjoy it?

COLIN
I enjoyed talking to people, even if it was
just about cleaning products. But my boss,
Mike… he weren't exactly patient. I used to
have this meeting with him every Monday
morning, bright and early. Me, and the rest of
the sales team.

We used to call them 'Beat up Mondays'. He'd
rant and rave at us for a full hour, about how
terrible we were, that we'd never meet our
targets and how we were all… well… worthless.
I dreaded driving in, knowing that I'd have a
battering in store to start the week. My head
would whirl, my stomach used to churn. I even
started getting these chest pains… come to
think of it, it must have been Monday morning
when I…

SALLY
You must have had a heart attack!

COLIN
That explains it.
    (Holds hand to chest)
No beat.

SALLY
It's the customers I don't like at my job.

COLIN
  What do you do?

SALLY
  Customer service for a toy company. Answering
  the phone mainly.

COLIN
  Do you like it?

SALLY
  It's stressful. Some really angry people call
  in, parents mainly. Angry that their kid broke
  one of our toys and furious we can't refund
  them. I say sorry but they don't listen, they
  just keep on shouting and screaming…!

TABITHA
  Sounds like you both need a good de-stress
  meditation. Shall we begin?

SALLY
      (Glancing at Colin)
  Yeah, why not?

TABITHA
  Close your eyes, both of you.

      Colin shuts his eyes. After a while, and a
      glance at Colin, Sally does too.

TABITHA
  I want you to visualise yourselves as small
  baby birds. And you're trapped inside a thick
  cage of string, with just your head popping
  out. All you can do is peck at your string
  prison with your beak. Pecking until slowly,
  piece by piece, the string starts to loosen.
  You peck a small hole in your string cage and
  you can feel the morning breeze flow through
  you. Then your chest and wings burst free and
  with one almighty gust, you fly. Free of your
  shackles you soar up into the air. Higher and

TABITHA (Cont.)
  higher you go as the sun rises. You feel the
  sun's warmth in the air as you
  absorb its life-giving energy. You're
  liberated from negative energy and cleansed by
  the sun's rays. You release anything weighing
  you down- your job, deadlines, your constant
  lust for human brains… Let it all fall from
  you…
      (A beat)
  Now, when you're ready, awake.

      Sally and Colin open their eyes.

TABITHA
  How do you feel?

SALLY
  So much better. Like I'm lighter!

COLIN
  Yes! I feel like a new… whatever I am.

SALLY
  From now on every-day I'm gonna take the time
  to mediate and relax. That'll stop me taking
  work so seriously.

COLIN
  I've always under felt pressure. To hit my
  targets when I was alive, to hunt for human
  brains in death… but now… I think I'll go
  vegan!

TABITHA
  I'm so proud of both of you. Amazing what a
  short stay at Detox Spa can do…

      A scream offstage.

TABITHA
  Oh my god!

SALLY
  What is it?

TABITHA
  One of the receptionists… Linda!

COLIN
  What's happening?

TABITHA
  Her face… They're- She's being eaten alive by…
      (looks at Colin)
  By one of you!

COLIN
  Oh, that's Carl. My grave neighbour.
      (Shakes his head)
  He's an absolute savage.

SALLY
  You'll protect us from them, won't you?

COLIN
  Tabitha can reform them. Like she did to me.

TABITHA
  But there's so many of them!

SALLY
  Gosh, you can see so much more now the fog's
  starting to lift…

      *A bang and loud groans. Tabitha recoils,
      Sally and Colin look out curiously.*

TABITHA
  We need to get out! They're getting closer!

SALLY
  There's nothing to worry about. You can calm
  them with meditation.

TABITHA
  I can't do a whole horde of them!

COLIN
  I think 'ravening' is the collective term.

TABITHA
  They'll eat us all alive! We have to get out,
  now!

SALLY
  No, we can stay. Like you say, Detox Spa is a
  Kingdom of Calm.

    More banging.

TABITHA
  Do you really think I can do it?

SALLY
  Of course.

TABITHA
  Can't you talk to them, Colin?

COLIN
  I don't think I speak their language anymore…

    A loud bang.

TABITHA
  They're here.

COLIN
  There's Carl at the front! Classic Carl…

TABITHA
  Shall we start?

SALLY
  Please!

TABITHA
        (She takes a deep breath)
    Close your eyes.

                                    LX - Blackout

    *Groans of the undead horde as they
    approach.*

                    END PLAY

Still Life With Grave Juice
By Jim Moss

CHARACTERS
  QUINCY - *Human, Mid-thirties to late fifties*
  SPUREB - *Sentient alien creature, Possibly male, Body made of segmented plates looking something like a lobster or armadillo*
  DEWLIS - *Spureb's child, A smaller version of their parent, with a higher voice, Any gender*
  ROBOWAITER - *A mechanical AI waiter or waitress*

SETTING
  Restaurant in a space station.

SPUREB and DEWLIS sit at one table facing
each other with plates of strange-looking
food in front of them. QUINCY sits at the
second table.

ROBOTWAITER enters and places a glass of
wine in front of Quincy.

ROBOWAITER
Your wine, sir.

QUINCY
This is the real thing? None of that synth-
sludge?

ROBOWAITER
Direct from Earth. Highest quality and price,
I assure you. You may access my Integriport to
confirm the-"

QUINCY
(Waving Robowaiter away)
Yeah, yeah, Thank you.

Robowaiter turns and exits.

DEWLIS
Pahdah, what is "wine?"

SPUREB
A drink for cannibals.

DEWLIS
Earthers are cannibals?

Dewlis turns to stare at Quincy.

SPUREB
Yes.

DEWLIS
(Turning back to Spureb)
Should we distance ourselves?

SPUREB
Don't worry, they only eat their kind.

QUINCY
I'm sorry, I couldn't help overhearing…
Perhaps you got some wrong information. Earth
people are not cannibals.

SPUREB
It is well known throughout the galaxy that
yours is a cannibalistic race.

QUINCY
You're wrong. I don't know where you heard
this propaganda, but it's false and insulting.

SPUREB
You deny you bury your dead?

QUINCY
We bury them, but we don't eat them.

        *Spureb smiles smugly at Quincy, then turns
        to Dewlis.*

SPUREB
Earthers bury their dead in the ground in
graveyards where the bodies decompose. They
sow their strange plant life into these yards.
The plants send their roots into the soil and
suck in the fragments of the dead. Then the
plant blooms and bears fruit. Fruit containing
bits of the dead. Fruit they then eat.

QUINCY
Where are you getting this nonsense? We don't
We don't plant fruit trees in graveyards.

SPUREB
Is not your 'wine' made of grave juice?

QUINCY
Ahh! Here's your confusion. Wine is made from

QUINCY (Cont.)
grapes not graves. Grapes are grown in
vineyards, not graveyards.

SPUREB
(Turning back to Dewlis)
Earthers have many words in their languages
that mean the same thing. They use these to
confuse others about what things really are.
When you point out their error, they complain
that it was a mis-understanding or a mis-
interpretation. Beware when an Earther says
mis.

QUINCY
You are not the authority on Earth languages,
Mis-ter. What is your name?"

SPUREB
Spureb. And this is Dewlis, my progeny, And
your name?

Robowaiter crosses stage.

QUINCY
Quincy, and I am going to prove you wrong.
(Calling to Robowaiter)
Waiter!

Robowaiter crosses to stand beside Quincy.

ROBOWAITER
Yes, sir?

QUINCY
Tell me where does this wine come from?

ROBOWAITER
Earth. France, the Bourdeux region.

QUINCY
(Sipping wine)
St. Emillion? Pomerol?

ROBOWAITER
  No sir, Graves.

      Robowaiter exits.
      Spureb points a digit at Quincy.

SPUREB
  Bah-Zah!

QUINCY
  No! Listen, that's just the name of the
  region. The waiter mispronounced it. It's
  pronounced 'grahv' with a short a. A different
  vowel sound. It's French for gravel. It's the
  name of a French wine growing region. It has
  nothing to do with graves. Don't mistake a
  vineyard for graveyard.

DEWLIS
  The Earther said 'mis' twice!

      Spureb and Dewlis laugh. Quincy, growing
      angry, pounds the table.

QUINCY
  Just stop and listen! A vineyard is a yard
  where grapes grow, a graveyard is a-

SPUREB
  They are both 'yards' then, a measured plot of
  land, yes?

QUINCY
  Yes and-

SPUREB
  Yet you pronounce the 'yard' in vineyard as
  'yerd'. A different vowel sound. Is this a
  mispronunciation?

QUINCY
  Uh… no, because, uh…

SPUREB
    So yard is a word pronounced two ways, but
    means the same thing."

DEWLIS
    Like 'grahv' and 'grave'

QUNICY
    No! They are two different things. You know,
    even if a vineyard was planted on top of a
    dead body, we don't eat dead flesh directly,
    so we're not cannibals.

SPUREB
    Suppose they are two different plots of land,
    as you say. You still contaminate your soil
    with your dead. If an insect eats a leaf from
    a plant in your 'graveyard' then flies into a
    'vineyard' and dies in the soil and the vin
    plants eat the soil with the dead insect, then
    you eat the fruit of vin plants - you have
    eaten pieces of your dead.

QUNICY
    No. Because what I've really eaten is
    molecular compounds. Someone dies, they're
    buried, they decay. Maybe a bug eats some of
    it. When the bug dies it decays into simpler
    molecules, water, proteins, amino acids. So a
    plant uses these nutrients and produces fruit
    that someone may eat. So what? Everything gets
    recycled. Broken down and recycled. It's the
    nature of the universe.

SPUREB
    That may be the nature of your planet, but not
    the universe.

QUINCY
    Oh, yeah? What do you do with your dead?

SPUREB
    Our dead become art. That is the proper way to

SPUREB (Cont.)
  honor them.

QUNICY
  Art?

DEWLIS
  My great Ahdmah won the Op Culbet for her work
  on great Pahdah.

SPUREB
  He's hanging in the Brachalach, our finest
  museum. And what a stunning piece! Great
  Ahdmah bent his spine into a semi-circle and
  beneath this, draped the flesh of his pale
  underbelly. Over this setting moon motif, she
  sprinkled the glittering shards of his
  shattered neck plate. His abdomen is broken
  open and from the center, strips of muscle are
  strung outwards like a blazer blossom. The
  left claw, stained in ochre bile, is curled in
  a fetal ball. The fourth digit, bent
  backwards, protrudes like a stamen. And no
  matter where you move to look, that digit
  seems to follow you. His head hangs upside
  down strung from a series of tendons like a
  rain basket that… Bah! I'm talking to a
  flabedah!

QUINCY
  A flabedah?

SPUREB
  You have no word in your language. It means
  one who does not understand or appreciate what
  art does for a soul.

QUINCY
  Uh-huh.

SPUREB
  Ah! I forget. You Earthers believe the soul
  leaves the body after the body is no longer

SPUREB (Cont.)
  self-animating.

DEWLIS
  That's silly! Soul is made of body. How can
  soul leave body? Silly!

SPUREB
    (Carefully)
  Dewlis, this is what Earthers believe. We
  should not ridicule their beliefs.

QUINCY
  Ha! You cut up bodies to make rain buckets. So
  you chop up souls.

SPUREB
  The soul may be divided, but it is not
  separated. It is recombined with the body into
  a more appealing form of art. Most souls find
  it agreeable.

QUINCY
  How do you know they find it agreeable?

SPUREB
  In the silent hours if we stand before our
  ancestors and relax our minds we can hear
  their voices whisper to us.

DEWLIS
  Zul Ahdmah whispers to me.

SPUREB
  Yes, she tells you to stop slumping so much.

DEWLIS
  No, she tells me I am entitled to extra
  Kerzyhisses, for I will molt large.

SPUREB
  She does not. You are only imagining that.

QUINCY
  Yeah, you creatures molt. You drop off chunks
  of body parts. What happens to the soul of
  those parts? You couldn't possibly save every
  single—

SPUREB
  We re-ingest them. That's what we're eating
  right now.

DEWLIS
  I don't like the taste of my lower abdomen.

SPUREB
  Well, you better eat it, or you'll be
  incomplete and never get displayed in a good
  museum.

QUINCY
  What do you do when your art decays?

SPUREB
  It does not decay. It is all how-you-say —
  varnished. We are not primitives that allow
  our dead to decay into pieces that end up in
  the food supply and get mixed in with other
  souls and eaten and-

DEWLIS
      (To Spureb)
  Is that why his abdomen is so large?

SPUREB
  Yes. That is where they would collect. No
  soul, even a piece of soul, wants to be
  expelled as waste.

QUINCY
  Alright, look, my… stoutness has nothing to do
  with souls in my body. Extra weight is caused
  by fat cells that accumulate because… Look,
  it's not souls, OK?

SPUREB
  You bury your dead in the ground, your plant
  life eats from this ground, breaking up souls
  and—

QUINCY
  Your information is ancient. Burial is hardly
  done on our planet anymore. Real estate is too
  expensive. It's more common that we cremate
  our dead.

DEWLIS
    (To Spureb)
  Creamate?

SPUREB
    (To Dewlis)
  Cream is a white goo. Earthers whip it up and
  serve it on their desserts.

QUNICY
  No! That's not what it is!

SPUREB
  Cream-ate… 'Ate' means that they've eaten it!

QUNICY
  No, no, no! In cremation the body is burned
  into ashes.

DEWLIS
  What do you do with the ashes?

QUINCY
  Scatter them in the wind.

    *A look of horror washes over Spureb's
    face.
    Dewlis notices and reacts with concern.*

DEWLIS
  Pahdah?

SPUREB
  Millions of Earthers die every year on your
  planet.
       (Horror, disgust)
  Your atmosphere is full of corpse dust. Your
  populace breathes in burned up pieces of
  souls!

QUINCY
  That's enough!
       (Pounds table, stands)
  There are no…
       (Catches breath)
  Souls in…
       (Breathing heavily)
  Dust!

DEWLIS
  Why is the Earther breathing funny?

SPUREB
  He appears to be experiencing withdrawal. Not
  enough soul dust in this atmosphere for his
  cannibal addiction. It appears the grave juice
  isn't enough.

QUNICY
       (Sputtering)
  You… No… Uh…

DEWLIS
  He spit dead Earther juice at my head!

SPUREB
  Move back, Dewlis. I don't understand what is
  happening. He may have angered the souls he
  has consumed by denying their existence.

QUINCY
  You puchh… You achh…

DEWLIS
  Look how red his face glows.

SPUREB
He is blushing. Earthers do this when they
have embarrassed themselves.
(Whispers to Dewlis)
It may not be proper for us to view his shame,
let us look away.

Quincy clutches at his heart. He stumbles.

QUINCY
Hep… Har… Ak…

*Quincy falls to the ground. Spureb and
Dewlis eat their food. Robowaiter enters
and rushes to Quincy's side.*

ROBOWAITER
Sir? Sir? Is there a problem?
(Examines Quincy)
No breath detected. System protocol – advise.
(Tilts head. Beeps)
(Places hand on his chest)
No heartbeat detected. Please advise.
(Tilts head. Beeps)
Initiating cardio-pul-monary resus-citation.

*Robowaiter begins performing CPR on
Quincy. Spureb and Dewlis turn around to
watch.*

DEWLIS
Pahdah, what is resus-citation?

SPUREB
I believe the waiter is trying to reset-
animate the Earther.

DEWLIS
What is cardio-pull-monary?

SPUREB
I don't know, but he's pushing instead of
pulling. They're so incompetent here.

>   *Robowaiter stops performing CPR, and*
>   *examines Quincy.*

ROBOWAITER
  Customer not responding to prescribed
  procedure. Please advise.
      (Tilts head. Beeps)
      (Taps button on shoulder)
  Clean-up crew, please immediately bus dead
  Earther at table four.

SPUREB
  Excuse me, but what will happen to the
  Earther's body?

ROBOWAITER
  It will need to be claimed in the next
  seventy-two hours, or it will be sent to the
  organic recycling center.

>   *Robowaiter turns to exit.*

SPUREB
  That poor soul!
      (Beat, turns)
  Dewlis, If no relative comes forward, I think
  I will claim his body.

DEWLIS
  Why?

SPUREB
  It is our chance to do something good, Make
  the Earther into art.

DEWLIS
      (Looking with disgust at Quincy)
  I don't want to make the Earther into art!

SPUREB
  Well, we don't have to do it. I think I can
  get Spiosac.

DEWLIS
  Spiosac!?

SPUREB
  Oh, he's very eager to work with other
  xenophylum. Can you imagine what he could do
  what such a creature? I wonder what his
  innards look like? Spiosac could create
  something phenomenal – perhaps a still life
  with grave juice.

DEWLIS
  What an honor for the Earther.

    Dewlis and Spureb turn to stare at Quincy.

SPUREB
  I'm sure he'll find it agreeable.

                    END PLAY

Sweet Ghoul Long Past
By Christine Emmert

CHARACTERS
  CHILD - *Female, played by an adult*
  GHOUL - *Male, horribly disfigured*

SETTING
  A pastoral setting.

*Lights up on a pastoral setting. A little
girl, CHILD, is tossing petals of a flower
into an imaginary stream.*

CHILD
He loves me, he loves me not. I don't even
know who "he" is… but adults know. I see my
sister do this all the time…

*After a long moment, there is a loud
crashing sound.*

CHILD
Oh no! They're coming to take me away… again.

*She watches as a large horribly disfigured
man, GHOUL, comes out of the bushes.*

CHILD
Oh, it's you.

GHOUL
(roars)

CHILD
No, that's no good. You tried that yesterday.
Want a candy?

GHOUL
(roars)

CHILD
I wrote about you last night in my diary.
That's what my sister does when she meets
someone. You are the stranger who appears…

GHOUL
I am not a stranger to those who know my
story. Do you know my story?

CHILD
I don't think I want to.

GHOUL
    (roars)

CHILD
  I'm sure I don't. So not the handsome
  stranger. My sister's strangers are always
  handsome. Were you ever handsome?

GHOUL
  There are those who think I am handsome now.
  Of course, they are all dead.

CHILD
  Well, you'd better stay off the road. There
  have been murders around here. The villagers
  are out looking.

GHOUL
  Do you think I am a murderer?

CHILD
  You have the face of one.

GHOUL
    (roars)

CHILD
  And the voice.

GHOUL
    (seductively)
  Have I hurt you?

CHILD
  No, but I'm just a little girl. People think
  twice about children.

GHOUL
  They taste the sweetest. Not that I've ever
  eaten one.
    (takes her hand)
  Like honey right from the honeycomb.

CHILD
  Will you take me to the cemetery again?

GHOUL
  Yes, my sweet.

CHILD
  And show me your grave?

GHOUL
  Oh, you will come and play with me!

CHILD
  Certainly. If you promise not to roar…

GHOUL
  Follow me.

          *Ghoul walks off. Child follows, drawing
          a long knife from behind her to strike.*

          From offstage, there is a long scream.

                    END PLAY

The Bus to Nowhere
By Cole Hunter Dzubak

CHARACTERS
  CHARLIE - *Recently lost the love of their life, intelligent but currently dazed by misery, Any gender, 20s-40s*
  TREVOR - *Has been missing for two years, quiet and thoughtful, Male, 20s-40s*
  LISA - *Caring and worried friend of Charlie, Female, 20s-40s*

SETTING
  A Philadelphia bus stop (night).
  The Bus to Nowhere (timeless).

NOTES

The Bus to Nowhere is the only mass
transit option for Philadelphia's lost and
hopeless. It is said that the bus appears
to those who are left truly distraught and
alone by the most tragic circumstances.
Passengers sit on the bus dazed by misery,
so much so they can't interact with others
or even acknowledge where they are. You
cannot leave the bus until you temporarily
break out of its daze and remember to pull
the cord and get off. Once you exit the
bus, you lose all memory of ever being on
it. Legend says that some ride the bus for
years before being able to leave, while
some never leave, whether by choice or
not, and ride the bus for all eternity.

SCENE ONE

*A Philadelphia bus stop bench. The space
seems baron and grey, there is a loud
silence in the air.*

*CHARLIE, a widow/widower, is sat on the
bench next to LISA, their friend. Both are
dressed in all black. They have just come
from a funeral. Lisa has her arm around
Charlie.*

LISA
  How you holding up?

CHARLIE
  About as shitty as you expect.

LISA
  Right… dumb question, sorry.

CHARLIE
  What am I supposed to do now…?

LISA
  Stay strong… try to move on-

CHARLIE
  I don't want to move on… I just want my wife
  back!

LISA
  I know, Charlie, I know.

CHARLIE
  You don't know! You're going home to your
  husband! How could you possibly know!?

  Lisa removes her arm.

LISA
  I'm sorry, Charlie, I really am.

CHARLIE
  I didn't mean to yell... Thank you for checking
  on me.

LISA
  Of course.

CHARLIE
  I just don't know what to do... She was my best
  friend...

LISA
  She was something special, that's for sure.

CHARLIE
  She looked beautiful, didn't she?

LISA
  Always.

CHARLIE
  I mean today, right... in her dress.

LISA
  Oh, of course, she did! She looked peaceful.

CHARLIE
  She always liked that dress... It was her
  favorite... That's why I wanted her to wear it.

LISA
  That was nice of you.

CHARLIE
  Fuck...

LISA
  Hey, hey, hey... It's alright... Let it out.

CHARLIE
  Lisa?

LISA
  What is it?

CHARLIE
  Could I get some time to myself?

LISA
  Of course, let's get you home and I'll

CHARLIE
  I mean… right now. I just need some space.

LISA
  Are you sure? I don't know if that's a good
  idea right now.

CHARLIE
  Please… I need to just… figure things out…

LISA
  Will you promise to call me if you need
  anything? And let me know when you get home.

CHARLIE
  Yes.

LISA
  Ok… Be safe, please.

CHARLIE
  Thank you…

        *Lisa gives Charlie a hug, who leans into
        it but doesn't move their arms. Lisa
        exits, looking back at Charlie as they do.*

CHARLIE
  God damnit… I'm sorry I let you down, Kayci…

  Why'd you have to leave me? Is this my fault?
  I know I shouldn't think that… I know it's
  self-destructive behavior to think like this
  but what if it's my fault you got sick?

CHARLIE (Cont.)
  What if karma paid me back… Maybe if I gave
  more to charity… Or if I wasn't such a piece
  of shit in high school… If I checked in with
  my parents more often you wouldn't have gotten
  sick…you always made me feel better… Always
  knew what to say…

  I don't know what I'm going to do without you…
  You were my everything… I'm trying so hard to
  keep it together, but I can't… I can't do this
  without you… we had our lives planned out… how
  am I supposed to do it by myself… Please,
  Baby… Give me a sign… Anything… I need you…
  I'll always need you…

    Charlie breaks down.

    *The sound of a bus approaches and pulls up
    by them. They look up and stand like
    they're in a trance.*

                    SCENE TWO

    *They enter the bus and the bench is
    replaced with a bus seat. Sitting on the
    seat is TREVOR, looking extremely tired
    and distressed. Charlie wanders the bus
    until they sit next to him. Trevor looks
    shocked to see Charlie enter the bus.*

CHARLIE
  Can I sit?

TREVOR
  Sure.

CHARLIE
  Thank you.

TREVOR
  Anytime.

CHARLIE
  Do I know you?

TREVOR
  Do you?

CHARLIE
  I don't know… I'm pretty out of it… Maybe, I'm
  seeing things.

TREVOR
  Guess I just have one of those faces.

CHARLIE
  Where are you heading?

TREVOR
  Nowhere, I guess.

CHARLIE
  Same here.

TREVOR
  Just needed to clear my head.

CHARLIE
  Me too.

TREVOR
  Why are you here?

CHARLIE
  Does it matter?

TREVOR
  To me… Maybe it does.

CHARLIE
  Why do you care?

TREVOR
  It seems we both need a friend right now…

CHARLIE
  My wife died.

TREVOR
  How so?

CHARLIE
  Cancer.

TREVOR
  I'm sorry to hear that.

CHARLIE
  Yeah… Me too.

TREVOR
  How are you holding up?

CHARLIE
  How do you expect?

TREVOR
  Right. Why else would you be on your way to
  nowhere?

CHARLIE
  She got sick so suddenly… It was too late by
  the time we caught it…

TREVOR
  I can't imagine how that feels.

CHARLIE
  No… You can't… It sucks…

TREVOR
  I'm sorry you're hurting.

        *Charlie now completely falls under the
        spell of the bus and breaks down.*

        Trevor watches for a moment.

TREVOR

I can't believe the bus found you… You were
one of the happiest people I knew… Nothing
could ever bring you down… I'm sorry about
Kayci… You two were perfect for each other… I
still remember your wedding night… You two
looked so happy… Why'd you have to be caught
alone this late? I know how bad you're
hurting… but damn it… Why'd you do this to
yourself… Why can't you hear me? Why can't you
snap out of it like I did? Maybe because I
accepted what happened… What I did…

I killed someone, Charlie… I killed some
random guy crossing the street… 'cause I was
drunk and got behind the wheel… I don't even
remember why I was drinking that night… hell I
can't tell you I decided to drive home… I get
drunk a lot, I'm used to walking home or
getting a cab… I know not to drink and drive
but for some reason… I was devastated, so I
ran and lived in the streets until the bus
came…

Charlie, you need to wake up… You can't stay
trapped here… You need to wake up… Live on and
remember Kayci's legacy… Keep her memory
alive… Charlie… CHARLIE!

*Trevor gives Charlie a push and they wake
up, no longer in a trance.*

CHARLIE
What?! Where am I? What am I…
Trevor? Oh, my fucking god, Trevor!

TREVOR
You need to calm down.

CHARLIE
Where am I?

TREVOR
  You're… on the bus…

CHARLIE
  The bus?

TREVOR
  The bus to nowhere.

CHARLIE
  That… That can't be… That's just a myth.

TREVOR
  Obviously not.

CHARLIE
  I don't even remember getting on any bus.

TREVOR
  Nobody does.

CHARLIE
  How long have I been riding?

TREVOR
  I don't know… Time moves differently here…
  Like, it doesn't exist…

CHARLIE
  Trevor… You've been missing for three years…
  We thought you were dead.

TREVOR
  You might as well be if you're here.

CHARLIE
  How do we get off?

TREVOR
  You're awake?

CHARLIE
  I'm talking to you, aren't I?

TREVOR
  Quick, pull the brake, get off before you fall
  under the spell again.

CHARLIE
  Ok. Pull the brake.

    *Charlie pulls the brake, the bus harshly
    comes to a stop.*

TREVOR
  You ok?

CHARLIE
  Yeah, you?

TREVOR
  Yeah, you need to go, now.

CHARLIE
  Come on, let's get outta here.

    *Charlie grabs Trevor's hand but he pulls
    back.*

CHARLIE
  Trevor?

TREVOR
  I'm not going.

CHARLIE
  What do you mean, you're awake?

TREVOR
  I've been awake… I'm not leaving.

CHARLIE
  Trevor, are you fucking serious? We have a
  chance here.

TREVOR
  I've yet to fall under the spell again since

310

TREVOR (Cont.)
  I've woken up… I try to do my best to wake up
  anyone else and get them off…

CHARLIE
  It's been three years, please.

TREVOR
  Nobody will miss me if it's three more…
  Somebody has to play guardian angel.

CHARLIE
  No, you don't.

TREVOR
  I've made up my mind.

CHARLIE
  Trevor, I-

TREVOR
  I'm so sorry about Kayci.

    Trevor pushes Charlie off the bus.

                SCENE THREE

    *The bus seat is replaced with the bench.
    Charlie looks confused as to where they
    are, now off the bus, they've lost all
    memory of what just happened.*

    *Lisa, now in regular clothing, enters and
    is shocked to see Charlie.*

LISA
  Charlie! Oh my god, Charlie, you're ok!

    Lisa runs and hugs them.

LISA
  It's been a week since we've heard from you, I
  thought something happened, that you-

CHARLIE
  Hey, hey… I'm ok.

LISA
  Where were you?

CHARLIE
  I don't know… I can't remember anything… I was
  sitting on the bench after you left then I
  woke up just now.

LISA
  You don't remember the past week at all?

CHARLIE
  No…

LISA
  I'm just glad you're ok… You gave me a heart
  attack… I thought we needed to plan another
  funeral.

CHARLIE
  Not yet…

LISA
  Come on, let's get you to a hospital… Make
  sure you're ok.

CHARLIE
  Yeah… I think I'll need that…

      *They begin to exit, but Charlie stops to
      look at the bench.*

LISA
  What's wrong?

CHARLIE
  I… had a memory…

LISA
  Of…

CHARLIE
  Do you remember Trevor?

LISA
  Trevor Jacobs…? It's been years since I've
  seen him.

CHARLIE
  I just had a strange memory of us…

LISA
  Must've been a dream.

CHARLIE
  It felt so… real.

LISA
  Come on, let's get going.

    They exit.

    Charlie looks at the bench one last time.

                              LX - Blackout

                    END PLAY

The Dark
By Janice Kennedy

CHARACTERS
  SALLY - *a woman, 20s-30s*
  MARK - *her husband, 30s-40s*
  FIRST WOMAN (SHADOW) - *an attractive woman, 20s*
  SECOND WOMAN (SHADOW) - *a woman who looks like Sally*
  MAN (SHADOW) - *a man who looks like Mark*

SETTING
  A City Apartment Kitchen with Bathroom adjacent.

*No lights are on in the kitchen area, but
there are a few small candles burning in
the bathroom. SALLY is in the bathtub with
a large towel draped across it so that
only her head and legs show. Her head is
tilted back, her eyes closed. Music plays
softly. Traffic can be heard through an
open window.*

*MARK enters the kitchen and flips on a
light. He's carrying books in one hand and
pulling his tie off with the other. He
throws the books on the table and crosses
to an air vent in the wall. He raps on it.*

MARK
  What? Is it out again?

  *Sally doesn't move. Mark opens the
  refrigerator door and not finding what he
  wants, slams it and enters the bathroom.*

MARK
  God, I'm tired of this. Is the A.C. out in the
  whole building or what?
    (pause)
  What are you doing?

  Sally rolls her eyes.

MARK
  No, I mean what's with the towel?

SALLY
  Was it William Carlos Williams who said there
  are fourteen ways of looking at a blackbird?

MARK
  Thirteen. And it was Wallace Stevens.

SALLY
  You were a good English Lit teacher. Really.
  It's just that when I was your student, I was

SALLY (Cont.)
    too busy looking at you, imagining things
    about you, to pay much attention to who wrote
    what.
        (pause)
    "I was of three minds,
    Like a tree,
    In which there are three blackbirds."

MARK
    Well, you remembered part of the poem anyway.

SALLY
    So there are thirteen ways of looking at a
    blackbird, but there's only one way a man
    looks at a woman with no clothes on.

MARK
    Oh really?

SALLY
    He looks with his body.

MARK
    You've never minded before.

SALLY
    Tonight, I do.

MARK
    God, Sally. Grow up.

SALLY
    I have, Mark. That's the problem. You like 'em
    young, don't you, Herr Professor?

MARK
    Come on. I'm really not in the mood for a
    fight.

SALLY
    You don't want to fight about anything
    anymore, have you noticed that?

MARK
  No. And I don't want to fight about that
  either.
      (pause)
  Come on, get out, we need to go get something
  to eat. If you want, I'll go into the other
  room.

      *Mark doesn't move. Sally stares at him for
      a moment. It's a standoff. Still staring
      at him, Sally prepares to stand up. As she
      grabs the sides of the tub: Blackout.*

                              LX - Blackout
                              SD - Silence

      *The small candles only add to the gloom.
      The kitchen is completely dark.*

MARK
  Damn it! No air conditioning, no lights! Don't
  we have any bigger candles than this?

      The sound of Mark walking into something.

MARK
  Shit!

      *Mark rummages through a kitchen drawer. He
      strikes a match and lights a fat candle,
      which creates a circle of light around the
      kitchen table when he places it at the
      center. As Mark does this, three SHADOWS
      covered in black drapes "materialize" on
      the outer edges of the candlelight. They
      settle into amorphous shapes.*

      *Mark sits, appearing not to notice the
      mysterious figures. Sally, wrapped in a
      towel, enters the outer circle of light.*

SALLY
  Do you feel it?

                      317

The shadows lean toward Mark.

MARK
  Feel what?

SALLY
  I think something happens when the lights go
  out like that.

MARK
  Happens?

SALLY
  Maybe it's the way your mind is suddenly
  surprised by the darkness. You haven't chosen
  it because you haven't flipped the switch and
  so you're not prepared for it. Your mind goes
  into a kind of shock. It reacts.

MARK
  Reacts?

SALLY
  It's as if your mind reaches into the darkness
  and tries to make sense of it. It goes into
  the gloom, becomes part of it. In the dark, do
  you think it's possible for your thoughts to
  become things?

    The three Shadows shiver.

MARK
  What do you mean?

    *As Sally speaks, the Shadows change their
    poses using slow, stylized movement.*

SALLY
  A tree becomes a man, a woman a bird. In the
  dark, your mind, in shock, creates its own
  reality. Can you feel it?

MARK
  Can I feel what? I don't know what you're
  talking about.

SALLY
  No, I don't think you do.

      Through the open window comes the
      plaintive, sad sound of a single musical
      instrument - perhaps a clarinet. Mark
      listens for a moment then turns to Sally.

MARK
  "Music is feeling, then, not sound;
  And thus it is that what I feel,
  Here in this room, desiring you,
  Thinking of you in your blue-shadowed silk,
  Is Music…"

SALLY
  Wallace Stevens again, isn't it? "Of a green
  evening, clear and warm, she bathed in her
  still garden." You used to quote those things
  to me and I would part my legs for you like
  they were water and you were Moses.

      Mark reaches out and takes her hand.

  That was before I realized you were just good
  at remembering other poet's seduction
  speeches.

      Mark withdraws his hand.

  Things you told me in the dark, I believed.
  Maybe it's because the darkness itself was so
  powerful, is so powerful. How little something
  like that candle does to cut through it. And
  when the light is so weak, it's as if your
  mind can bend it into a new dimension, like
  you do in your sleep when you're having a
  nightmare.

The three draped Shadows shiver.

MARK
  You want to know about a nightmare? It's
  coming home to find there's no fucking air
  conditioning, there's not a damn thing to eat
  in the house and you're in the fucking tub
  soaking your tush under a towel because you
  don't want my body to "see" yours.

SALLY
  But, we've already discovered you're always
  thinking about sex, aren't you?

  *One Shadow throws off their drape to
  reveal FIRST WOMAN, scantily dressed. She
  walks around the table.*

  *Mark is transfixed, but Sally doesn't
  appear to see the apparition.*

MARK
  No, I'm not.

SALLY
  Get rid of her.

  *The Woman drapes herself again and settles
  back into an amorphous shape.*

MARK
  What? What are you talking about? Get rid of
  who?
      (pause)
  Look, I think we need to get something to eat.
  Things are getting a little crazy and I'm
  starving. How about Harv's? That's at least
  seven blocks. They've probably got
  electricity.

SALLY
  Why are you so late tonight?

MARK
  What do you mean? Why are you looking at me
  like that? You knew I had a faculty meeting.
  God, it went on forever.
      (pause)
  All right. I stopped off at a bar on my way
  home.

SALLY
  What bar?

MARK
  I don't know. A bar.

SALLY
  Why?

MARK
  Why what?

SALLY
  Why did you stop?

MARK
  What do you mean, why? Because I wanted a
  moment of peace. Because I wanted to think.

SALLY
  About what?

MARK
  Things. Just things. For Christ's sake.

SALLY
  When the poem says:
  "A man and a woman,
  Are one.
  A man and a woman and a blackbird are one,"

  What does it mean?
  Can three things- a man, a woman and a
  blackbird- make one? And when a man and woman
  marry, as you and I did, and the ceremony says

SALLY (Cont.)
  you two are now one, can there be another who
  enters into that? And can the three of you-the
  man, the woman, and… can the three of you then
  be one as well?

MARK
  Three?

    *The First Woman undrapes and walks around
    the table again. She stops and freezes in
    a sexy pose.*

SALLY
  A man and a woman and his-

MARK
  -Don't.

SALLY
  A man, a woman and his… blackbird.

    *Another of the three Shadows undrapes to
    reveal a SECOND WOMAN, who looks very much
    like Sally. She's even wearing the same
    towel. The Second Woman goes to Mark,
    pulls out a butcher knife from under the
    towel and mimes stabbing him.*

                                    LX - Strobing

    *Mark does not appear to see the Second
    Woman, but Sally does.*

MARK
  Stop this!

    *The Second Woman steps back, redrapes and
    settles back into an amorphous shape at
    the edge of the circle of light.*

SALLY
  Stop what?

MARK
  This attitude you've developed. All right,
  you're right, I didn't stop at a bar.

SALLY
  What's her name? A man, a woman and...?

MARK
  Look, it's just that... I don't know how to
  explain it.

      *The First Woman moves toward Mark. She
      caresses his face and sits on his lap. He
      smiles nervously.*

SALLY
  I think I get the picture.

MARK
  You probably want to kill me, don't you?

      *The Second Woman emerges and walks around
      the table again, stopping at Mark. She
      pulls out the knife and brings it back and
      freezes. Sally stares at her.*

SALLY
  I keep wondering about your conscience.

      *The third Shadow undrapes to reveal a MAN
      who looks very much like Mark. He is, in
      fact, dressed exactly like him. The Man
      takes out a noose and stands behind Mark,
      the noose hanging over Mark's head.*

SALLY
  Do you have one?

      *Mark scratches the back of his neck, but
      seems unaware that anyone -or anything- is
      standing behind him.*

MARK

A conscience? Yes, yes, of course I do. I know
how I must have hurt you.

*As Mark is shaking his head "yes," the Man
with the noose is shaking his head "no."
He puts the noose around Mark's neck and
tightens it. Mark coughs and stands up,
dumping the First Woman off his lap. The
Man removes the noose and all the Shadows
go back under their drapes. Mark is still
coughing as he takes the candle and goes
to the refrigerator.*

MARK

You know, there's never any goddamn beer.
Maybe I should go get some. Maybe the corner
store's still open. Hey, maybe they're having
an impromptu sale because of the blackbird, I
mean the blackout.

SALLY

There's beer in the back.

MARK

Hey, so there is. But I should go get some
more. There's only two. I bet you're out of
smokes. I can get those, too.

*Mark brings two beers out and sets one in
front of Sally.*

SALLY

Like the urban myth.

MARK

What myth?

Mark opens his beer and takes a swig.

SALLY

About the man who pops out for a pack of
cigarettes and never comes back.

MARK
   Look, we need to talk.

SALLY
   Do me a favor first? Get me those smokes?

MARK
   Sure. Sure. And when I get back, I'll explain
   everything to you. I think maybe you're a
   little confused. It's really not what you
   think. I just, well, you know these things
   happen. And, mostly, they don't mean anything
   and that's what we're talking about here. So
   I'll just pop out and be right back, okay?

SALLY
   Be careful.

MARK
   Of what?

       *Mark moves toward the door and is
       surrounded by the three Shadows, who
       "swallow" him with their drapes.
       Sally shrugs.*

SALLY
   The dark.

       *Sally calmly opens a drawer in the kitchen
       table and takes out a full pack of
       cigarettes. She unwraps the package and
       lights one, inhaling deeply. She blows out
       her match.*

                           LX - Kitchen
                 SD - Music and Traffic

       Sally sits smoking.

                           LX - Fade to black

           END PLAY

The Demon Speaks
By Rebecca Holbourn

CHARACTERS
  MOLLY - *Any age, any gender*
  DAMON - *An unseen demon, hiding under the bed. Any age, any gender*

SETTING
  A single bed.

A single bed. MOLLY lies propped up under the covers, resolutely not asleep.

MOLLY

Dreams are such weird things. Weird places. Weird situations. Is it any wonder that we push them away when we wake up? That we can't hold onto the memories. Those brief few seconds of the brain creating what seems to be an entire day of activity just before you wake up.

Sometimes, I don't want to leave it and I wake up so angry that I've been forced into the real world. A world of no control. A world of constant sleeping, waking, eating, sleeping, waking, eating, sleeping…

Well, you understand…

Sometimes, I wish I didn't have to sleep. More often, I wish I didn't have to wake.

Which world would I most want to exist in? The dreamworld where anything is possible? The real world where everything is tangible?

DAMON
    (unseen)
Will you shut up?

MOLLY
What the hell? Who- Where?

DAMON
I'm under your bed. Could you just shut up and let me have my fun?

MOLLY
Fun?!

DAMON
Yes, I'm a dream demon. You can call me Damon.

MOLLY
  Can I indeed?

DAMON
  Yes… That's my name.

MOLLY
  Well, could you come out and talk with me?

DAMON
  No, I can't be seen by the human eye.

MOLLY
  Oh, well, could you go away then?

DAMON
  I thought you wanted to dream.

MOLLY
  I do.

DAMON
  If I go, then you won't.

MOLLY
  What?

DAMON
  I work with your mind to create a dream. I'm
  an artist.

MOLLY
  And everyone has their own personal dream
  demon artist?

DAMON
  No, a lot of people can't appreciate it so we
  just give them an easy dream or nightmare.
  Depends who's on call for the quick draw.

MOLLY
  Every dream is from a demon?

DAMON
    Yeah, that's why you're always so unfulfilled.

MOLLY
    Thanks.

DAMON
    You're welcome.

MOLLY
    So when I had a dream about an infestation of
    spiders who were actually dressed like
    sailors…

DAMON
    Haaaa, that sounds like Malcom.

MOLLY
    And the time that I thought my Mum was
    actually a ladybird prime minister?

DAMON
    Oh, that was me, yeah.

MOLLY
    What is wrong with you?

DAMON
    Nothing.
    What's wrong with you?

MOLLY
    Nothing!

DAMON
    Hmm…

MOLLY
    What?

DAMON
    You want to exist in the dreamworld I create
    for you and not wake up.

MOLLY
  Do I?

DAMON
  Yes, what's so wrong about the waking world?

MOLLY
  Nothing.

DAMON
  Hmm...

MOLLY
  What? Tell me!

DAMON
  Well, if you liked the waking world so much,
  then, you never would've heard my voice.

MOLLY
  How come?

DAMON
  We can only talk when you're sleeping.

     Silence.

MOLLY
  Oh, for crying out-

                                   LX - Flash

     Molly sits upright.

MOLLY
  LOUD!

     She glances around.

MOLLY
  What...?

     Confused silence.

Molly stares out at the Audience.

MOLLY
  Was I awake then or awake now?

She continues to stare.

                              LX - Fade to Black

                    END PLAY

The Ex-Files
By Jamie Mcleish

CHARACTERS
  DAWSON - *A youngish guy, in the first flush of romance with Joey*
  JOEY - *A youngish woman, smitten with Dawson and ready to take the next step*
  TRACEY - *Dawson's ex-girlfriend who may not be all she seems*

SETTING
  A living room with sofa and coffee table.

*DAWSON and JOEY are snuggled on a sofa
with a glass of wine.*

JOEY
  This is nice.

DAWSON
  Happy one-month anniversary.

JOEY
  Happy anniversary to you!

  Dawson and Joey nuzzle.

                           SD - Doorbell

JOEY
  Who's that?

DAWSON
  Dunno. I'll get rid of them.

  *Dawson pecks Joey on the lips and exits to
  check who it is. While he is gone, Joey
  checks in her bag and seems reassured by
  what's in there.*

  *After a while, TRACEY enters, closely
  followed by Dawson. Joey looks bemused.*

TRACEY
     (To Joey)
  Pardon me for barging in but it's like I said
  to Dawson; two's company but three's allowed.

JOEY
  Isn't three 'a crowd'?

TRACEY
  Don't be daft.
     (Beat)
  I'm Tracey. Nice to meet you.

JOEY
  I'm Joey.

DAWSON
  I see you two have already met.

JOEY
  Er… Yes. Who… Who are you?

TRACEY
  Me? I'm nobody. Although I was somebody,
  wasn't I, Dawson?

DAWSON
  Tracey is my er… my friend.

TRACEY
  Friend? Friend!
      (to Joey)
  If he gets up to what we got up to with all
  his friends I'd watch out if I were you, Joey!

JOEY
  You and Dawson know each other well?

TRACEY
  Very well. We were-

DAWSON
  -Partners.

TRACEY
  Lovers.

DAWSON
  Briefly.

TRACEY
  Well it was briefly with you.
      (to Joey)
  Catch my drift?
      (to Dawson)
  Put the kettle on, Dawson. I'm parched. Or if

TRACEY (Cont.)
  you've got any more of that wine, I'll have a
  glass.

DAWSON
      (tetchy)
  No! There's no more wine left, I'm afraid. And
  I'm out of tea and coffee, so…

JOEY
  I'm sure I can find something, Dawson. You two
  stay here, I'll have a look.

      *Joey stands and picks up her bag before
      exiting to the kitchen.*

DAWSON
      (seething)
  What are you doing here!

TRACEY
  Aren't you glad to see me?

DAWSON
  No, I am not! I want you out of here! Remember
  what I said?

TRACEY
  I remember everything. All too well!

DAWSON
  I thought I made myself clear!

TRACEY
  Crystal. But like I said… We've unfinished
  business.

DAWSON
  You're crackers! Always were.

TRACEY
  Come on, don't be like this, Dawson! There's
  no reason we can't be friends.

DAWSON
  I've got enough friends! Now why don't you
  just fu-

     Joey enters, carrying two glasses of wine.
     She places them down in front of Dawson
     and Tracey.

  -nnily enough, I was just thinking that I
  should return your copy of Prince Harry's
  autobiography. I've finished it.

TRACEY
  You can keep it. Or give it to charity, if
  there's one you don't like.

DAWSON
  Either way, I think you should be going now.
  Joey and I were just about to-

TRACEY
  To what?

JOEY
  Watch TV.

DAWSON
  I've also got something simmering on the hob,
  so…

TRACEY
  I hope it's not a bunny!

JOEY
  What?

TRACEY
  Joke.
       (Beat)
  I take it you two are…?

DAWSON
  That's right. Joey's my girlfriend.

TRACEY
  Aww! That's lovely. It really is. Dawson and
  Joey. It's like that TV teen drama… Beverly
  Hills 90210. Dawson, Joey… and Tracey.
      (Beat)
  Tell me Joey, does Dawson still like it when
  someone does that thing to his-

DAWSON
  -Goodnight, Tracey! It's nice to see you again
  but I must ask you to leave.

TRACEY
  Keep yer hair on! Jeez! I only called in as I
  was passing because I need the loo.

JOEY
  The loo?

TRACEY
  I've got a touch of cystitis.

DAWSON
  Cystitis?

TRACEY
  Burny piss!

DAWSON
  Right. Yeah. You know where it is.

TRACEY
  Thank you! I'm bursting!

      Tracey hurries offstage.

DAWSON
  I'm so sorry about this! I had no idea she'd
  call round.

JOEY
  You used to go out with her?

DAWSON
Yes. I finished it a while ago. She was…
overbearing. After a while, she became more
than overbearing, she was unhinged! She was
obsessed with me, wouldn't leave me alone.
She's dangerous!

JOEY
Oh my God! Dawson, that's awful.

DAWSON
I haven't seen her for a couple of months. I
thought she'd finally accepted it was over.

JOEY
Can you get rid of her?

DAWSON
I hope so! She's not spoiling tonight for us!

JOEY
I hope not. With it being our one month
anniversary, I was hoping that you and I could
take things to the next level. I was planning
on going… all the way, with you.

DAWSON
You mean sex?

JOEY
I don't mean 'to Blackpool'.

DAWSON
      (flirty)
Funny you should say that, because when I'm
with you I'm like a stick of rock.

JOEY
Twisted?

DAWSON
Hard.

JOEY
  I know this is embarrassing but I've... I've
  never done this before. You're very special to
  me and I want you to be my first.

DAWSON
  Your first?

JOEY
  Yes. Is that alright? I've brought what I
  need, in my bag. You know, for protection.

DAWSON
  I'm flattered. I would love to be your first.

JOEY
      (breathy)
  Oh, Dawson...

      Tracey bustles back in.

TRACEY
  Christ, that stung like a bitch.

JOEY
  I've heard that cranberry juice can help.

TRACEY
  Tried it.

  Lay on my back, put my legs in the air and
  poured it all over it but all I did was ruin
  my sheets. Waste of time.

DAWSON
  Aren't you supposed to drink it?

TRACEY
      (to Joey)
  Get Dr. Hilary there!
      (to Dawson)
  When did you last manage a yeast infection?

DAWSON
  Never.

TRACEY
  Exactly! You stick to your bits and I'll stick
  to mine… Which is what's been happening
  lately.

      Tracey rearranges her crotch.

DAWSON
  I think I'll just nip to the loo myself…
  Clean the seat.

      Dawson exits.

JOEY
      (awkwardly)
  So… Do you have any other… conditions?

TRACEY
      (serious, ignoring the question)
  Listen carefully to to me, Joey. You need to
  get out of here.

JOEY
  What?

TRACEY
  You're not safe. With Dawson.

JOEY
  Dawson? Why not?

TRACEY
  There's no time to explain but I've been
  watching this house for months, waiting for
  him to bring someone home. I'm here to warn
  you, you have to go. Now!

JOEY
  Dawson said you were unhinged but-

TRACEY
    Im sure he did! I'm sure he told you a
    wonderful story about me being clingy and
    desperate, maybe a little bit crazy.

JOEY
    Yes! He did!

TRACEY
    He probably told you that he got sick of me
    and broke it off. You mustn't believe him! It
    was me who left him!

JOEY
    I don't understand?

TRACEY
    I fell hard for him and I overlooked the signs
    at first but he's not right, Joey! He's
    dangerous!

JOEY
    Dangerous? How?

TRACEY
    It started off with small things at first,
    minor ways to assert himself but things slowly
    started to escalate until he was dominating
    me. His behaviour became so controlling and
    manipuliative that I lost who I was for a
    while. I was lucky to get free of him when I
    did. I don't know what he would've done If I'd
    stayed much longer.

JOEY
    You left him? But he's so lovely!

TRACEY
    He was with me, too! At first. You can believe
    me or not but I'm telling you, Joey, do
    yourself a favour and walk away!

JOEY
But if you were obsessed with him this is
exactly the kind of thing you'd say.

TRACEY
I can't deny that. But I also can't sit back
and let a sister suffer like I did. When I saw
he was dating someone new, I had to act.

JOEY
This is all-

Dawson enters.

DAWSON
All what?

TRACEY
        (light)
All a bit awkward, really! What am I doing? I
should go. You two obviously want to be alone.

JOEY
You're going? Leaving me?

TRACEY
Yes. But it was nice meeting you. I hope you
remember what I said.

DAWSON
And what was that?

JOEY
Oh, just that she and I obviously have good
taste… in men.

DAWSON
Yes, you do. But Tracey's right. It's time she
left.

JOEY
Maybe I should be going, too. I mean, it's
late and-

DAWSON
  You can't drive now, Joey. You've been
  drinking. And I've had a couple as well so I
  can't give you a lift.

TRACEY
  She can get the bus with me.

DAWSON
  Please, don't go Joey. I was looking forward
  to… to getting to know you better.

JOEY
      (torn)
  I don't know what to do for the best.

TRACEY
  The offer's there, Joey.

      Dawson spreads his arms.

DAWSON
  And the offer's here, too.

JOEY
  I think that maybe I should go home.

DAWSON
  But I thought that you and I…

JOEY
  I dunno, I mean…

TRACEY
  Well, I'm off. Joey?

DAWSON
  Joey?

JOEY
  How about we all have one more drink then
  we'll see?

TRACEY
  It'll have to be quick, my bus comes in ten
  minutes.

DAWSON
  The quicker, the better.

    *Dawson picks up the two drinks brought in
    by Joey, hands one to Tracey and keeps the
    other himself. Dawson and Tracey down
    their glasses of wine.*

TRACEY
  Cheers.

DAWSON
  Slainte.

JOEY
  Good health.

TRACEY
  Good health? You didn't even have a drink!

JOEY
  No. But you both did.

    *Dawson and Tracey retch and splutter as
    they stagger backwards and fall to the
    floor, dead. Joey looks at them both for a
    few seconds before kneeling next to
    Dawson.*

JOEY
  Gentle Dawson. Don't worry, I didn't believe
  that crazy bitch. I didn't do this because of
  her. This was always going to happen tonight.
  Like I said, I so wanted you to be my first.

    Joey looks over to where Tracey is lying.

  Sorry, love. You weren't meant to be here. But
  everyone loves a bargain and two for one is

JOEY (Cont.)
    too good to pass up.

      Joey stands and looks around the room. She
      picks up her bag and removes a small
      bottle of poison.

You're both just so, so dangerous. Lucky I
brought protection.

      The theme song from 'Dawson's Creek' -
      Paula Cole's "I don't Wanna Wait", kicks
      in as Joey makes her way offstage.

END PLAY

The Frog Prince
By Marzia Dessi

CHARACTERS
  FROG PRINCE - *a prince who is a frog*
  GREDA - *a young girl*
  HENRY - *the prince's manservant*

SETTING
  A pond.

GREDA, a young girl, finds a frog by a pond.

GREDA
  Only one.

FROG PRINCE
  The season is over.

GREDA
  You can talk?

FROG PRINCE
  Of course.

GREDA
  Frogs don't normally talk.

FROG PRINCE
  I do.

GREDA
  How come?

FROG PRINCE
  Because I have something to say. Isn't that
  why everybody talks.

GREDA
  I don't know some people talk just to fill the
  space.

FROG PRINCE
  I don't like those people.

GREDA
  But you never really answered my question.
  Most frogs don't talk.

FROG PRINCE
  Most frogs don't have anything to say.

GREDA
  I find that hard to believe.

FROG PRINCE
  It's true.

GREDA
  Did you asks them?

FROG PRINCE
  I'm afraid I'm not local so I don't speak the
  local ribbit.

GREDA
  There are different dialects of ribbit? How
  many variations are there?

FROG PRINCE
  Ribbit

GREDA
  Sorry, don't speak ribbit.

FROG PRINCE
  Ribbit.

GREDA
  Are they like different languages too or how'd
  you come about speaking English and what
  dialect of ribbit do you know?

FROG PRINCE
  Ribbit.

GREDA
  I heard sometimes witches turn people into
  animals, is that how you came to talk?

FROG PRINCE
  Ribbit.

GREDA
  Not much of a talker are you.

FROG PRINCE
  Ribbit.

GREDA
  Well, none of those people want to become
  animals but you seem to want to be one.

FROG PRINCE
  Ribbit.

GREDA
  Isn't that very odd?

FROG PRINCE
  Are you always this annoying.

GREDA
  Maybe.

FROG PRINCE
  Fine. Just don't scare away any of the flies.

GREDA
  Don't you want to become a person again?

FROG PRINCE
  No.

GREDA
  You'd have a great palace?

FROG PRINCE
  I have a great log.

GREDA
  How come you talk to me if you didn't want me
  to find out?

      Silence.

FROG PRINCE
  I suppose I was lonely.

GREDA
  You'd have plenty of interesting people to
  talk to at the palace.

FROG PRINCE
  I significantly doubt that. And I am not that
  lonely.

      Silence.

FROG PRINCE
  Would you prefer to become a princess?

GREDA
  Of course. I don't like it here.

FROG PRINCE
  It's very peaceful here.

GREDA
  It smells of manure.

FROG PRINCE
  I'd prefer to never have to blink and never to
  think.

GREDA
  But frogs live much shorter lives.

FROG PRINCE
  How do you know?

GREDA
  I've dissected them before, and I read about
  it.

FROG PRINCE
  I am only a tiny bit concerned about this now.

GREDA
  Don't worry I won't dissect you.

FROG PRINCE
   That is only mildly comforting.

GREDA
   I can't learn about the frog dialect if you're
   dead.

FROG PRINCE
   That is marginally worse.

GREDA
   I would like to try kissing you…
      (pause)
   For scientific purposes, of course.

FROG PRINCE
   Scientific purposes of course.
      (Contemplates)
   You are not a princess so I suppose it doesn't
   do any harm.

      *The girl kisses the frog. The frog
      magically became a prince.*

FROG PRINCE
   What have you done?

GREDA
   It worked. You're really a prince?

FROG PRINCE
   I told you as much, but what have you done?

GREDA
   You're a prince.

FROG PRINCE
   But I don't want to be one. How did this even
   work when you're not a princess. We'll have to
   find the witch to turn me back. I knew I
   shouldn't have taken any chances. I knew you
   were trouble.

Henry rushes in.

HENRY
  My lord. You're alive. I rushed here as soon
  as I heard the news.

FROG PRINCE
  Oh no. Do people know that I'm alive.

HENRY
  No, it's just me. I never thought I'd have the
  honor of seeing your majesty in all your
  princely glory again.

FROG PRINCE
  Thank goodness. Help me re-locate the witch.

GREDA
  Hi, nice to meet you, I'm Greda.

HENRY
  The witch's daughter. I've heard all about
  you.

GREDA
  That's not very nice calling my mother a
  witch.

HENRY
  Grendalia Grentag Wisteria. That's your mother
  right?

GREDA
  She's a witch?

FROG PRINCE
  No wonder your dissecting toads nothing but
  trouble brewing around me. Humans. This
  simplifies things take me to your mother and
  have her turn me back.

GREDA
  Okay. I really have a lot of questions to ask.

HENRY
But, my Lord, you no longer have to turn back;
you are now the sole heir to the throne. Your
brother is dead.

FROG PRINCE
Solomon is dead?

HENRY
Yes, he died at the hands of the Dragon of the
East.

FROG PRINCE
That's very sad to hear but does do wonders
for my personal safety. Him trying to kill me
and all. But changes nothing. I still want to
be a frog.

HENRY
Well, if you, my Lord, are becoming a frog I
want to become a frog too.

FROG PRINCE
Why?

HENRY
Because I wish to go wherever you go. I waited
so many years for you to return. And now I get
to finally see you again, my Lord.

Frog Prince takes Henry's hands.

GREDA
Alright then let's get you both turned back
into frogs.

END PLAY

The Ghosts of the Doomed Circus Train
By Joseph Galata

CHARACTERS
  CIRCUS FRONT MAN - *Male*
  ALONZO - *Circus Train Engineer, Male*
  LUCKY BUCKY - *Circus Clown, Male*
  HENRIETTA HARLEQUIN - *Porcelain Masked Dancer, Female*
  SPECTRAL RINGMASTER - *Male*
  VIOLETTE - *Circus Violinist, Female*

SETTING
  A long-abandoned circus near old railtracks.

The stage is dimly lit. Low echoing circus music is heard. ALONZO, a middle-aged man wearing 1918 train engineer overalls, cap, and a red handkerchief around his neck appears lost, while weaving around LUCKY BUCKY, The Prancing Clown, HENRIETTA HARLEQUIN wearing a porcelin mask and ballerina outfit, SPECTRAL RINGMASTER dressed in a top hat and crimson suit, and VIOLETTE playing a violin which emits no music. Seated at the front of the stage is CIRCUS FRONT MAN addressing the audience.

CIRCUS FRONT MAN
In the heart of a small, forgotten town, there is a long-abandoned circus, it's faded tents and weathered banners concealing chilling secrets. Once a place of laughter and wonder, it is now said that the ghosts of performers killed in that doomed circus train, roam the grounds, trapped by their love for the spotlight.
102 years ago, a circus train crashed into an on-coming train. Eighty six circus employees, including children of the lead clown, killed. Since then, on the anniversary night, high school pranksters, enter the old grounds, hoping to see the spirits of the once-upon-a-time merrymakers. Boastful proclamations that have circulated as gossip, transforming into legendary anecdotes, persistently provoke debates between believers and skeptics.

Among the supposedly seen spectral inhabitants is Lucky Bucky in tattered clown attire, forever trapped in a never-ending pantomine act. His translucent body spins through the air with an otherworldly clumsiness.

Reportings of Henrietta Harlequin, her porcelin mask hiding her face. She dances through the moonlit ring with ethereal grace,

CIRCUS FRONT MAN (Cont.)
    her pirouettes casting eerie shadows that
    seemed to dance with a life of their own. Her
    silent melodies are played by Violette the
    Violinest filling the air with invisible
    notes.

But the most prominent of all the dead circus
performers gossiped about by the pranksters is
the Spectral Ringmaster, a towering figure in
a tattered top hat and crimson coat. He wields
an invisible whip, cracking it through the
darkness, and summons performers from under
the Big Top.

Teenagers who dare to enter the circus grounds
at midnight would issue self-proclomations of
witnessing these spectral performers, their
haunting acts a testament to the circus's
tragic past. Many have claimed to have taken
photos of their peer's dressed in replica
costumes, faces frozen in awe and terror as
they claim to peer into the realm of the
ghostly spectacle.

Legend has over the past 102 years that the
circus performers are cursed, bound to the
mortal realm where the circus once
entertained. Their only hope of finding peace,
their spirits and souls moving onward to the
cemetery where their bodies lay, in the hands
of a brave soul who would dare to unravel the
mystery and set their spirits free. Quite a
few pranksters, psychics, exorcists, and self-
proclaiming human angels have tried to be the
hero or heroine who releases them from the
eternal cycle of nostalgic entrampment.

And so, the old circus grounds remains a place
of both wonder and dread, a haunting spectacle
that draws the curious all in search of the
circus performers in the afterlife.

CIRCUS FRONT MAN (Cont.)
Why, I often ask, does no living mortal on the anniversary nights of the doomed train circus train wreck, report they see the spirit of the Alonzo the train engineer?

ALONZO
They're coming again. I hear their footsteps. They're walking. Over the gravel, over the stones, over the train tracks. How many pranksters this time?

Blow, wind. Keep blowing. Blow the fog away. Yes, yes, I see a girl. She's so thin, rather tall, dressed as a circus ballerina. How dare she be so insensitive! There's a laughing boy prancing around her. Is he trying to play or disrupt her? He's dressed as a circus clown, no less! So disrespectful. And another girl, angry, wearing the circus costume of a violinest.

What's wrong with these teenagers? Have they no decency, no respect for the 86 circus performers who died here? No respect for the souls of Bucky Lucky who was sleeping in Train Car Number 12? Henrietta Harlequin who was practicing her new dance in Train Car Number 18? Spectral Ringmaster who, as always, was winning the poker game in Train Car Number 32? And the mysterious Violette the Violinist who was sitting in Train Car Number 53 playing - what she always claimed - was the favorite music of Vivian the elephant?
Do they believe it was an accident? Have they forgiven me?

Oh, a second boy, wearing... what? He's wearing the costume of a Circus Ringmaster. Come here, you rascal! Give me your whip! I will show you what pain feels like when the burning walls of the train, the flaming crates filled with costumes, the frenzies of tigers and lions and

ALONZO (Cont.)
wolves and birds and elephants and horses are
being thrown in every direction!

Have you pranksters have no decency?! What do
you want from me? It was an accident! Do you
think I purpoeflly caused the train to crash?
I wasn't drunk! I fell asleep for two minutes!
Have none of you kids ever fallen asleep for
just two minutes when doing your homework or
listening to the radio?!

Oh, none of them know the suffering I'm
enduring. Why don't they see me? Why don't
they hear me? I'm here! I'm not buried in the
cemetery like the clown, and ballerina, and
violinist, and ringmaster. I survived! I'm
here! Look at me! Listen to me! It was an
accident!

Now they're tiptoeing again. Where are they
going? They are struggling to see through the
fog. The leaves attacking their faces. Don't
to yet! Don't leave! Help me! Take me to the
train station!

LUCKY
        (pointing)
Look, Henrietta! The kids are coming!
Showtime!

HENRIETTA
        (stops dancing, prances towards Violette)
The children are here! Play happy music so
they can get their parents to quickly buy the
popcorn and candy cotton while the kids take
their seats on the bleechers!

RINGMASTER
        (cracking the whip)
Boys and Girls! Welcome to the greatest circus
on earth! Lions and tigers! Acrobats and
trapeze artits flying through the air at

RINGMASTER (Cont.)
dangerous neck breaking speed! The spectacles
you are about to witness will burn in your
memories forever!

ALONZO
It was an accident!

I keep repeating those words everytime they
come here, as I did at my trial, outside the
courthouse, and in jail… for… what was it?
Manslaughter! My trial for manslaughter.

I told the judge, yes, I told him day after
day in his courthouse. Your Honor. I don't
know how many lions and elephants were killed.
There's talk of placing elephant statues
overlooking their cemetery plot. It was an
accident, Your Honor.

I am waiting for one of you kids to take me to
the train station! It's too dark! There's too
much fog! I can't find my way to the train
station through it all. I've been trying,
really trying! That is where I belong. Even
though I was found innocent and even though I
was fired from the train company, I can prove
to them that I can still carry out my
responsiilities like I did for all those years
before I … before I…

I can't stay here. I can smell popcorn. I can
smell burning costumes. I can hear laughing. I
can hear screaming. I can see parading. I can
see flames. As if I live in two yesterdays.
The yesterday of entertainment. The yesterday
of tragedy.

If you don't want to take me to the train
station, then go home, you rotten pranksters!

Go home and tell everyone it was an accident!

CIRCUS FRONT MAN

There was never another circus that came to
this small town. Perhaps that's why, year
after year for 102 years, so many high school
kids come to these old haunting grounds -
creating their own urban legend circus type
entertaiment.
Mystical entertainment. Magical entertainment.
Myterious entertainment. When I was the Circus
Front Man, well, that's how I would write up
the newspaper and radio announcements, design
the posters and flyers. Mystical! Magical!
Mysterious Entertainers!

82 people perished in that train wreck.
Elephants. Tigers. Wolves. Birds. Horses.
I always remind myself that as one of the
survivors, I have a duty to tell the story of
the doomed circus train. Alonzo shouldn't have
fallen asleep while driving the train. He
deserves to be forgiven. I try to tell the
pranksters when they go to the old circus
grounds. But they don't listen to me. They
just ignore me as if I'm not here.

Alonzo was a nice man. The circus performers
trusted him. He engineered the circus train
back and forth from town to town, state to
state. Just one mistake. We all make mistakes.
I forgive him. I hope he's in Heaven. And
Lucky Bucky the funniest clown any circus ever
had. Henrietta Harlequin, so beautiful and
delicate. The extraordinary Spectral
Ringmaster who cracked that whip and brought
the audience roaring with cheers. Violette the
Violinst, a little crazy with all that musical
passion. May they all rest in peace despite
what the crazy teenagers in this town think. I
miss them. They were so much fun.

Then again, I'm thankful I survived that train
crash. As the Circus Front Man, I just have to
keep telling the story. Perhaps if I do, one

CIRCUS FRONT MAN (Cont.)
day, another circus will come here. We can
start entrtaining once again.

I hope when my time finally comes to die, I
get to see them again - in whatever realm is
beyond this realm.

LUCKY
    (shouting)
The kids are leaving! Do you think they
enjoyed seeing me perform? Did I make them
laugh loud enough for their bellies to ache?

HENRIETTA
    (dancing)
Oh, seeing the girls watch me dance makes me
so happy. I always hope that one of them will
become a ballerina. Not in the circus, but in
am opera house where I always hoped to dance.
I'll just keep hoping. Hope. Dance. Hope.
Dance. Always. It's my life.

SPECTRAL RINGMASTER
    (bowing)
Come back again, Boys and Girls! Another great
show from the greatest circus on earth eagerly
awaits to entertain you once again! Thank you!
Thank you! Thank you for coming! We will be
here waiting for you!

ALONZO
    (whispering)
Take me with you! Take me to the train
station!

                    END PLAY

The Haunted Geese Goose Gift for Blind Brenda

By Rebecca Holbourn

CHARACTERS
  MIKE - *Male, middle-aged*
  THERESA - *Female, middle-aged*
  BRENDA - *Female, blind, elderly*
  GEESE GOOSE - *A goose lamp/Offstage*
  CHILDREN - *Offstage*

SETTING
  The very messy living room of a middle-aged couple, including a sofa.

A messy living room of a middle-aged couple. THERESA sits squeezed on to the sofa playing on her iPad.

MIKE walks in.

MIKE
    (Jokingly)
  Alrigh', love?

Theresa doesn't look up.

MIKE
  Playing that Farm click game?

THERESA
  The what?

MIKE
  Where you match 3 fruits or whatever.

THERESA
  Oh, yeah. Where have you been?

MIKE
  I went to visit Blind Brenda.

THERESA
  You can just call her Brenda.

MIKE
  No. There's also Bank Brenda and Brenda from HR.

THERESA
  Couldn't think up a B word for her?

MIKE
  Called her Barmy Brenda 'til she gave me a right old bollocking.

THERESA
  Charming.

MIKE
  Barmy.

THERESA
  Got you down to a tee though.

MIKE
  Hey!

THERESA
  Urgh, I lost again.

MIKE
  Why do you play that so much?

THERESA
  They've introduced real-life prizes if you win
  the special challenge without dying.

MIKE
  Making a fortune off advertising I'm sure.

THERESA
  Probably.

MIKE
  So, what do you win?

THERESA
  I'm not sure. They just said a topical mystery
  prize.

MIKE
  Fair enough. You'll never know if you don't
  win then.

THERESA
  No…

SCENE TWO

Nighttime. Mike sits on the sofa playing on the iPad. Theresa walks in.

THERESA
  Are you still playing that? It's 3 in the morning.

MIKE
  I made it to the last level, but the farmer used his pitchfork and I got covered in hay.

THERESA
  That is a weird level.

  She moves some stuff off the sofa and sits down next to him.

THERESA
  It looks a bit creepy.

MIKE
  You think?

THERESA
  Yeah.

MIKE
  I'm getting into it though.

THERESA
  So I can see.

MIKE
  I think I'll have it this time. Look, the owl just distracted the farmer and he didn't use his pitchfork.

THERESA
  This is a super weird level.

  They both stare at the screen.

MIKE
  Come on chain reaction. Come on…

THERESA
  So close…

     They both cheer loudly.
     A dog outside starts barking.
     They laugh and see what the screen says.

MIKE
  Cool, so I just need to email our address and
  they'll send us our mystery prize.

     Mike starts typing away.

     Theresa stands.

THERESA
  Great, now, let's go to bed.

MIKE
  I'm well chuffed.

THERESA
  Bed!

     Mike stands up as ordered and follows
     Theresa, still typing away and trips over
     a pile of stuff causing it to topple.

THERESA
     (half-jokingly)
  You alrigh', love?

MIKE
  Yeah. I'll fix it in the morning.

THERESA
  Sure you will…

SCENE THREE - HALLOWEEN

There is now a skeleton sitting on the sofa, plus a couple of bowls of chocolates are placed around the room.

SD - Doorbell Ring

CHILDREN
(*offstage*)
  Trick or treat?

SD - Front Door Closes

Mike and Theresa enter. Theresa flops down on the sofa next to the skeleton who falls over onto her.

THERESA
  Oh, hello to you too, Fred. Bit handsy tonight?

MIKE
  Well, it is his favourite night of the year.

THERESA
  When he's allowed out of his box?

MIKE
  Exactly!

She nods and makes Fred wave at Mike who waves happily back.

SD - Doorbell Ring

Theresa sighs.

THERESA
  Isn't it past their bedtimes now? I don't think we were allowed out past 8, let alone getting on for 10.

MIKE
    Stay there, I'll go.

        Mike heads out of the room.

                            SD - Front Door Opens
                            SD - Front Door Closes

        *When no children call out, Theresa sits up
        curious. Mike steps secretively into the
        room.*

MIKE
        (whispers loudly)
    It's Blind Brenda.

        Theresa stands up.

THERESA
    What?

        *In hobbles an elderly lady, BRENDA, with a
        walking stick in each hand.*

MIKE
    Brenda, you remember Theresa?

        Brenda nods.

BRENDA
    Where can I sit down?

THERESA
    Oh! Over here.

BRENDA
    You'll have to guide me. As young Mikey said,
    I'm blind, dear.

THERESA
        (stares, mouthing)
    Young???

Mike gently takes Brenda's arm and leads her carefully around the messy room to the sofa.

MIKE
It's not far now.

Brenda sits down on the sofa and Fred falls on her. She feels the boney arm and yells in fright.

THERESA
Oh, I'm so sorry, Brenda. That's just Fred.

BRENDA
Fred?! A skeleton?

THERESA
Yes. I would barely call him a friend really.

MIKE
Never trust someone you can see through, eh?
(loud silence)
Sorry, I'll move him… Would you like a cup of tea?

Mike picks up Fred and puts him down in a corner.

BRENDA
No, thank you, or I will be up all night.

THERESA
So, how can we help?

BRENDA
Some boys were banging on my bungalow.

MIKE
Banging boys, Brenda? Naughty.

Theresa shoots daggers at Mike and they both try not to laugh.

BRENDA
  They were demanding sweets but I didn't have
  any. I didn't want to be alone.

MIKE
  No, of course not.

THERESA
  Our sofa is yours as long as you need it.

BRENDA
  Thank you. I might just close my eyes for a
  little bit, if that's okay?

    Brenda closes her eyes.
    She's gently snoring quickly.
    Theresa and Mike exchange looks and shrug.
    They tiptoe out of the room.

                SCENE FOUR

    Brenda wakes with a start and a yell.

    Mike comes crashing into the room.

MIKE
  What? What's wrong?

BRENDA
  I thought I was being attacked by a budgie.

MIKE
  A budgie?

BRENDA
  Yes, I've always wanted a bird, but the budgie
  began bludgeoning me with it's beak.

    Theresa follows Mike into the room.

THERESA
  Are you okay now, Brenda?

BRENDA
  Yes, thank you. I should probably go home.

  *Mike nods and Theresa nudges him in the
  side.*

MIKE
  If you're sure? I'll walk you home.

BRENDA
  That's very kind of you, thank you, Mikey.

  *Mike smiles. Theresa nudges him again and
  points to her eyes. Mike remembers.*

MIKE
  Happy to help. I'll just put some shoes on and
  grab my coat.

  Mike leaves the room.

THERESA
  Would you like a hand to the front door?

BRENDA
  Yes, bless you.

  *Theresa helps Brenda to her feet and then
  guides her offstage.*

SCENE FIVE

  *Theresa is curled up on the sofa alone.
  There is the sound of keys in the lock and
  then some awkward scraping sounds. Theresa
  turns to look at the door almost scared.*

MIKE
  I know it's midnight, but we've had a
  delivery.

  *Mike walks into the room carrying a large
  cardboard box, plonks it down on the sofa.*

371

THERESA
  It's midnight on Halloween and you're bringing
  in a random parcel?

MIKE
  It's addressed to me and it's got that game
  logo on the label.

THERESA
  Halloween eve is the right time for a topical
  mystery prize?

MIKE
  Apparently so.

THERESA
  Maybe it's haunted.

MIKE
      (slightly high-pitched)
  Why would you say that?!

THERESA
  Wimp.

      Mike coughs and plumps up his chest.

MIKE
  No, I'm not.

THERESA
  You are a bit.

      Mike sighs and nods resignedly.

THERESA
  You gonna stand there all night or are you
  going to open it?

MIKE
  Alright, alright, keep your hair on.

He opens up the top of the box with his keys from his pocket.

MIKE
  There's a card.

He pulls it out and opens it.

MIKE
  Congratulations to completion our special game. Please enjoy the Geese Goose in all it's unique glory.

THERESA
  What on earth does that mean?

MIKE
  I don't know.

THERESA
  Get it out then.

MIKE
  Alright, hold the box.

Theresa takes hold of the box and Mike pulls out a polystyrene box. He opens it up to reveal a goose lamp.

THERESA
  Weird.

He puts it down on a nearby table and plugs it in.

GEESE GOOSE
  HONK!!!

Mike jumps away, falling over a pile of random stuff and looking directly up into Fred's skull. He yelps.

THERESA
  Wimp.

MIKE
  You're telling me you didn't jump?

GEESE GOOSE
  Honk honk.

THERESA
  Not like you!

MIKE
  Well, you weren't two inches away from it.

GEESE GOOSE
      (like laughing)
  Honk honk honk!

THERESA
  Turn it off?

MIKE
  Now who's scared of it?

      Theresa glares at him.
      Mike crawls over and unplugs it.
      The light stays on.

GEESE GOOSE
  Honk!

THERESA
  What on-

MIKE
  -No. What the hell?

GEESE GOOSE
  Haaaaaaa-onk!

      They both stare at the goose.

GEESE GOOSE
  Honk?

MIKE
  Is it just me or-

THERESA
  Is it trying to talk to us?

    *Mike grabs the box it arrived in and goes
    to put it over the Geese Goose.*

GEESE GOOSE
  HOOOOONK!

THERESA
  It knows!

MIKE
  How can it know? It's a light.

THERESA
  Maybe it is a haunted light. Maybe there was
  no courier, it just transported itself?

    Mike drops the box over the goose.

MIKE
  Nonsense.

THERESA
  You're scared.

MIKE
  So are you.

THERESA
  No.

MIKE
  Don't lie.

THERESA
  Yes, I'm scared. A creepy goose-

GEESE GOOSE
  -HOOOOONK? HONK! HONK! HONK!

    They stare at the noisy box.

MIKE
  Be quiet and we'll uncover you.

    The Geese Goose goes quiet.

THERESA
  Are you kidding me?

    Mike lifts up the box.

MIKE
  No more honking.

    The Geese Goose stays silent.

THERESA
  You know who was just saying that they wanted
  a pet bird?

MIKE
  Blind Brenda.

    They look at each other.

THERESA
  It would be perfect for her, all alone in her
  house.

MIKE
  Help to scare off any naughty boys.

THERESA
  We'd just be being good neighbours.

MIKE
  Absolutely.

GEESE GOOSE
  Honk!

    They stare at the Geese Goose again.

MIKE
  We're going to bed now. Please don't make a
  noise. We'll take you to Brenda's in the
  morning and you'll have a new friend.

GEESE GOOSE
  Honk.

MIKE
  Great. Lovely to meet you. Goodnight.

GEESE GOOSE
  Honk honk.

    *Theresa stares at Mike who leads her out
    of the room, unable to look away from the
    Geese Goose.*

SCENE SIX

    *The living room, the same as the night
    before, but without the Geese Goose
    lamp/boxes. Mike and Theresa walk into the
    room.*

THERESA
  Do you feel a little mean, giving Blind Brenda
  that goose lamp?

MIKE
  No, she'll love it.

THERESA
  Hmm… I hope so.

Mike plonks himself down on the sofa.

MIKE
  I barely slept last night.

THERESA
  I know, you kept asking me if I was still
  awake.

MIKE
  And you were!

THERESA
  You kept talking to me!

MIKE
  Doesn't normally keep you awake.

THERESA
  Well, you also kept poking me and I was
  slightly terrified that the goose would appear
  in our room.

MIKE
  Now, who's the scaredy-cat?

THERESA
  Still you.

MIKE
  Hope the Geese Goose is happy with Brenda.

                              LX - Blackout

THERESA
  Mike?

MIKE
  Yes, Theresa?

THERESA
  Why did the lights go out?

MIKE
  Probably a power cut.

THERESA
  Yeah… You don't think it's because we
  mentioned the Geese Goose, do you?

MIKE
  That's crazy.

    *The lights start to come back on, starting
    with beyond the living room door. Theresa
    and Mike turn to look, then look back
    around the living room where the Geese
    Goose has suddenly reappeared.*

MIKE
  You said you'd stay with Brenda!

GEESE GOOSE
  HOOOOOOOOONK!

    Theresa and Mike stare at the Goose.

                                    LX - Fade

                  END PLAY

The Monster
By Jacquelyn Priskorn

CHARACTERS
  SCARY MONSTER - *any age, any gender*
  PERSON - *any age, any gender*

SETTING
  A dark place.

*A dark place. SCARY MONSTER corners
PERSON.*

SCARY MONSTER
  You're mine now!

PERSON
  Um, what?

SCARY MONSTER
  There's no escape

PERSON
  From?

SCARY MONSTER
  Me, you foolish person! I'm going to peel off
  your skull and eat your brains!

PERSON
  Wow.

SCARY MONSTER
  There's nowhere to run.

PERSON
  So you said. Before the peeling and the
  eating, can I ask you something?

SCARY MONSTER
  Ask me something?

PERSON
  Yes. Why?

SCARY MONSTER
  Why?

PERSON
  Why would you want to peel and eat me?

    Scary Monster laughs.

SCARY MONSTER
  You question me? Your little life means
  nothing to me!

PERSON
  See, now that just doesn't make sense to me.

SCARY MONSTER
  Silence!

PERSON
  No, really. If my life means nothing to you,
  what's the big deal if you peel me or not?

SCARY MONSTER
      (laughing)
  You're going to die.

PERSON
  What's so funny?

SCARY MONSTER
  What?

PERSON
  You keep laughing. What is it with you
  monsters? You're always laughing at something.
  Why?

SCARY MONSTER
  You keep asking questions of me when I'm going
  to kill you. You should be screaming! Grrrr!!!

PERSON
  "Grrr"? I wonder what makes that sound a fear
  inducing sound...

SCARY MONSTER
  I should shut you up!

PERSON
  And yet you still stand here, "grr"ing at me,
  discussing your unmotivated, homicidal desires.

SCARY MONSTER
  What?!

PERSON
  I really want to know what it is that makes
  you want to kill me.

SCARY MONSTER
  I'm just… Going to kill you!

PERSON
  Fine. I'm sure you have your reasons.

SCARY MONSTER
  NO!
  There are no reasons!
  I'm a monster!
  We've met in a dark corner!
  Now, I'm supposed to kill you!

PERSON
  Says who?

SCARY MONSTER
  Shut up!

PERSON
  Okay. There's no need for shouting.

SCARY MONSTER
  Yes! There is! Now cower before me!

PERSON
  Instead of the peeling and eating?

SCARY MONSTER
  No! You cower while I peel your skull and eat
  your brains!

PERSON
  Well, this wasn't what we originally
  discussed.

SCARY MONSTER
  There was no discussion! Why am I talking to
  you?!

PERSON
  Good question. What do you think?

SCARY MONSTER
  I don't believe this!

PERSON
  How do you think I feel? You think I woke up
  this morning planning a discussion with a
  scary monster?

SCARY MONSTER
  This isn't a discussion!

PERSON
  Whatever you say.

SCARY MONSTER
  That's right!

PERSON
  Thank you.

SCARY MONSTER
  What?!

PERSON
  Thank you for acknowledging that I—

SCARY MONSTER
  Stop it!
  I'm not acknowledging you. I'm not having a
  discussion with you. I am simply frightening
  you and then peeling your skull and eating
  your brains.

PERSON
  I'm sorry, but that's not true.

SCARY MONSTER
  Are you kidding me?

PERSON
  No, seriously. You're not frightening me. I'm
  sorry to disappoint you.

SCARY MONSTER
  You're stupid. .

PERSON
  That's not true, either.

SCARY MONSTER
  I can't take much more of this. Are you ready
  to die?

PERSON
  To be perfectly honest, no, I'm not. Does that
  really make a difference to you, or was it
  just a rhetorical question?

SCARY MONSTER
  Um… The second one?

PERSON
  Oh. Okay. I just wanted to make sure before I
  went into a big, long—

SCARY MONSTER
  You know something? My mistake. You're not the
  one I'm supposed to eat.

PERSON
  Well, to be fair, you weren't planning on
  eating me. Just my brains. Unless that's
  changed, too?

SCARY MONSTER
  Yeah. Yeah. Everything's changed. It's dark.
  Things are crazy…

    They look at each other…

385

Scary Monster bolts.
Person looks at the audience.

PERSON
  And they said I'd never do anything with a
  degree in philosophy.

  Person laughs maniacally and exits.

                    END PLAY

The Return
By Abhisek Bhattacharya

CHARACTERS
  BOB - *Scientist, Male, 50 yrs*
  LIZ - *Bob's daughter, Female, 20 yrs*
  ELENA - *Bob's wife, Female, 30yrs*
   ~STELLA - *Actress, Female, 30 yrs*

SETTING
  The waiting area in front of Bob's
  laboratory.

The waiting area in front of Bob's laboratory; a room or a corridor that has seen better days. There are a few chairs and a coffee table. Some newspapers and (science) magazines are on the table. Many sandwich wrappers, empty packets of chips, soda cans, and discarded, torn pieces of paper and notebooks litter the whole place. BOB is holding a gun to his temple.

LIZ

Papa! Please, papa, don't do this, please.

BOB

I am done, Liz. I am sick and tired of waiting. I've been sitting here in front of my laboratory for almost twenty years, hoping to see Elena emerge from that time capsule. Every day, I tweak some parameters, recalculate, recalibrate, re-make the whole thing. Each night I go to bed hoping that tomorrow will be the day; tomorrow, I will activate the time capsule and… and she will be there. But nothing, nothing ever happened! It's my fault that she left the way she did, and I can't bring her back. I am an utter failure.

LIZ

She died from cardiac arrest, Papa! There's nothing you could do.

BOB

I wasn't there when she needed me! And I did the same with you. I'm sorry, Liz.

LIZ

No, Papa… please.

BOB

I should have taken better care of you. Liz, I've never been with you at any stage of your life. Not for parent-teacher meetings, not for field trips, not even for your graduation.

LIZ
  You were busy with your experiments.

BOB
  The time capsule had become my life, Liz, my
  hope, my identity. I dream of freezing time…
  to recreate our last days… I love you, Liz.
  You remind me so much of your mom, it's almost
  painful to look at you. You are her perfect
  image.

LIZ
  Then don't leave me! Stay with me, Papa.

BOB
  There's nothing, Liz. Nothing left for me to
  do. All for nothing. I spent my entire life
  waiting for something that could never happen.
  Nobody can do this, Liz. It's impossible.

LIZ
  It was always impossible, Papa… That's why
  nobody could do it. Nobody but you.

BOB
  And I can't either. I couldn't stop her from
  going, and I can't bring her back. The time
  capsule is a myth, it never works, Liz. All
  these years, I was trying to do something
  that's beyond all the laws of physics.

LIZ
  You did it because you love her, Papa. You
  love her so very much.

BOB
  Liz, I thought this time capsule would be a
  unique time barrier. A small area inside which
  time will never move. She will always remain
  alive, holding you in her arms.

LIZ
  Holding me?

BOB
  That's the date I chose, Liz. The day you were
  born, the day she passed away.

      *Liz nervously removes her hair, tucking it
      behind her ear.*

LIZ
  Papa, please, please!

BOB
  I just wasted my life, your life… all the time
  we could have spent together… all the time I
  could show you the world, teach you, learn
  from you, and tell you about your mom. I hope
  I will see her again, Liz, and when I do, I
  will tell her how proud I am of you… our
  little girl…

      Bob's about to pull the trigger.

LIZ
      (screaming)
  No! Papa…

      Elena enters wearing her blue bathrobe.

ELENA
  What's going on here?

LIZ
      (feigned ignorance)
  Who are you?

BOB
      (slowly dropping the gun)
  Elena! How? How…

ELENA
  You look… old, dear. What's up, Bob?

BOB
  How did you…

390

LIZ
    (forced enthusiasm)
  Papa! That's Mom, Papa, isn't she? Your
  machine worked, Papa, your machine worked.
  You are a genius!

BOB
  How are you here? I mean, even if the machine
  worked, you should not be able to leave the
  time capsule… How did you come out of it?

ELENA
  You tell me, dear. You are the scientist.

BOB
  I don't know! It should not be possible! And
  what about baby Liz? That's a paradox…

LIZ
  Why does it matter, Papa? You did it! You
  really brought Mom back!

BOB
  I did! Didn't I?

LIZ
  You sure did, right… Mom?

ELENA
  You look different… frail… exhausted. Why,
  Bob?

BOB
  I'm sorry, Elena. I'm so sorry. I should've
  been there. None of this would have happened.

ELENA
  You went to the cafeteria, Bob. I went to the
  restroom and had a cardiac arrest. There's
  nothing you could do about it; there's nothing
  anybody could do about it.

BOB

I miss you! I can't live like this… every
minute of every day, all our plans, all our
dreams… I can't live without you… I can't even
look at her. Every time she talks, turns her
head… every time she removes her hair from her
forehead and tucks it behind her ear… I see
you, only you. She is your mirror image,
Elena. I can't bear this anymore. And it's all
my fault.

ELENA

Stop living in your guilt, Bob! That's the
worst kind of life… especially imaginary
guilt. It howls inside your head, eats your
heart. Continue wallowing in guilt and self-
hatred, and they change you into something
different, something you're not. See for
yourself, a scientist, an inventor, Bob- and
twenty years of guilt turned you into a
killer! It's time for you to leave the past
and learn to live in the present.

BOB

I don't have a present. Without you, I don't
want to have a present, Elena. I told you when
we were teenagers, and I still stand by what I
said. You are my present, my future, Elena;
you are my everything.

ELENA

Is that why you want to bring me back and cage
me inside that capsule? Twenty years of guilt
made you a trapper too?

BOB

I… I just want to stop you from going.

ELENA

Freeze time and imprison me in a moment? All
because you want to hold me captive and spend
time with my fake self? That's not like the
Bob I knew.

BOB
　　Elena… I… I…

ELENA
　　Bob Agassi, who saved every single cent of his
　　daily allowance so that he could buy Aston's
　　Macaw… No, no, dear Liz, not to own it, but to
　　release it in the forest. Here is my Bob, who
　　fought Andrea and her brother even though they
　　had a perfectly legal permit to hunt a
　　whitetail buck. You never were much into
　　caging animals, Bob. Now you changed so much
　　that you would like to cage me?

BOB
　　I want you back… it hurts, Elena… it hurts so
　　much… I cannot let you go…

ELENA
　　And you don't have to, Bob. Nurture the
　　memory, reminisce about the time we spent
　　together, and teach her…

　　　　Elena brings Liz in front of Bob. Liz
　　　　nervously fiddles with her hair and then
　　　　tucks it back behind her ear.
　　　　Bob and Elena smile; Bob ruefully, Elena
　　　　merrily.

ELENA
　　See! She is me, Bob, she is mine, she is ours.
　　She is our greatest treasure.

BOB
　　Elena… I… I…

　　　　Elena fiddles with her hair and then
　　　　tucks it back behind her ear.

ELENA
　　And focus on your students, your job… your
　　science. You have the whole world to explore,
　　Bob. Things to invent…

Elena looks expectantly at Bob.

BOB
    (smiling ruefully)
  Stuff to build…

ELENA and BOB
  The universe to explore.

    *Elena starts laughing, Bob caresses her
    hair.*

ELENA
    (wrinkling her nose)
  But you should start with a shower, Bob. And a
  fresh meal, a few nights of sleep…

BOB
  Shall I see you again?

    *Elena points at Liz, who nervously tucks
    her hair behind her ear.*

ELENA
  I'm always here… Don't you see me, Bob? My
  eyes… My smile… My gestures…

BOB
  Elena.

ELENA
  Yes, dear?

    Bob slowly cups Elena's face in his hands.

BOB
  Is this real? Are… Are you real? Or am I just
  imagining things? Is this all happening inside
  my head?

ELENA
  No, Bob. Your lab, your instruments,
  calculations… your time capsule, your ideas

ELENA (Cont.)
  about freezing time… those are the things that
  happen inside your head. We live here…
    (Elena touches over Bob's heart)
  I… Our daughter… deep inside your heart.
  That's what makes us so special, so very real.

BOB
  I will see you again, won't I?

    Elena kisses Bob's fingers, slowly
    removing them from her face.

ELENA
  Yes, but not soon. You have things to finish,
  stuff to invent, and the whole world to
  explore with our daughter. But first…

BOB
  A shower… A shower will be good. Some food
  too…

ELENA
  And sleep, dear. You need to sleep. But go
  take the shower first.

    Bob kisses Elena and leaves.
    Elena smiles.

LIZ
  I… I don't think I can tell you how grateful I
  am, Stella. I know, I know! You're a
  professional actor, and I will be paying you.
  Aunt Jemima was right; you're brilliant. You
  completely creeped me out.

    Elena caresses Liz's hair and kisses her
    forehead.

ELENA
  You do look like your mother, you know…

LIZ

Please, Stella! You are already freaking me
out. I know you have the photos, so I can
understand the blue bathrobe. But how do you
even know about the macaw? And that buck
thingy about… what's-her-name…

ELENA

Andrea.

LIZ

Yes, Andrea! I don't know any of these. How do
you… oh! You spoke with Aunt Jemima, didn't
you? That explains a lot! She was very close
to mom. Thank you, Stella. Without you, I
don't know what would have happened today.

ELENA

My pleasure, dear.

LIZ

But I don't have cash on me. After calling
Aunt Jemima, I was going to go to the ATM, but
then papa got into one of his episodes, and…
Do you want me to go to the ATM now? I can
give you a check, but you told me you don't
like checks. Or I can meet you at your
apartment within a couple of hours. Yes, that
will be good. I will get the money and go to
your place. Again, thank you, Stella, thanks a
lot.

> *Elena smiles and nods. Liz's cell phone
> starts ringing. As Liz picks up the
> phone, Elena leaves.*

LIZ

Oh, Aunt Jemima… Easy, easy… Yes, he's okay.
Stella got your message… Yes, she came right
on time. Papa was going to shoot himself… No,
I don't even know where he got the gun…
Without Stella, he might be… Yes, I will call
the doctor, but you know Papa, he hates

LIZ (Cont.)
doctors… He doesn't even think he has any
problem… Yes, yes. I will try to make him go…
Thank you, Jemima, I really appreciate your
help… See you soon, Aunty. Bye.

STELLA comes running in.

STELLA
An' here you 're, gal. O' Liz, I came as soon
as I could…

LIZ
Hi, Stella. Did you forget something?

STELLA
Gal, I'm so sorry! I was at the grocery store
when Jemima called, an' I tried ter come
immediately, but muh car broke down… Gotta
wait for the bus, ya know how the public
transport is…

LIZ
Your bathrobe… Oh! You left it somewhere! Let
me find it before Papa…

STELLA
Yeah. I've questions abou' that. The photo ya
gave me only shows the fron'. How abou' the
back? Anythin' there? Real-life actin' ain't
easy, gal, and when ya tryna be somebody's
wife… I don' know if I could do it, Liz. I
don' know nothin' abou' yer mom… Ya need ter
tell me…

LIZ
What are you talking about? You did an
excellent job!

STELLA
I jus' arrived! Jemima called an' gave me this
address. Is this a kinda science laboratory?

LIZ
  You helped Papa! He was about to shoot
  himself...

STELLA
  I didn' do diddly shit!

LIZ
  You just came... You had that blue bathrobe... You
  talked about the macaw... the buck... and the
  girl, what's her name... Andrea...

STELLA
  Ya high or somethin', gal? I understan' ya
  stressed an' shit goin' crazy... I mean nobody
  in 'em right mind would pay an actor ter dress
  up as her mother...

      *Liz is completely shaken. Bob enters, he's
      freshened himself up.*

BOB
  Mother! Is she still here, Liz?

LIZ
  Yes... I mean, no, Papa.

BOB
      (notices Stella)
  Um... Hi! Are you... Is she your friend, Liz?

LIZ
      (still shaking)
  No. I mean yes... Yes, Papa. She is. She looks a
  bit like mom, but she is not mom, absolutely,
  she is my friend.

BOB
  You okay, Liz? Looks like your mom! Maybe in a
  dark room, if you squint really hard. No
  offense, young lady.

Stella shrugs, Liz flings herself into Bob's arms.

LIZ

It was really Mom, Papa... She came!

BOB

Easy, Liz. Easy. Yes, she did.

LIZ

No! You don't understand. It was really Mom, like actual Mom...

BOB

I know, Liz. It was really her. I'm already missing her. But I'm not going to cry and shut the world out. I promise I will make it up to you, Liz. Now if you can order some deep fried chicken, some chocolates... Oh! I almost forgot! What's your name, dear?

STELLA

I'm Stella...

BOB

Hi, Stella. I'm Bob, Liz's father. Nice to meet you.

STELLA

Nice ter meet ya...

BOB

Liz, would you like to invite your friend for lunch? Maybe, we will get to know each other over some food. How does that sound?

STELLA

Wouldn' say nah teh food.

BOB

Yeah! Warm, fried, very unhealthy food, and lots and lots of chocolates. To a new beginning. Right, Liz?

LIZ
Yes, Papa, to a new beginning.

Bob and Liz embrace.

Stella smiles, removes the hair from her forehead, and tucks it behind her ear.

END PLAY

Times Lost Forever
By Roderick Millar

CHARACTERS
  ALHASIK - *Male*
  URPHORG - *Male*
  GHOST - *Female*
  GHOST 2 - *Female*

SETTING
  A tomb.

A tomb. Enter ALHASIK.

ALHASIK
Not twenty years have passed since I
The body of my beloved
Kankiy here did lay. The moon's up.
If I wait here, old memories
Perhaps will flock, echoes of our
Happy past, times lost forever.

He kneels. URPHORG approaches.

URPHORG
Who is this who intrudes thus here
Trampling and disturbing the
ground?
Who dares defile this sacred place?
You seem like one from far away.
Why do you visit this bleak place?

ALHASIK
I am Alhasik, a merchant.
In years gone by I traded here,
Where died my lover, good Kankiy.
So I mourn, not the past but now,
The present, what's happening now.
Please forgive me if I do wrong.
I did not mean to. I will go.

URPHORG
No, you may stay. Others come here
And disrespect the area.
You seem different somehow to me,
Gentler, humbler, perhaps truer
Of purpose. So you may remain.

ALHASIK
Also I am much wealthier
Than people you normally meet.
But seeing you, I'm reminded of
Kankiy - are you perhaps her ghost?

URPHORG
    Let me settle your worried mind.
    No ghost am I, but a humble
    Servant of this place, a sweeper
    Put upon by the mighty and the
    Lowly both the same. I travail
    Ill-tempered, outraged; attending
    On thoughtless bothersome poxy
    Repellent antisocial terse
    Loathsome uncooperative
    Dismissive nosy impertinent
    Foul-mouthed overpaid obnoxious
    Banal listless disengaged harsh
    Worthless members of the public
    So I'm not a ghost. As you thought.

ALHASIK
    You bear a resemblance to her-

URPHORG
    -I'm not her!

ALHASIK
    Your jawline-

URPHORG
    Listen!

ALHASIK
    Your nose from a certain angle-

URPHORG
    -I am not the ghost of your wife!

ALHASIK
    Oh.
        (Silence)
    Had to ask.

URPHORG
    They all say that.

403

ALHASIK
  Sorry, I'll bother you no more.

URPHORG
  Don't worry - it goes with the job.

        Urphorg sweeps. Ghost enters.

GHOST
  Excuse me…

ALHASIK
  Psst! The sweeper is busy.

GHOST
  I wish only to-

ALHASIK
  -Can't you see
  He doesn't need your incessant
  Querulous queries and questions
  Annoying comments and helpful
  Critiques of how he does his job.
  He's only human. Go and throw
  Your litter where it should belong
  In the bin.

GHOST
  I only wonder

ALHASIK
  Something

GHOST
  Why are you so disapproving?
  A shiftless ghost I haunt this place

ALHASIK
  Oh ghost now is it? How many
  Disguises have you donned to persuade
  The gullible? I'd say many!

GHOST
  Oh, where is my husband? Will he
  Come back to me. I'm so alone.

ALHASIK
  Who do you think you're fooling then?
  I for one am not taken in.

GHOST
  He was so morose when I died,
  So overcome with heavy grief.

ALHASIK
  You're consistent, I'll give you that.

GHOST
  He was a merchant, who traded here.

ALHASIK
  So you give your tale specifics - A merchant -
  ha ha ha - how smart
  And yet painfully obvious.
  It also is…

GHOST
  What? You have stopped.

ALHASIK
  A double-take I think I do
  As the scales horrifyingly
  Drop from my eyeballs. Can it be?

GHOST
  Can what be?

ALHASIK
  Can it be - no!
  No!

GHOST
  What? Can it be what? Let me know!

ALHASIK
  Can it be you, Kankiy, returned?

GHOST
  What - you think I am your dead
  wife?

ALHASIK
  Who did die here.

GHOST
  Not on your life.

ALHASIK
  Pardon?

GHOST
  You think I'd have someone like you
  To have and to hold? Not likely.
    (laughs very broadly)
  To be fair, that's the biggest laugh
  I've had all day. Thanks. Everything's
  Better when you can have a laugh,
  That's what my husband always said.
  Don't worry, I won't bother you
  Any more. Our anniversary
  Is today but he didn't show.
  What a total fricking tosser!
  Typical failed broke ex-merchant!

    She goes.

ALHASIK
  Farewell, poor ghost.

URPHORG
  Sweeping's done now.
  Time to clock off. You find your
  ghost?

ALHASIK
  No, sadly it was the wrong one.

URPHORG
That's funny! Like I always say
Everything's better when you can
Have a laugh. Anyway, goodbye!

He heads off very quickly.
Alhasik is lost in thought.

ALHASIK
She was his wife. If only I'd…

He ponders some more.

ALHASIK
Time to return home, having not
Performed my due. In another
Ten years I'll return. Probably.
  (Wanders off)
It all happens for a reason.

Enter GHOST 2.

GHOST 2
I'm always late. Is he still here,
My husband the merchant? Oh no.
He is gone and I must pine.
Ahhhhhhh.

She sinks to the ground and pines.

END PLAY

Voodoo Doll Syndrome
By Clinton Festa

CHARACTERS
  KATHY - *Moderator of the support group, Jeffrey's mother*
  MATTHEW - *A man with VDS*
  RON - *A man with VDS*
  LAUREN - *A woman with VDS*
  JEFFREY - *A teenage boy or young man, Kathy's son*

SETTING
  A support group meeting location such as a room in a local community center.

A room inside a community center.
KATHY, MATTHEW, and RON sit around a ring
of chairs. Kathy holds a clipboard.
Matthew and Ron sit apart from each other.

KATHY
We're expecting one more, so we'll just wait
another minute for her to show up.

MATTHEW
(Handing Kathy an envelope)
Before I forget, Kathy, here you go.

KATHY
Thank you, Matthew. Did you get a haircut this
week?

MATTHEW
Yep. Trimmed my nails, too. All the clippings
are in there.

KATHY
Great. I'll make sure these don't fall into
the wrong hands. Ron, do you have anything for
me?

RON
(Folded arms)
Nope.

KATHY
Ron? We've talked about this. We're here to
support you.

RON
Sorry. I'll bring them next time.

MATTHEW
Look man, they go through your garbage.
If they keep getting locks of your hair and
stuff, they can control you forever.

RON
No, you look! There is no they. Nobody's
controlling us. We got problems, but we are
the problem! It's all in our heads!
(Slaps self)
It's all us!
(Slaps self again)

KATHY
Ron, are you all right?

RON
I'm fine. I just had a little episode there.

LAUREN enters.

LAUREN
Hello? Am I in the right place?

KATHY
I think you are. Are you Lauren?

LAUREN
Yeah. I'm looking for the support group for
people who are controlled by voodoo dolls.

RON
People who think they're being controlled by
voodoo dolls. Welcome to the looney bin,
Lauren.

KATHY
Now Ron, remember, we're not doctors. We don't
get into that here. Everyone is free to
believe whatever they want about Voodoo Doll
Syndrome. Lauren, here at the VDS support
group, our mission is not to judge, but to
support each other so we can live the most
normal lives possible.

MATTHEW and RON
(Together, droning)
To control all that we can while accepting all

MATTHEW and RON (Cont.)
　　that we can't.

MATTHEW
　　　　(To Lauren)
　　You're in the right place. Come on in, grab a
　　coffee, and have a seat.

KATHY
　　Matthew?

MATTHEW
　　　　(To Lauren)
　　I'm sorry. If you choose, you are welcome to
　　join us. We are not forcing you to do
　　anything.

　　　　Lauren sits with the group.

KATHY
　　Lauren, do you wish to introduce yourself to
　　the group?

LAUREN
　　Hi, my name is Lauren.

KATHY, MATTHEW and RON
　　Hi, Lauren.

LAUREN
　　About a year ago, I started getting a pins and
　　needles sensation in my feet, but I thought it
　　was just my circulation. Then I started
　　getting stabbing pains in my side, but I
　　thought it was just gas. Then I started doing
　　ninja moves in the checkout line at Trader
　　Joe's, so I went to see my doctor. He said it
　　was Voodoo Doll Syndrome, so here I am.

MATTHEW
　　Any idea who has the doll?

RON
  There is no doll, Lauren. It's all in our
  heads.
      (Slaps self)
  It's all in our heads!
      (Slaps self)
  Okay, okay, stop it! It's real! It's all real;
  just stop it!

KATHY
  Ron, would you like to tell us about your
  week?

RON
  No, thanks.

MATTHEW
  Come on, Ron. Just tell us.

KATHY
  Matthew?

MATTHEW
  Sorry.

KATHY
  Ron, do you choose not to tell us about your
  week? Because if you want to talk, we're here
  to listen.

RON
  All right, I'll go. It was terrible. Another
  awful week. I had an episode at my cousin's
  wedding. I started doing the chicken dance. In
  the middle of the ceremony, not the reception.

MATTHEW
  Ron, that's great! Your puppet master might
  have been at the wedding. You may have just
  narrowed down who it could be!

RON
  Puppet master? Matthew, when are you going to

RON (Cont.)
    admit it? Voodoo isn't real. We're all just
    crazy. I don't have a puppet master. I did the
    chicken dance because I'm nuts.
        (Slaps self)
    There's no puppet master!
        (Slaps self)
    There's no PUPPET MASTER!
        (Slaps self)
        (Weeping)
    Okay, okay… you're real… Wherever you are,
    you're real… just leave me alone.

KATHY
    Thank you for sharing, Ron. That sounds very
    difficult. Matthew, do you wish to tell us
    about your week?

MATTHEW
    Oh, my week was awesome. I went to the pool
    and jumped off the high dive. My doll handler
    must have been in a good mood, because I was
    doing all kinds of flips, and twists, and tons
    of cool stuff. Moves I could never do on my
    own. People were cheering, and clapping… it
    was like I was in the Olympics.

        Ron scoffs.

MATTHEW
    Oh, and you know what I did yesterday? I
    walked right into my boss' office, turned
    around, and mooned him. I pretended I was
    having an episode, but it was allll me. And
    the best part? There's nothing he can do about
    it. He knows if he tried to discipline me,
    he'd have a real big lawsuit on his hands.
    VDS, baby!

RON
        (To Matthew)
    You disgust me.

MATTHEW
  Well, isn't that what this group is all about?
  Living life to the fullest, and not letting
  Voodoo Doll Syndrome control you? Maybe you
  need to show your puppet master a little more
  respect, Ron.

KATHY
  Now, gentlemen…

        *Ron involuntarily stands, walks over to a
        chair in front of Matthew and bends over
        with his butt in the air.*

RON
  Uh-oh.

KATHY
  Ron, are you okay?

RON
  Yep, just having a little episode here.

MATTHEW
  Ope, me too. Here we go.

        *Matthew involuntarily gets up, stands
        behind Ron and spanks him.*

MATTHEW
  Dude, I'm sorry. I don't mean to be doing
  this.

RON
  It's cool. I know you can't help it.
        (Sticks thumb in mouth, garbled)
  Annnd there goes the thumb.

MATTHEW
        (While spanking)
  You know, Ron, despite all of our differences,
  I really do respect you.

RON
     (Garbled)
  Thanks, man. You too.

MATTHEW
     (While spanking)
  I mean, you really are a fighter. It's not
  easy having our condition, wherever it comes
  from. But you're a real man about it. You
  haven't given up on the hope of a nice, normal
  life, and I respect that.

RON
     (Garbled)
  You really feel that way?

MATTHEW
     (While spanking)
  I sure do, bro. You see, I'm more of an
  opportunist. I exploit my condition. You? You
  resist it. You don't make any excuses. I
  admire you, and I consider you my friend.

RON
     (Garbled)
  Thanks, Matthew. You too.

     *Matthew and Ron regain control; the
     spanking stops, Ron's thumb comes out of
     his mouth, and both return to their seats.*

KATHY
  Well I think this was a very productive
  session.

LAUREN
  Thanks for having me. I'm so glad I found you
  guys.

MATTHEW
  Well, then you need to come get a drink with-
  I'm sorry. Would you like to come get a drink
  with us?

LAUREN
   Sure! I'll chooooose to join you.

MATTHEW
   Great! Kathy, you coming?

KATHY
   Uh, I'll meet you down there.

        *Lauren, Matthew, and Ron leave together.
        Once they're gone, JEFFREY comes out from
        hiding behind a closet or curtain with
        four voodoo dolls in his hands.*

JEFFREY
   Did you get the clippings, Mom?

KATHY
   I got some. Here you go, Puppetmaster.
        (Handing Jeffrey the envelope)
   Matthew and Lauren would make a nice couple,
   don't you think?

JEFFREY
   You wanna see them together? I could make that
   happen.

        *Jeffrey takes two of the dolls and joins
        their hands together.*

KATHY
   Jeffrey, do you mind if I go out with them for
   a drink? Just this once.

JEFFREY
   Oh, come on, Mom! You said you'd take me to
   McDonald's!

KATHY
   Do I have a choice?

*Jeffrey waves a voodoo doll in Kathy's
face. Kathy's body follows the movements
of the doll.*

JEFFREY
    (Bratty)
  No! Take me to McDonald's!

KATHY
    (Sighs)
  Well, at least you're not playing video games.

                        LX - Blackout

          END PLAY

With Love, Your Ghosts
By Mike Brannon

CHARACTERS
  OLIVE THOMAS - *Female, already a ghost*
  DANNY KETCH - *Male, becomes a ghost*
  SAMARA MORGAN - *Female, not yet a ghost*
  RODRIGO ROGERS - *Male, not a ghost*

SETTING
  Danny's living room, in an average
  apartment building, somewhere in an
  averaged-sized town.

Danny's living room, in an average
apartment building, somewhere in an
averaged-sized town. A sofa is down-left,
with small end tables and brass lamps on
either side. There's a small coffee table
in front of the sofa, with a few dirty
dishes splayed across. A staircase is at
back, and a door outside is stage left,
with a kitchen door stage right.

DANNY and SAMARA are sitting on the sofa
stage left, frozen in mid-discussion.
OLIVE is set in a spotlight stage right,
watching them both with a mild look of
disdain.

OLIVE
How long does someone have to be dead before
they notice that they're dead? You'd assume
they'd figure it out after a while, with the
translucency and that whole "floating
weightless" thing…

Olive sighs, and then snaps her fingers.
Instantly, Danny and Samara resume their
conversation – Danny is recounting one of
his more epic adventures in the world of
database analytics; Samara is clearly
bored, and keeps surreptitiously glancing
at her cell phone.

DANNY
The data wasn't anywhere close to third normal
form, so the OLAP software just treated it as
flat-file…

SAMARA
Mmm-hmm.

DANNY
And of course they want to script it entirely
in Python, even though I've been using R and
RStudio since graduate school…

SAMARA
  Ugggh! Stop! Please!

DANNY
  What is it, Samara?

SAMARA
  No more programming talk. No more programming
  talk. You're killing me, Danny. Literally.
  Killing me.

DANNY
  I don't understand. You asked me how my day
  went.

    *Samara in her standard dull cadence and
    Olive in a mocking sing-songy fashion say
    the next phrase together.*

OLIVE and SAMARA
  "You asked me how my day went."

SAMARA
  Please. As if.

OLIVE
  He can be such a dweeb sometime…

SAMARA
  I was just being, you know, polite…

OLIVE
  He's still cute, though. Like a nerdy marathon
  runner. With a slide rule.

DANNY
  A slide rule?

SAMARA
      (puzzled)
  What?

OLIVE
     (excited)
  What?!?

DANNY
  You said I looked like a marathon runner... with
  a slide rule...

OLIVE
  That was me! Danny! Hello?!? That was me!!!

SAMARA
  What's a slide rule? You know, whatever. Not
  really part of my life.

     Samara puts her phone in front of her face
     and resumes texting; Danny stands and
     takes a few steps towards Olive, who waits
     breathlessly.
     Then Danny shakes his head, and turns back
     to Samara.

DANNY
  Hey, you hungry? You want some pita chips and
  hummus?

SAMARA
  Sure, I guess. I could eat some hummus.

OLIVE
  Aaaaaargh, no. No! Come on! We were so close!

     Olive snaps her fingers and the lights go
     out stage left. She begins pacing, clearly
     agitated.

OLIVE
  It's been forever since the accident. He just
  keeps going on and on, reliving the same
  boring days from his same boring life. Always
  with that girl. That Samara girl. Ugh.
     (Takes a breath)
  All right. Let's try it again.

Olive snaps her fingers, and the lights go out. Almost immediately, the lights come back up again, with all three of them back in their starting positions – Danny and Samara on the sofa, and Olive stage right.

DANNY
  The data wasn't anywhere close to third normal form, so the OLAP software just treated it… as… flat-file…

  Danny hesitates as he speaks, feeling the ebb and flow of déjà vu.

SAMARA
  Mmm-hmm.

DANNY
  They want to script it… entirely in… Python… wait, have I said that before?

SAMARA
  Ugggh! Stop! Please!

DANNY
  Hold on. I…

SAMARA
  No more programming talk. No more programming talk.

DANNY
  …I said that before. I said that before! You've…

SAMARA
  You're killing me, Danny.

DANNY
  …said that before.

SAMARA
  Literally. Killing. Me.

DANNY
    You've said that before!

        *Samara freezes in place; Olive walks
        slowly over to Danny, who suddenly
        recognizes her. As they speak, the lights
        fade to black on Samara and the living
        room.*

DANNY
    Wait. Olive? Is that you? What are you…?

OLIVE
        (shyly)
    Hi, Danny.

DANNY
    This… this can't be happening… you're…

OLIVE
    Your… your ex-girlfriend. Yes.

DANNY
    That's not what I mean. You're… you're…

OLIVE
    It's all right, Danny. Just keep calm.

DANNY
    You're dead. You're dead! You died! Right here
    in this house!

OLIVE
    Danny, the most important thing is to be calm…

DANNY
    What do you mean, be calm! You're dead! And I
    can see you! And that means that… that means
    that I…

        *Danny seizes up, realizing for the first
        time his own predicament. The lamps on the
        end table shake a small amount.*

DANNY
How did it… How did I…?

OLIVE
     (shrugging, trying to act casual)
You fell down the stairs and broke your neck,
Danny. You died instantly. It happens. The
important thing…

DANNY
How long ago was that?

OLIVE
Danny…

DANNY
How long ago was that? How long have I been
dead?!? Answer me!

     The lamps quiver and bounce even more
     noticeably. Olive speaks in an even, calm
     voice.

OLIVE
Three months. It's been three months since
the… accident.

DANNY
Three months? But… but I was just talking to…

OLIVE
Samara, yes. The new girl. That's not present
day, Danny. Those were memories you were
exploring. You can do that. You can go back
and relive some of those moments. Not any of
the happier stuff… but… you can look at the
past.

DANNY
I don't want to look at the past, Olive. Show
me.

OLIVE
  I'm not sure you're ready...

DANNY
  I need to know, Olive. I need to see. What's
  going on? What's happening with Samara? Show
  me. Show me the present day.

      *Olive stares a bit at him, and then sighs
      and shrugs her shoulders. She snaps...
      And the lights come up on Samara and
      RODRIGO making out on the living room
      sofa. Danny stares at the scene in horror.*

SAMARA
  Mmmm, Rodrigo, you're an amazing kisser. Much
  better than any man I've ever been with.

RODRIGO
  Come, my love. Let me feast upon your lips.

      *Samara and Rodrigo embrace again; Danny
      looks from the two of them and back to
      Olive, uncomprehending.*

DANNY
  I don't... I don't understand. It's been... three
  months? How could she...

OLIVE
  Well, duh. She was seeing this bronze-plated
  douchebag on the side. Obviously.

DANNY
  She was cheating on me?

OLIVE
  Oh, like you have any grounds for outrage.
  Like you weren't seeing this Samara chick all
  the time that we lived together. Get real,
  Danny. You know what they say - "once a
  cheater..."

DANNY
  It... It wasn't like that...

OLIVE
  Uh-huh. I'm sure it was different with her. It
  was puppies and sunshine and rainbows and all
  of the rest. That true love bullshit. Right?
  Right? Is that what you had? You and your
  precious Samara???

  While Olive has been saying all of this,
  the contents of the house begin quaking –
  lamps clanking, plates and cups
  clattering. Samara leaps to her feet and
  turns to Rodrigo.

SAMARA
  What's going on? Some kind of earthquake?

RODRIGO
  In Minnesota?!?

SAMARA
  Quick, Rodrigo – we have to get out of here!

  Samara and Rodrigo exit stage left.

  Danny stares at Olive in disbelief, even
  as she starts taking deep breaths to calm
  herself down.

DANNY
  What was that? What's going on?

OLIVE
  OK. OK. I'm going to level with you, Danny.
  Here we go. So, we're ghosts.

DANNY
  Ghosts? Ghosts? Like, in the movie Ghost? With
  Patrick Swayze?

OLIVE

Sort of. Cross the movie Ghost with
Beetlejuice and The Sixth Sense and The Woman
in Black and… well, you get the idea. They get
some parts right, they get some parts wrong.
Let's see. As a ghost you are invisible,
inaudible, and incorporeal… and your emotional
state can affect your physical environment, so
it's important to keep a level head.

DANNY

Wait. The lamps shaking and stuff. That was
you?

OLIVE

I can get a little worked up at times –
especially when I see you with a skanky bitch
like Samara – but, well. I'm sure you remember
how passionate I am…

DANNY

(under his breath)
Sure… if by *passionate* you mean *psychotic*…

OLIVE

(continuing)
I mean, we definitely loved each other, right?
I took care of you. Cooked you eggplant
parmesan. Bought you those Funko figurines and
Star Wars phasers…

DANNY

(still muttering)
Star Trek, Olive, not Star Wars. There is a
difference…

OLIVE

I tried to make you happy, Danny. Was it
really all bad?

DANNY

Of course it wasn't all bad. Some of it – a
lot of it – was really good. It's just that…

427

*Samara and Rodrigo enter back into the
living room, holding hands.*

DANNY
  …Wait a minute. They're coming back in.

RODRIGO
  None of the neighbors said that they felt the
  earthquake. That's really weird…

SAMARA
  What's really "weird" is how many people
  around here are at home in the middle of the
  day. It's like we're living in a sitcom
  neighborhood…

RODRIGO
  Aren't we at home in the middle of the day?
  What does that make us?

SAMARA
  Well, me, I'm in mourning from my clumsy ex-
  boyfriend…

    *Danny tenses up; Olive puts a hand on his
    shoulder.*

SAMARA
  And you… Well… I guess you're just too pretty
  to work.

    *Samara crosses and starts kissing on
    Rodrigo again; he indulges for a while,
    and then pushes her away.*

RODRIGO
  You got anything to eat in this house? I'm
  starving.

SAMARA
  I can make you a sandwich in the kitchen.
  Maybe we even have potato chips.

RODRIGO
Sounds good, sweetie. See if you have any
ranch while you're at it.

*Samara kisses him and heads out the door
stage right into the kitchen. Rodrigo
pulls out his phone and begins texting.*

RODRIGO
Whoa, it's Tina. That girl is hot as fire.
"Hey there, Rodrigo, you free to come over?"
Oh hell, yeah! Tina is DTF as they get, man.
Let me just text Samara "Hey girl… save… that…
sandwich… for me…"

Rodrigo *quickly types out a message,
clicks "send", and then darts toward the
door.*

RODRIGO
        (talking and texting)
"Yo, Tina, I'm on my way." Better believe I'm
going to hit that…

Rodrigo exits.
Danny looks after him in disbelief.

DANNY
Can't believe Samara is hooking up with that
guy…

OLIVE
It's all right, Danny. Look at it this way –
you don't need her anymore. We're together
again. Together forever…

*Danny glances at Olive, an odd expression
on his face, then he's struck by a
realization, and he backs away from her in
horror.*

OLIVE
What?

DANNY
  You said your emotional state can affect your
  physical environment. When you get mad, you
  can move things around.

OLIVE
  Yeah, well…

DANNY
  And you called Samara a skanky bitch.

OLIVE
  She is a skanky bitch. She knew you were
  taken, that you were living with me!

DANNY
  Olive… we broke up! Granted, I was still
  living with you when I met Samara, but… the
  two of us had broken up. We'd been broken up
  for weeks!

OLIVE
  You just needed time to come to your senses…

DANNY
  When I told you I was moving out, you slit
  your wrists! You killed yourself in the
  upstairs bathroom…

    *Samara comes walking out of the kitchen,
    holding a sandwich on a plate.*

SAMARA
  We didn't have any potato chips, so I gave you
  Fritos…

OLIVE
    (angrily)
  What choice did I have? You said you loved me!

DANNY
  People change, Olive!

SAMARA
    (looking around)
  Rodrigo? Are you here?

OLIVE
  People change! People change! You said you'd
  be with me forever! Well, guess what? I made
  that happen.

    *Olive suddenly realizes what she's said,
    and falls silent. Danny begins to get more
    and more upset, and as he does, things in
    the house begin to go "bump".*

DANNY
  What do you mean, you made that happen?

OLIVE
  Danny… Sweetheart…

SAMARA
  Hello??? Is somebody there?

DANNY
  Don't you "sweetheart" me. What do you mean,
  you made that happen?

OLIVE
  Like I said, you just needed more time. When I
  saw how miserable you were with that woman…
  when I realized that I could have you to my
  own…

    *Still carrying the sandwich, Samara roams
    around the living room.*

    Danny turns on Olive, livid.

DANNY
  It wasn't an accident, was it? When I fell
  down the stairs. You pushed me. You saw me
  there, you saw me with Samara, you got upset,
  and… you…

OLIVE
  Danny, I…

DANNY
  You pushed me. You killed yourself, then you
  killed me, and for what? So you could pretend
  that you'll have me to yourself? Forever?!?

OLIVE
  I will have you to myself forever!

DANNY
  You think so?

SAMARA
      (rounding the front of the sofa)
  Rodrigo?

OLIVE
  Yes, I do!

DANNY
  Fine!

OLIVE
  Fine!

        With a large "thunk", the coffee table
        flies out and strikes Samara on the shins.
        She stumbles – the sandwich goes flying –
        and we hear a loud "cracking" sound as she
        falls to the ground.

        Danny and Olive walk slowly over to
        Samara's body and stare at it. Samara is
        not moving.

        The lights go out. Danny and Olive are lit
        again by a single spot. They continue to
        stare down, and then stare at each other.
        Finally, they are joined in the spotlight
        by Samara, who looks at them both oddly.

*The three of them look at each other for a
long, uncomfortable amount of time before
Samara speaks.*

SAMARA
  Well, this is awkward.

                    END PLAY

Monologues

An Audience At The Crossroads
By Dominic Palmer

CHARACTER
  MARY REDMOND - *Female*

SETTING
  Crossroads.

MARY REDMOND

I was standing alone outside the bar on the crossroads of Kings Street and Barrack Street the first time the stranger spoke to me. Waiting for my father to finish his swilled wallowing inside. Ten years old, terrified he'd never come back out. As I stood there, the slurred sounds of the bar oozing from the cracks and windows, looking for his face each time the door opened, heart leaping, I became gradually aware that I was not, in fact, on my own.

I fancied I couldn't so much hear their breathing, as feel it around me in the thick air.

At last, the stranger spoke. How can I describe this voice? All at once terrifying and beautiful, a white noise fugue of frequencies, a rasp without obfuscation. Performative. Narcotic. Operatic.

"I'm sorry for your loss. What can I do to help you?" What could they do to help me unburden myself of this terrible pain? I was ten years old, couldn't begin to put voice to it. The stranger understood. "Grief can rob us of expression. Return to these crossroads when you have an answer. I'll be waiting." In a blink, they were gone, I alone once more. For a long time after, they drifted into a nostalgic dream. Life – as is often the case – got in the way of the dreams, the stranger disappearing into the hazy alcoves of my recollection. It would be another nine years before I heard that voice again, on those very same crossroads. By then, I knew what to ask for.

Well, but, I'm getting ahead of myself a little bit. I can't tell you my story if we've never met. So, let's introduce ourselves.

Here stands before you Mary Redmond, for a time the greatest Soprano in Wexford. Born in this town on the 11th October, 1941, to my mother, Oona, nineteen years old, and her husband, my father, Thomas Redmond, a twenty-one-year-old never-was whose own father, in a terrible case of mistaken identity and reprisal for an anti-treaty execution he had no part in, had been dragged from his local Enniscorthy bar by free state jackboots, beat to death, his bloodied pulp of a corpse draped across the riverbank walls as a grisly warning. With retaliations firing all around them, Thomas' remaining family escaped to Wexford town until the drama ended. In my father's mind, I don't think that chip ever fully left his shoulder.

For a time, we were happy. I was born into a house of constant music. My mother, a passionate behind closed doors singer, had a keen ear and voice for opera. She kept a small but expansive collection of itched second-and third-hand records, some bought, most gathered from the refuse of those wealthier neighbourhoods for whom she washed and cleaned, all of which cycled through the record player. My father sneered that it was 'just people shouting over each other in a busy bar.' But those grandiose swells of orchestra, cannon-ball thrusts of sensuality and brutally public declarations of love and hate transcended all for her. She would sit me on her knee and we would pore over tragic deaths, revenge, angels and demons, singing along; she with her gently powerful lilt, me at first a joyous gurgling child. As time passed, she began to teach me, in her own way, how to sing these songs. It was to me an abandon of pure joy.

And then in 1951, when I had just turned ten, Oona took ill with Tuberculosis, a most

villainous illness that stole her of her song.
She spent her remaining months alive and dying
in an ancient sanatorium, passing away alone
at the age of twenty nine. Buried in a
pauper's grave.

Grief consumed my tiny family. And without her
to care for us, we both slipped into a
complacent despondency that stole me from my
studies, and drove him to the bar where first
I met the stranger. The passion for my mother'
operas became an obsession, and alone I would
sing alongside them, forming words I barely
understood in a voice that sweetly echoed
hers. Oh, those arias and duets, sopranos
weeping for their lovers, and baritones
cursing the gods and the Earth, these were my
solace, and singing my escape. Drink and a
quiet fury, my father's.

By fifteen, I was working for the bar my
devastated father had begun frequenting the
day of her pauper's funeral, and seemed to
have never left.

My two joys were the moments where my
confidence got the better of my timidity, and
I sang for the few regulars remaining as night
melded to morning, and - my greatest joy - the
annual opera crowd spilling in when all other
bars had closed, listening to their money-
drunk chatter as they pored over at first
recordings, and later luxurious shows. Time
passed, and like dust, I settled, whiling away
the next few years entertaining the bar
patrons with song. I was happy for their
attention, allowing myself to enjoy the
crooked melody of my voice in front of this
grateful audience of damaged men who knew
nothing from a good tune, and a perfect one.

I continued serving my father and men like
him, despite all efforts becoming a mirror to

my poor passed mother, sensing Thomas'
resentment grow into something edging towards
a kind of wild hatred for the daughter who
reminded him so immediately of his loss. I
kept a distance from him, but that distance
acted as a rueful form of rejection in our
tiny cage of a home. Time passed, and like
dust, I settled into something akin to
contentment, even finding a kind of
confidence, whiling away the next few years
entertaining the drinkers and storytellers
with my song, we all becoming lost souls in
the music. It was our joy. It made me happy.
It could have stayed this way, if not for
Jenny O'Rourke, that most famous of Irish
divas. Twenty five and filled with the hubris
that a singular skill admired by many can
breed, someone had told Jenny of my flights of
musical fancy from behind the bar, and in a
whisk of delight, she bade me sing for her
party of debauched and drunken hangers on, the
year the opera house returned from
hiatus.

I didn't have the wit to see it for what it
was, as I nervously climbed onto a proffered
chair, hand held gently by Jenny as I did so,
to sing for a group of people who had
lustfully set me up for cruel mockery. The
drill of drunken laughter, the sneering
bitchery, oh, the humiliation. For the famous
Jenny O'Rourke had chosen to show me up,
singing across me, her powerful voice finding
trained notes I could never hope to, curving
up through the air with a solitary beauty that
robbed me of my own breath and left me red
faced and ashamed, standing, raised on that
dunce's chair, the sting of mortification and
fury prickling my eyes as I held back the
tears. Climbing back down, no one to hold my
hand this time, I returned to the bar, where I
found myself fantasising revenge. It was only
invention of the mind, the night passed, and

I fell into the rhythm of the bar once more.
Perhaps time could have killed this
humiliation and the resentment it bore.
But humiliation is a terrible muse. As is
grief.

Unfortunately, ladies and gentlemen, this
being that most Irish of tales, I need to warn
you that this story is about to take a very
dark and ugly turn. It can't be helped. These
are the facts of my life. But I'll warn you
nonetheless, because although the more
fanciful tinges to my fable can make it feel
like a fairytale, the truth is my story is not
a kind one.

On the day of my nineteenth birthday, not one
week from my humiliation, my father took his
own life. He was forty years old. I've since
heard some remark that he did so in spite. He
was a great many things, Thomas Redmond, but I
think that it takes more than a mean spirit to
drive a person to leave this plane of
existence by their own hand. What I had
mistaken for anger in my childish sentiment
had in fact been a terrible, furious anguish
that had finally overwhelmed Thomas. I
couldn't have known. Well. But of course,
modern attitudes have no doubt changed greatly
in the intervening years, but then what would
euphemistically be referred to as a 'tragic
death' for fear of naming the devil, meant
shame for family and community, and of course,
divine rejection. My father could not be
buried next to his wife. Shunned, instead his
two brothers, one cousin, and I took his body
into the countryside, held a secreted service
heated by drink and sorrow, and buried him in
an empty spot in a forgotten field before
returning to the town, more drink, and more
sorrow.

And so we returned to the bar that seemed to

be the centre of my woes, where that same
opera crowd were winding down. This particular
night, it appeared I was not alone in drowning
my sorrows. Jenny O'Rourke had given a bad
performance. She could not be consoled, seemed
beside herself with a grief even the passing
of my father had not brought out in me,
lashing out at all around her. After one drink
to quell the tradition of the wake, I escaped
outside, perversely basking in the sounds, my
loss, and I confess, a little element of
schadenfreude. I whispered to the air: "Why
her and not me? Why does she have everything,
and I nothing? What can you give me! Where are
you now?" What can you possibly offer me now?"
And as I stood there, swaying a little with my
own imbibement, I became almost sensually
aware that they were once more standing
nearby. That numbness crawled over me, not
quite fear, and certainly not calm. Invasive,
but externally so. Sweet, in some way I could
never explain.

As they had so many years ago, the stranger
responded in that cracked honeycomb voice.
"What is it that you want?" "Just once," I
told the air, "I want to be the greatest
soprano in Wexford." "There is a way," they
said. "But it comes at a cost." I couldn't
help but laugh. I had nothing left to lose.
"Tell me." That clouded figure appearing in
the dark, leaning in to whisper vaporously:
"Death, and rebirth. Usurp her. Take her voice
from her. You'll get what you want, I promise
you. But it will steal something back from
you." Let it, I thought.

On cue, Jenny O'Rourke stuttered from the bar,
her eyes drifting across me with a lazy
disdain, before losing her balance and
dropping to one knee with an anguished,
tuneless squeal. I - feigning a kind of
innocent shock at seeing her so ill - offered

442

to assist my bane, suggesting we walk the
quay, breathe the air. I led her down the old
Viking streets, Jenny, feeling the flush of
regret for her treatment of me, slurring an
apology. I felt a desire to comfort her. This
emotion I crushed. I knew that if I accepted
her apology, for her it would be all right.
For people of privilege it's always all right.
For people like me, only consequences. We
reached the ocean. I whispered: "How I would
love you to sing, Jenny. Just for me." She
turned, unsteady, beaming with childish
delight and, perhaps taking this as a sign of
redemption for her, began to sing for me, the
song she had fumbled on stage earlier that
night, angelic across the grey, churning
ocean. I cherished each pristine note.

But I knew what I had to do. Usurp her. Death
and rebirth. My hands felt swollen and cold,
as I reached up and wrapped them around
Jenny's throat. For a moment, I suspect she
thought I was offering affection, and started
to turn, to reject or accept, I'll never know.
I tightened my grip, dug in my nails, and
strangled the song from her throat. I knew
what I had to do. Drunk as she was, she still
tried to fight back, but my desire was
stronger than hers, and I continued to tighten
my grip in a flurry of thrill and seasick
nausea. What had once been beauteous song had
turned to a terrible gurgling, a desperate
plea in her eyes.

But I knew what I had to do, and so I did it.
I held on until she no longer could, and as I
watched her life diminish before me, I felt no
guilt, only elation. It was my turn. She had
had her moment, and now it was mine. As her
life left her body, I fancied I could feel an
ebb and flow of something new enter mine. I
pushed her, then, into the ocean she had sung
across before this intimate violence, for a

moment the sea salt fizzing around her, before she succumbed to the water's gentle but firm pull, drifting on her back, hair floating out around her. Even in death, she was hatefully beautiful. And then she was gone and I, once more, alone and waiting for a miracle I suddenly realised might not be forthcoming. Had I really believed what this stranger had told me? Or had I just wanted to believe, to excuse my desire for vengeance against Jenny O'Rourke? Were they even here, now, with me, as I had imagined? Had it been worth it?

I stood there, once more alone, in a state of exquisite calmness. Time would tell.

Having composed myself by the sea, I returned to the bar. Her peers had not cared for Jenny's behaviour, had been relieved to see her leave, one of the more coarse crew members declaring, "Wouldn't it be grand if she fell into the sea!"

I luxuriated in my private knowledge. Gaining courage, and driven by drink and the cheers of those who only nights ago had bayed for my humiliation, I stood up and sang. And oh, my friends, my voice was stained glass beauty. Be it spiritual or merely confidence gained by my ugly deed, I had never sang more powerfully. Each time I finished, they begged for more, and each new song I sang, received better than the last. I held my audience enraptured and I clung on to each moment. The night, already broaching morning, finally succumbed to it, and those hail and hearty performers and lifters carried me out on a cloud of cheer as they caterwauled back to their lives. As I watched them disappear into the still dark air, alone once more on those crossroads, I thought of my beautiful mother, her song taken so painfully, and my poor father and his inconsolable grief.

"Well? Was it worth it?" the stranger asked me. I could not see them, was only vaguely aware of their presence in the air around me. Inside my mind, where perhaps they had always been. "You were the best soprano in Wexford. For a night." I smiled. "Just once," I told them, realising how I had sealed that fate with my own words. "Just once." And so, ladies and gentlemen, here stands before you Mary Redmond, for the briefest of moments the greatest soprano in Wexford.

Now, ladies and gentlemen, we all know this old, old story. It's been told with many variations. Marlowe made it popular, and blues brother Robert Johnson made it legendary, even if on reflection there might have been a little plagiarism involved in the former's tale, and just a touch of racism in the latter's, an inherited legend that sought to obscure a talented performer's incredible and incredibly influential skill, and attribute it instead to the dark arts.

Had it really been this stranger's gift that had given me this moment, this perfect moment in time, had I sold my soul to some devil for the ability to, if only briefly, shine bright, if only once? Or was it the immaculate confidence I had gained in an instant of wild debauchery? I have never desired to find out. So I never sang again.

Now. You've heard my tale. Be honest. If any one of you could sell your soul to the spiritual for power, I think most of you would at least consider it. Just like the least spiritual of us will turn to God in moments of despair. So don't stand on judgment here. We are all of a one in art, are we not?

"Was it worth it?"

I stood there on the precipice of understanding and found myself crying, not tears of misery, despite the day that had been. No, I was weeping tears of joy.

I could barely breathe, such was my elation. Yes. It had been worth it, despite the cost. My audience of one silently applauded me.

Yes.

It had been worth it.

END PLAY

Claustrophobic
By Emma C. R. Skinner

CHARACTER
  UNNAMED - *Deceased*

SETTING
  A dark space.

UNNAMED

Is this your grave, or is it mine?

No, no, don't look at me like that. Don't run
away. Stay right where you are. Stop. That's
better.

I'm a little confused, you see, and I'm trying
to figure things out. The last that I
remember, Charlotte and I were standing
together at the edge of a precipice. She had
brought me up there because she thought I
would like the view. And I did, of course. The
sun was low in the sky, and sunset was
starting to bleed across the clouds…

I was so enraptured by all of it. She would
have known that, of course.

The next thing I remember, there were hands on
my back, shoving me forward, roughly, and then
the air was whistling past me and the clouds
were flying further away and then -

Everything was dark, and I was lost in an
ocean of dirt.

I don't know how long I was down there. But I
heard your footsteps, just a moment ago.
Clomping around on top of me, all rough and
loud. Why did you detour over it? Don't you
have any respect? That seems rather rude of
you.

So, I thought I'd make my way up here to talk
to you. To ask you if you know what happened
to me. Have you ever met Charlotte? Did she
say what happened? Or had she already
forgotten about me?

I don't want to be down there. I don't belong
down there. I like heights. I deserve to be up
at the top of a cliffside or the peak of a

mountain. Not down in the ground with that
headstone that's been eroded away.
I don't really remember my name. Maybe that's
why?

Would you like to go down there in my place?
You probably don't hate small spaces as much
as me. It probably won't be as painful for
you. And after all, you owe it to me, don't
you? You walked over the grave and woke me up.
So don't you owe me a favor in return?

The name has eroded away. No one can read it.

It could just as easily be your grave instead.

                    END PLAY

Ghost Whisperer
By Melvin S. Marsh

CHARACTER
  PARANORMAL INVESTIGATOR - *Any gender, any age*

SETTING
  A haunted house.

PARANORMAL INVESTIGATOR
Hello?

If there is anyone here who would like to talk
to us, can you make your presence known to us
please?

If that was you making that noise and you were
trying to get our attention a few minutes ago,
here we are. We aren't trying to hurt you, we
just want to communicate with you and find out
why you are still here.

This is a K-II meter, it will help you
communicate with us if you are willing. You
can come closer to it and it will light up
some of these lights here. It has already
showed us that someone is in here.

I'm going to set it right here if that is ok?

I was wondering if you could come closer and
see how this works?

A two… Ok, that is perfect. Can you make it go
back to zero or one please?

Perfect. Thank you.

May I ask you a few questions?

Thank you.

Is there more than one of you here living in
this house?
Ok… that looks like a yes

Two of you?

Yes…

Three of you?

Ok, only two of you then.

Are both of you present right now?

No...

Are you the one who also moves the doors and rattles the cupboards?

No...

We found a reference of someone named John who used to live here but whose body was found in the basement mangled, locked from the inside. Was that you?

Yes...

You're John?

Yes...

No-one is sure who killed you as the murderer was never found and there is a rumour that a ghost killed you.

Was your murderer alive at the time of your death?

...

Were you killed?

Yes... ok.

Was your murderer alive at the time of your death?

...

Silence again? A No?

Ok... were you killed by something not alive?

Wow it's running up to a 5… That's a definitely strong yes.

Is your murderer in this house?

Yes…

…Did you hear that? I'm not sure where that sound came from…

Is the other one making that noise?

Yes…

Jesus, what on Earth was that? It sounds like it is in the same room as us. Is the other one here now?

Damn… Well, that's a yes.

Ummm… Is that axe on the wall… wiggling?

Yeah, you didn't have to answer that it was rhetorical!

I think it definitely doesn't want us here…

You can stop answering rhetorical questions, I didn't even ask anything.

I think we better get out.

RUNNNNN!

END PLAY

My Friend Audrey
By Greg Lam

CHARACTER
  ISABELLA - *Female, 8 years old*

SETTING
  A childs bedroom.

Isabella, an 8-year old girl, plays alone with a doll. She talks straight to the audience.

ISABELLA
Audrey is the ghost who lives in my room. When I first moved into this house she was kind of scary, but she's OK now.

I leave my toys around when I'm not around so she can play with them, too.

She died in the 50's I think, but she doesn't want to talk about it much.

Neither do my parents. I don't talk to them about Audrey anymore.

Audrey doesn't leave my room ever. I asked her why not, and she said she's scared.

"About what?" I asked. She said she's cared of the ghosts that are out there.

"That's silly," I said. "You're a ghost, how can you be afraid of ghosts?"

"Well you're a person," she said. "Aren't you ever afraid of other people?"

"That's a good point," I said.

A beat. Isabella turns to the side.

I said you made a good point, Audrey!

Isabella turns back to the audience.

Anyway, Audrey's nice...

Most of the time.

Staring into the Portal
By Katy Lever

CHARACTER
  RESIDENT - *Any gender, any age*

SETTING
  A living room.

RESIDENT

Staring into The Portal… The lights and sounds
were like nothing I had seen or heard in any
life before.

It had taken me 10 years to find its exact
location, by using a system of mirrors, spells
and bells.

I'd always heard them, the whispers in the
house calling my name, conversations replayed
like the house's internal voice recorder.

At first, they were shy, only tapping me on
the shoulder when I did the washing up, but
when I turned around there was no one there.

As time went on, they got bolder, maybe they
trusted me more?

And then I started to see the other people in
the house.

A glimmer at first, of a woman in a bustle, a
slow walk across the corner of my eye, and the
woman disappeared up the stairs that were
built 100 years ago.

The shimmering people at night who stood by my
bed, sometimes getting in -maybe wanting to
talk- but the wall between us was too thick to
hear them.

The woman in the bustle had once been brazen
and moved across the room right in front of
me, but the moment I blinked- she had gone.

The animals had first alerted me to The
Portal.

One by one over the years they had sniffed,
stared, growled and howled into it.

Which really freaked me out while trying to watch Coronation Street.

A good witch who lived across the road had given me the mirrors to reflect dark energy.

This worried me as I never thought the energy was dark.

It was just an old house replaying moments like a projector.

But now, I'm looking directly into the portal and I can clearly see something staring directly back at me.

END PLAY

Tell-Tale
By Peter Dakutis

CHARACTER
  ALLAN - *Male, late 20s-early 30s*

SETTING
  A law enforcement interrogation room.

ALLAN

True, I'm nervous. I've always been very, very
nervous. But why would you think I'm mad? The
nervousness heightens my senses. Makes me
sharper, more focused. That's why I'm very
good, brilliant really, at coding.

The incident at my last job was just
nervousness, nothing else. No one was
permanently injured, and they were more than
generous in buying out my stake in the
company. Which I used to find a quiet place
here in the mountains. Working remotely on
projects that come my way.

See how calmly I'm relating my story? If I
were some kind of madman, would I be so…
collected. It's impossible to say how the
thought of killing him entered my brain, but
it wasn't madness that put it there.

I liked the old man, Cliff, well enough. His
was the only cabin that I could see from mine,
and there was a wooded area between us. I'd
wanted total privacy, but Russell, the real
estate agent, said Cliff kept mostly to
himself. When I'd go out on the deck to smoke,
I might see him working outside, and we'd
wave. Or we'd say hello down at the mailboxes.

One day at the mailboxes, he said Russell had
told him that I knew computers. And would I
look at his? I got his number and said I'd
call later and stop by. As I suspected, it was
a malware issue. Old people don't know what
they're doing on computers. It didn't take
that long to deal with it.

I didn't want to spend too much time there. He
didn't talk much, which suited me. The place
was pretty dirty and smelled funny, and there
were piles of junk all around, but none of
that bothered me.

No, it was his hand. His right hand. It was
hideous. Twisted and gnarly, it looked more
like a claw. Like it belonged to some monster
in an H.P. Lovecraft story. Something about it
was evil to me and made my blood run cold.
That is why I needed to get out of there.
Whenever I'd seen the old man before, he was
wearing gloves. This was the first time I'd
actually seen it. It.

Of course, once Cliff had my number, he was
often texting me, asking for more assistance
with his computer or his phone. I tried to
face my fear and not be revolted by his hand,
but gradually I began to dread it more and
more. Every time I received a text from him, I
could see that hideous claw pecking out the
words.
One day, I was helping him at his computer,
and he leaned over me to take the mouse. His
hand— that thing—touched me. I pulled my hand
away quickly in fear and disgust. It was as if
I'd been touched—no, marked—by a demon.

I told him I'd been startled, that it was just
nerves. But I knew then that I was going to
have to kill him in order to rid myself of
that thing forever.

Now, you think I'm some kind of madman. That I
don't know what I'm doing. But you should have
seen how I went about it. I was as nice as I
could be in the days leading up to his death.
I spent as much time as I could in his cabin,
learning the layout, learning his habits,
learning his routine.

Cliff had showed me a path from his cabin to
mine through the wooded area separating us,
and I learned that path as well as I could. I
wanted to be able to walk it in the dead of
night, using only starlight to see. The plan
was to murder him in his sleep. Make it seem

like he died of natural causes. Once I had all the data I needed, I went about it very methodically.

At midnight, I would make my way carefully to the old man's cabin. Like a lot of people up here, he never locked his doors. I knew he slept soundly. One of his meds knocked him out every night. And he was hard of hearing, so it was no trouble to creep up on him. The first night, I just stood there at the door and watched him, taking in all the details I could. I was in no hurry to kill him.

The next two nights, I did roughly the same, staring at him, getting used to the surroundings. Moving closer and closer to him. That's where the nervousness helped. I could make myself very still, using my senses to be attuned to every single stimulus around me. It was almost as if I could feel my synapses firing, sending all the information to my brain to be processed.

The fourth night, I made slight noises to see if they would wake him up. They didn't. The next night, I leaned over him as close as I could, even blowing gently on him. He would not be easily roused. The next two nights were similar. I would get as close as possible, imagining just how the deed would take place.

During the day, the old man said nothing about receiving midnight visits. Nor did he suspect that I would be his executioner.

On the eighth night, the last night, I stood near his bed, holding a pillow from the other bedroom. I was barely moving, barely breathing. Until that night, I hadn't realized just how powerful I was, how in control I was. I could feel a sense of triumph flowing through me, like an electrical current.

At that moment, something woke the old man. A bad dream, perhaps. A feeling of doom, of death approaching. I stayed as motionless as possible. He didn't get up. He didn't really move. But I knew he hadn't fallen back to sleep. We were both motionless for almost an hour. And then he let out this long moan of despair from the bottom of his soul. I knew the sound well. I've woken up many nights, making a similar wail from a feeling of hopelessness.

As the old man moaned, I used this as an opportunity to carry out my plan. I pressed the pillow against his face and threw myself on him to pin him down. I didn't want there to be signs of a struggle, and I wanted to make sure that right hand didn't touch me. He resisted a little, but my weight was too much for him. Then it felt like he was just giving up, resigning himself to his fate.

After I was sure that he was dead, I used as little light as possible to survey the scene and ensure that it looked like the old man had died undisturbed in his sleep. Now, if I'd been a madman, I would have cut that evil hand off. And burned it or buried it. But no, the demon that had touched me was gone. That's what had driven me, not madness. There was no need to think any more about it.

And so I put it out of my head. I went home and slept like a baby. I had a new work project that was going to be very intensive, and I spent all my time focusing on that. When I went out on the deck to smoke and looked at Cliff's cabin, I didn't even think about what had happened there. I just completely forgot about it.

About a couple of weeks later, I was out on the deck and saw a couple of sheriff's deputies over at Cliff's cabin. I waved, and they motioned that they would be driving up to my cabin. I went inside and put on a fresh pot of coffee.

When they arrived, I invited them in and offered them coffee, making a joke about not having any donuts. They said they'd received a request for a welfare check on Cliff from his niece and found that he had died in his sleep. I extended my condolences to the niece, explaining that I hadn't been here too long and didn't know Cliff that well, except to assist him with computer issues.

The deputies said they'd checked Cliff's phone and seen the messages. They speculated that I might have been the last person to see him alive.

"That's too bad," I said. "Our visits weren't that social."

They asked if I'd keep an eye on the cabin until the niece arrived to take care of things. They said a Mrs. Johnson swore that she'd seen something moving around the cabin in the middle of the night, but she "liked to drink" and wasn't a reliable source of information. They also warned me that they were airing out the cabin and that I may occasionally get a whiff of something unpleasant.

The deputies started to leave, but I was feeling triumphant, and I invited them to stay and have some more coffee. One of them asked if I had Wi-Fi, and I said, yes, they could use it.

I set them up at one end of my dining table, and I sat with my laptop at the other end. I could afford to be magnanimous because my plan

had clearly worked. I was getting away with
it. They talked quietly, and I focused on my
project, feeling good about myself. Then my
phone vibrated.

(Makes vibrating noise)
I assumed it was from my client.
I was stunned. A text had come from Cliff's
phone: "They know," it said. I thought it must
have been a mistake or some kind of joke.

Then another arrived:
(Makes vibrating noise)
"They know you murdered me."

I sat as passively as possible, not letting
the deputies see my nervousness. Fortunately,
they weren't paying attention. I needed to
pull myself together.

(Makes vibrating noise)
Another arrived: "They're onto you."

(Makes vibrating noise)
"They're playing with you."

This had to be a trap the deputies were laying
for me. But I was smarter than that. I would
simply ignore the texts until they left.

(Makes vibrating noise)
"They're like a cat toying with a mouse."

(Makes vibrating noise)
"Torturing it."

I pictured a cat with a mouse, but the cat had
the old's man hideous claw. I could feel my
heart racing, pumping faster and faster. My
head pounded. I could feel the blood draining
from my face. One of the deputies looked my
way and smiled, giving me a thumbs up.

(Makes vibrating noise)
"Torturing it."

I started picturing the old man's claw sending the texts. Then it was coming for me. I was feeling deathly ill, and it was all I could do to sit quietly.
(Makes vibrating noise)
"Torturing it."

The deputies were pretending that there was nothing wrong. They were mocking me.

(Makes vibrating noise)
"Torturing it."

The same text over and over again. My ears were ringing. I could barely swallow.

(Makes vibrating noise)
"Torturing it."

I couldn't take any more of it. I jumped up. "Stop it. Stop the texting. I did it to never to see that gruesome thing again." The deputies looked confused.

(Makes vibrating noise)
Yet another one.

"Stop it, you demons! Just stop the texting, and I'll admit it. I killed the old man. I killed him."

END PLAY

The Butler
By Jamie McLeish

CHARACTER
  INVITEE - *Male*

SETTING
  A bare, sparse room.

INVITEE

I didn't recognise the writing on the envelope
and as I am not overburdened with letters,
curiosity quickly stole over me and led me to
open the letter. It was a single card, printed
on one side; an invitation of some kind. There
was no name but after scanning the text I
understood I had been invited to attend a
reunion at the School I had attended many
years ago.

Initially sceptical of accepting the
invitation, one singular fact aroused my
interest – that the location of the reunion
was not to be the Main School building which
was home to the vast majority of boys and had
housed me for five years but the ancient
Briary which had served as my scholastic home
for the first two years of my secondary
education.

This grand building had once been the Grammar
School's one and only building. An impressive
Victorian structure, built to educate Catholic
boys in the region who were either rich or
academically gifted enough to win a coveted
place on the School's register.

Of the seven years I had spent in Secondary
Education these first two were by far the most
interesting and rewarding – in no small part
due to the atmospheric setting of my lessons.
Whilst I didn't blossom academically, I found
the whole experience of being taught in such a
magnificent setting to be thrilling.

After overcoming my initial intimidation of
the old place, I found that I enjoyed the
ambient surroundings and thrived on the
history that emanated from the wood and brick.
During the autumn months, after trawling the
surrounding road for conkers which had fallen
from the overhanging chestnut trees, I would

often arrive at the School from the East
entrance which led to the new, main School
building with its typical comprehensive
façade. This would then require me to walk
through the tunnel which was at the head of
some steps at the far end of the new
playground. This tunnel was the connection
between the school of today to the one of
yesterday. Around 200 feet long, it ended in a
series of steps which seen from a distance
(say, from the entrance of the tunnel by the
eyes of an eleven-year-old boy) looked like
giant logs, stacked one on top of the other in
a seemingly insurmountable pile.

Hopefully, the one electric light on the roof
of the tunnel in its centre would give a
comforting glow, if not, you fixed your eyes
on the daylight at the end and marched
forward. I would hurry through this tunnel but
never run. To run was to give in to the
creeping sense of being watched, of being
followed. To run was to let your mind snap and
admit that you were scared, terrified; yet it
was terror that mingled with excitement until
the moment when you emerged at the other side
and scaled the steps to the soft, earthen path
that was shaded by thin trees and heard the
birds singing and felt the air on your face
again. Then you might laugh to yourself - a
nod to your own cowardice and bravery -
acknowledging the gratitude and admiration you
felt at being on 'safe' ground again.

My young mind often embarked on flights of
fancy and it almost felt as if the old place
whispered as I walked alone through its
corridors and hallways to class. This was no
doubt due to the story all boys were told of
the Butler who hung himself in the loft of the
Briary around the turn of the last Century.
Looking back, I'm certain this tale was an
ingenious ruse to discourage boys from roaming

the more secluded parts of the school and to
keep them in groups, heading straight to
whichever class they were meant to be going.
At the time though, I, as well as every other
boy, felt a sense of disquiet as we passed the
steps leading from the east corridor up to a
small locked door, as this was rumoured to
lead to the very loft in question. The fact
that this door was forever locked only
increased its reputation.

Yes, the School was decrepit but it was also
awe-inspiring and emanated a sense of
importance and grandeur which impressed me
greatly at the time.

Having made up my mind to attend the function,
I made my way through the well-remembered
streets and my feet seemed to find their own
path as my mind recalled the hundreds of
identical journeys I had taken to this place.
The early October evening suffused the
approach to the school with a golden light as
the trees which formed a natural canopy from
either side of the road swung their branches
and shed their leaves.

As I stopped at the entrance of the grounds,
the gateposts reared above me on either side.
Yet I almost didn't enter. Years of nostalgia
had created an unrealistic memory of the
place. What if the building was just stone and
mortar? What if the other-worldly character I
perceived as a boy had lessened as my own
character matured? I was certain I would be
disappointed with my own history and felt a
sudden urge to turn and flee reality,
preferring to keep my vision of the past. But
my curiosity and affection for the old place
was stronger than my fear of anti-climax. With
an intake of breath, I crossed the threshold
and took my steps towards the building itself.
I walked slowly, taking in the atmosphere of

the grounds - even the air smelled differently to what it had a few steps back.

Although light was showing from several windows I could not see or hear any sign of any other guests and so I decided to savour the moment of anticipation and delayed my entrance to the building - instead turning left to take in the playground I had ran in years ago.

This delighted me as I found that while it was indeed smaller than memory measured, it still maintained its sense of space. I was still filled with the feeling that it was a place I could relax in, a place I had earned after working hard in class. I walked around the yard with its grey tarmac and red-brick walls. I recalled the many games I had played here and listened for the enthusiastic shouts of years ago but was met with silence. My thirst for reminiscing slaked, I didn't linger and headed for the school doors.

The handles were still the same - golden, weather beaten but still retaining their ornate style, offering a reassuring sense of quality in their solidness. As I pulled one of the double doors open, I was greeted with a rush of age and that familiar, unforgettable scent of school. I was inside.

There was still no noise to assail my ears. There was no sight or sound of any other guest and I checked my watch to make sure I hadn't miscalculated the time. The light in the hallway seemed insufficient, casting a dull, orange glow in the deepening dusk. I walked tentatively forward and placed my hand on the old-fashioned radiator - it was warm.

I was puzzled - doors unlocked, lights and heating both on yet no sign of anyone. I began to wonder if perhaps I had mistaken the day. I was not a little disquieted. I thought of turning around and leaving – the sudden sense of unease I felt directed all of my thoughts to the exit.

My legs however, seemed to lead me forward into the dimness of the corridor, past the old art room and through the double doors to the bottom of the east staircase. This led up to the upper floor, where my old First-Year classroom was located. It also led up to the Butler's last, grisly abode. I was curious to see my old classroom and plunged forward up the stairs, past the statue of the Virgin Mary – arms outstretched in supplication.

Upon opening the doors to the upper corridor, I was immediately faced with the small door to the loft. Cast in shadow it seemed tiny and insignificant yet I felt a shudder as I passed it, trying not to increase my pace. To my joy, I found the door to my first-year classroom unlocked. As I surveyed the room, I cast my mind back thirty years to a time when it was full of small, excitable boys, all animated with talk and laughter.

I remembered the numerous times we had been sent home in winter as the ancient heating system had given up the ghost. I can't recall ever feeling the cold in the place (possibly a result of so many small bodies generating heat) but I noticed it now. The classroom was icy. The desks and chairs were now modern, tough metal and plastic, ergonomically designed – a far cry from the creaking, wooden antiques on which I sat. There were many times when I would nip the skin of my thighs in a crack in the wooden chairs or receive a splinter in my hands from the desk lid. Even though my original desk had long gone I still could not resist taking a seat in the same position I used to sit and raising my hand as if to ask a question of the teacher.

It was just as I raised my hand that I heard the double doors in the corridor open and close. With a start I stood, hesitating a moment while my mind played out all of the scenarios that could have caused the sound. My logical brain ascertained that it must have been the arrival of another guest. I stepped to the door of the classroom and proceeded beyond, readying myself to greet an old face from my past. There was nobody there. I hurried to the double doors and gazed through the glass to the staircase – there was no sign of anyone.

Retracing my steps, I dashed along the corridor to see if anyone had already passed my classroom. There was nothing. My stomach lurched as the overhead light began to flicker. Before I could shout a hello, the light extinguished – and with it my courage. It was as if the atmosphere of the place had infected my senses.

Suddenly, I was imagining spectres and ghouls to appear from the corridor ahead of me or for a cold, skeletal hand to grab my shoulder from behind. Lost in a paroxysm of childish fear I dashed for the staircase – past the small door to the attic which suddenly resounded with a sound as if heavy knuckles were rapping on its surface from the opposite side. My feet carried me with a speed I did not know I possessed down the stairs, back along the ground floor corridor and out of the main doors.

However, as I ran the short distance to the school gates, I found they were closed, a solid padlock fastening the bolt. I did not stop to consider how this could be when barely twenty minutes earlier they had been standing open, unlocked. In the thirty years since my boyhood I knew I had lost the ability to scale the school gates and perimeter walls and thus fled to the only exit I could remember – through the tunnel to the main school and freedom.

The old, worn path to the tunnel seemed more gnarled and weather-beaten than ever and daylight was clinging to the earth with its fingertips as darkness stole silently over the grounds. Memory enabled me to navigate the path safely until I arrived at the stone steps to the tunnel where I stopped in my tracks. My fear of the unknown back at the school was matched by my fear of the known ahead of me. I was Eleven years old again on a dark and lonely morning, faced with a long walk through my childhood nightmare. I steeled myself to push onwards, stumbled down the steps and plunged into darkness.

I fear I must have been either physically or mentally sick. How else could I explain the sweat which began pouring from my brow, the weakness in my legs or worst of all – the sounds I heard in my head? Whether real or imagined, I cannot say. My ears were assailed by a deep, low throbbing which increased to a crescendo of guttural groans as if the very walls of the tunnel themselves wept with misery. My head dizzy, my legs shaking, I careered through the tunnel, praying that the light at the end would soon wrap me in its safe, warm arms. Suddenly my progress was halted and my journey through the tunnel was a realisation of every nightmare I had had of being chased.

It seemed that no matter how quickly I lifted and planted my feet, however desperately I wanted to progress, I remained virtually motionless, moving barely an inch for every frantic stride I took. I did not - could not - look back. I was as Lot's wife and knew that if I looked back, I would look into the abyss and never return. My physical and mental strength sapping and snapping, I made a last, agonised push for the tunnel's exit, forcing myself through with my mind rather than my body.

Then I was out. The air around me was cleaner, free of chilling sounds. No, that was not quite true. There was one chilling sound, a sound that chilled me so deeply that it finally made me aware of what I must do. I heard the sound of the wind through a branch. The East entrance of the tunnel - from which I had longed to emerge - had no foliage, only the concrete mass of schoolyard which belonged to the main building.

I was back at the entrance of the tunnel, on the same gnarled path with the same trees swaying overhead. Impossible as this seemed I turned to look back up the tunnel and saw a miniature version of what I was looking at now. The tunnel had kept me at the Briary, prevented me from escape and forced me into understanding. The truth was clear to me now - I would not be allowed to leave this place until I had done what it wanted me to do. I must enter the attic.

With a heart as heavy as the atmosphere, I slowly trudged back along the dirt path and re-entered the school. The darkness outside melted before the brilliance of the lights in the school corridor which now blazed. The double doors at the end of the ground floor corridor were open, awaiting me and beckoning me on. I felt none of the fear I had felt when 1 ran from the building - the certainty of my task had galvanised me into fortitude. I walked with purpose along the corridor and back up the stairs to the door of the attic.

As I stood outside of the door, my new-found courage disappeared along with the light which was silently extinguished to leave the entire building in blackness. What I had previously thought to be the rapping of knuckles upon the door was no longer to be heard as silence hung heavy in the air. I could barely find the dull sheen of the door knob as I forced my hand forward and flexed my fingers around the metal.

The door opened soundlessly and I was confronted with an acrid smell. Faced with several stairs which led to a raised platform around head height, I could see dust motes floating in front of me – obviously having been disturbed by the opening of the long-closed door. I took my first tentative step and then pushed my thighs onwards to mount the steps which may have been as high as a mountain for the energy they drained me of.

As my eyes reached the level of the top riser my mouth fell open in a silent scream. Imagination could not have created a more gruesome sight then that which greeted me in the attic. Swinging from a beam not twenty feet in front of me was the Butler. Only it was not the Butler, but Daniel Butler. After all these years I still recognised the boy I had once mercilessly bullied at school, whose life I had made a misery for two years. He was obviously dead – the blue skin and sickening angle of his neck testified to this fact – but his eyes remained open, fixed upon me with a look almost of mirth.

How I wish I had not made those final few steps. The course of my life would most surely have taken a more fortuitous turn.

As it was… is…

I must finish this now. My sentence is to be
passed anon and I do not wish my jailors to
see me as dishevelled and debased as I feel. I
pray my strength holds for the final few
moments of my life.

As my protestations of my innocence fell upon
deaf ears I have no other recourse but to hope
this tale finds its way into sympathetic hands
so that at least my name and reputation if not
my physical self may be redeemed.

I still cannot understand nor quantify how the
body of evidence against me in the death of
Daniel Butler came to be; my fingerprints on
the rope, my blood on his shirt. How did these
things come to pass?

Coupled with my prior acquaintance with the
victim and the appearance of several witnesses
at the trial who testified to our less than
friendly past, my jurors took less than one
hour to find me guilty.

Now it is I who will swing from a noose this
very morning. I commend myself to fate's whim.

I must go… I can hear them coming for me, led
no doubt by that brute, Warden Butler.

                        END PLAY

The "Haunted House"
By Ryan Vaughan

CHARACTER
  PARENT - *Any gender, any adult age*

SETTING
  A car on a Fall night.

Parent sits in a chair on the stage. There is a chair to their right and two chairs behind them. In the beginning they pantomime rolling down the window of a car and calling out to their children.

PARENT

Would you two please get in the car? Leave that mummy alone! No, I'm not waiting so you can get the bride of Frankenstein's autograph. You know why? Because she's an actress! Her name is probably Karen or something. Hey! Do not make me drag you into this car!
    (Beat)
Finally, thank you. Now, will one of you two hooligans, please, tell me why I just paid $25 per person for us to go to an old house with cheap "scary" decorations, FAKE blood, and actors who couldn't manage to book a show right now so are instead working here? I mean COME ON! One of those newbies popped out and screamed the "B" word.
    (Beat)
No, not that "B" word! I'll wash your mouth out with holy water when we get home for saying that, mister. "Boo" the actor said "Boo." Everybody knows saying boo doesn't scare anyone."
    (Pause, then, jumps as if scared)
Well, that time doesn't count. I was driving! Anyway, what I'm saying is that if you two wanted to experience a "haunted house" we could have just stayed home. Because oh, I don't know…

WE'RE GHOSTS!
    (Beat)
Ok, alright, hold on. I'm sorry. Please, don't cry. It wasn't all bad. Seeing the kid's face at the ticket booth when $75 just floated towards him was priceless. He went white as snow! I know! It's like he'd seen a ghost. Oh wait, he did!

(Beat)
So, hey, I'll tell you two what, how about we
scare the cashier at the gas station when we
each pick a few treats for dessert?

END PLAY

The Rescue
By Debs Wardle

CHARACTER
  STORYTELLER - *Female, 50s-60s, British*

SETTING
  A medieval castle with a roaring fire and
  a dog curled up on a rug.

STORYTELLER

Marguerita's turret was not cosy. Small? Yes.
Cosy? No. They hadn't wanted her to get too
comfortable while she waited for a hero to
rescue her. It wasn't how these things were
done, they had said.

For five long years, Marguerita sat in her
turret waiting to be rescued. She tried to
accept her fate with good grace, but good
grace was not something that came naturally to
her.

No, try as she may, what Marguerita felt was
resentment. Resentment for the townsfolk who'd
locked her up here and regularly forgot to
feed her. Resentment for her own beauty,
whatever "beauty" was, that had seen her be
chosen as The Damsel. And resentment for the
hero who had yet to show up and rescue her.

One rainy Tuesday, that had started just like
any other, with the crushing tedium of her
reality hitting her mere moments after waking;
Marguerita heard a sound. It wasn't a sound
she remembered hearing before, a sort of
scratching sound.

As she listened, the sound grew louder and
closer. She wondered what it could possibly
be, birds nesting in the masonry below? A
horse stomping about in the neighbouring
field? No, neither of those seemed right. Then
a thought struck her. No, it couldn't be that.
Could it?

Marguerita gingerly leaned out of the window
and looked down. She nearly fell out with
shock – there was a man climbing up the wall
of the tower, heading straight for her turret.

Her hero had FINALLY arrived!

She ran to the mirror, and half wished she hadn't. Her hair was all matted, there were large gloops of sleep dust in the corners of her eyes, and the nightgown she was still wearing had definitely seen better days. Marguerita sprang into action – grabbing her hairbrush, she made a dash for her tiny bathroom. At least she didn't have to decide what to wear, she thought, the "rescue dress" the townsfolk had selected for her was still carefully wrapped up in the box it had arrived in. She hoped it would still fit.

Once she was vaguely presentable, she returned her attention to the man she was about to meet. She'd only caught a glimpse of him, only really enough to ascertain that a) he was a man and b) he was climbing up her wall. She wondered if he was handsome. She wondered if he was kind – surely he must be if he was the sort of person who would go out on a mission to rescue a damsel.

She continued wondering for some time and conjured up quite the image of manhood, a paradigm of non-toxic masculinity – kind, brave, noble, funny, moral, loving, strong, supportive. Marguerita eventually roused from her daydream and realised that it had been some time and her hero had not yet appeared. What was taking him so long?

She poked her head out of the window again only to find he was gone. Had she imagined him? It had been a couple of days since she was last brought food, hallucinating wasn't entirely out of the question. She was still fixated on the man-free wall below her when all of a sudden there was a loud noise as somebody broke down the door to her room. She whirled round and came face to face with her hero. She hadn't imagined him after all, he'd simply found a way in and come up the stairs!

She'd spent much of the past five years
anticipating this moment and imagining how it
would play out. But now it was here, the
nerves took over and she realised she didn't
know what to do. How does one greet one's
hero? The townsfolk hadn't covered that part.
Should you curtsey? Bow your head? Shake
hands? Embrace? She honestly had no idea so
she stood and waited in the hopes that he
would give her some kind of sign. But the man
in front of her didn't seem especially
concerned with the social etiquette of
introductions.

He was cold and angry and beady eyed, and not
at all what Marguerita had anticipated. "Girl"
he said, after regarding her for a minute or
two. Marguerita wondered if she ought to give
him her name, but something told her that he
wouldn't be interested. "Girl, I am your
rescuer. You are to come with me." Her hero
stalked off down the stairs, only stopping
briefly to check she was following.

This wasn't how it was supposed to go at all.
Her hero was supposed to take her lovingly in
his arms and tell her how beautiful she was
and kiss her passionately. She wondered
fretfully whether she could reject her hero;
but quickly concluded that wouldn't be the
done thing. So follow him she did.

Their wedding was small and quick. Marguerita
wasn't sure the townsfolk had even been
notified of her rescue – certainly none of
them were there to witness her nuptials. There
were no flowers, no doves, no cheering
bystanders; she hadn't even been given time to
change out of her rescue dress and into
something more bridal.

She spent much of her wedding night scrubbing
the floor of her hero's hall, while he was

locked in his office – a room he'd wasted no time in forbidding her from entering.

Marguerita found her married life to be just as lonely as her turret, and now she had so much housework to do. Her hero never really noticed what cleaning she did, but got horribly cross if he thought she hadn't been doing it. They dined together most evenings, and the conversations over the table were one sided and difficult to navigate. Marguerita was expected to listen to him, support him, and offer help wherever she could; but she often seemed to get it wrong, which would result in him breaking things, which she'd then have to clean up.

As she lay in bed listening to his footsteps pass by her door – half relieved, half hurt – Marguerita wondered when the love was supposed to begin. They'd said that these things often don't happen right away, that they can take both time and work, but nobody'd offered any pointers on precisely what work might be required.

Perhaps, there was something wrong with her.

One morning, he stalked into the room she was cleaning. "Girl, I have business in town, and I won't be back until late." He went into no further detail and promptly left. As she heard the front door close behind him, a sense of relief washed over her – she was alone for the first time since the rescue. But relief was entirely the wrong thing to be feeling, she thought, surely she should miss her hero when he wasn't at her side?

Marguerita put away her mops and cloths, sat down, and closed her eyes. A short while later she opened them again, an idea brewing. Perhaps the reason she was struggling to feel any affection towards her hero was that she didn't actually know much about him. Who was he? Where was he from? What did he do for a living? She had, of course, asked him these questions but he either hadn't heard her, or hadn't felt like answering.

Now she was finally alone in the house, what was to stop her from having a look around? She could get some answers and, so long as she was careful to put everything back exactly as she'd found it, he'd never have to know.

She went through his wardrobe first, opened every box and bag then went through his pockets. She found nothing so moved on to the dresser, then under the bed, then the bathroom, then all of the cupboards, then the bookshelves, up the chimney, and behind the sofa. Having still found nothing, her feet took her to the last room. The room she had promised him never to enter. The room that she couldn't enter because it would almost certainly be locked. Wouldn't it?
Marguerita tried the handle.

Yes, it was locked. How do you get through a locked door? There must be a key, she supposed, but he'd probably taken it with him. She wondered how you pick a lock – she knew it was possible, but also knew it probably wouldn't be a skill she could teach herself in one afternoon. Then it hit her: the window. The office had a window looking out onto the garden!

The window was small and forbidding, but the frame was old and gave way quite easily. Marguerita was able to drag herself through without too much trouble and was soon standing in her hero's forbidden office. Like the rest of the house, it was sparsely furnished with just a desk, a chair, and some shelving.

Marguerita sat on the chair, needing to take a moment before beginning her search. This would be where she would finally get to know her hero. Perhaps she might find something to explain why he was so cold towards her, perhaps some piece of information contained in this desk might even make him lovable.

She took a deep breath and began, the thrill of discovery pulsing through her. There was very little on the top of the desk save for a few pens and a large, oddly sharp looking paper knife, so she quickly turned her attention to its drawers.

The top drawer held nothing surprising – household receipts, writing implements, ledgers, etc. The second drawer down was a little more interesting, its contents seemed to indicate that he was some kind of merchant, but she couldn't make sense of what was being traded. The third, final, and largest drawer contained, amongst other things, a large leather document holder.

Leafing through it, she realised that she was looking at the details of various damsels. Her heart rose as she read their names and descriptions, realising that he must have read through them too and, out of all these wonderful sounding girls, he had chosen to rescue her. Here, in her hand, was the proof she had longed for – she was special to her hero after all! How could she ever have doubted her rescuer?
And that might have been that. Marguerita might have put everything back where she'd found it and climbed back out of the window, but something else in the wallet caught her attention.

On closer inspection, she found it was a marriage certificate. Perhaps it was a parent's or a sibling's, she thought, but no. The name on it was his. And then Marguerita found another marriage certificate, and another, and another – and the wives? Why did she recognise their names too?

With a start, Marguerita realised that she was not his first damsel. Not even close. That wasn't how this was supposed to work, she thought, you're supposed to rescue one damsel, then go and live your happily ever after with that damsel; you don't just go about collecting damsels. Another, less comfortable thought followed a moment later: what had happened to the other damsels?

The answer had to be somewhere in this desk, she thought as she started frantically rummaging. At the bottom of the drawer, she found a little black book full of newspaper articles. She read each one carefully. A suicide. An accident. A disappearance. Missing body parts. Disfigurement. Torture. Every fibre of her being was screaming that he'd killed them. He'd killed them all and got away with it. He'd killed them all and she was next.

With her hands shaking, Margurita closed the book and went to put it back where she'd found it -put everything back exactly as she'd found it- but then the door flew open and there he was. Her murderous hero, standing in the doorway.

Marguerita froze. "You were the one person I thought I could trust" he said. She wanted to tell him that she was sorry, that she wouldn't do it again, that she would be good now; but her mouth was suddenly so very dry.

In an instant he'd crossed the space between them. "This is the one thing you promised me you'd never do" he grabbed her by the throat "you're just the same as the others, using me, draining me of my generosity". Marguerita struggled, desperate to break free, but his grip grew tighter and tighter "I rescue you, open up my home to you, and this is how you repay me?"

From the corner of her streaming eye, Marguerita saw him reach for something shiny on the desk with his free hand. The paper knife! Her struggles intensified. "Ungrateful girl, you drove me to this!" As he went to plunge the knife into her, she dredged up all her strength - strength she didn't know she had - got her foot against his thigh, and kicked him hard away. He staggered backwards, releasing his grip on her as he tripped over the corner of the desk.

Marguerita stumbled to the other side of the room gulping in air. She blinked the tears out of her eyes and looked about to see which direction the next blow would be coming from - but her hero had not got back up. He was laid on the floor where he had fallen, wheezing, something shiny in his side.

"Girl! Save me!" he ordered as his blood began to pool on the floorboards. She remained motionless. "I am your rescuer - it is your duty to save me!" Her head inclined ever so slightly to the left as if she were considering this point, but still she made no move to come to her hero's aid.

This continued for some time, he insisting that she had no choice but to help him and her making no effort to do so. Eventually his demands grew weaker and before too much longer there was silence. Through all this, Marguerita did not move a muscle.

As she watched his cooling corpse, she tried to decide what it would be appropriate to feel at this moment. Sadness? Regret? Guilt, even? She felt none of those things, in fact the thing Marguerita felt was laughter bubbling up inside of her. She knew that laughing at a time like this would be improper, but the laughter would not, and could not, be contained.

And so, Margurita laughed.

A joyful, ringing laugh that made her heart swell and her cheeks ache and her head light.

She laughed until tears streamed down her face.

She laughed until her ribs ached.

She laughed until she was seeing stars and gasping for breath.

She laughed until eventually, she could laugh no more.

Once her breathing returned to normal Marguerita found herself leaning forward and grasping the handle of the paper knife that was still sticking out of her hero's side. Firmly and deliberately, she pulled it out. Thick, dark blood oozed from the now open wound, and she watched it for a moment, transfixed. Her eyes flickered up to meet his, which were already becoming glassy. She wiped the knife clean on his tunic and turned away.

Marguerita was not heard from again, although there are many rumours regarding what happened to her.

Some say that she had acquired a taste for revenge and for many years following her

disappearance any grizzly death with no
obvious culprit was attributed to her,
especially if the victim was a hero who had
proven to be undeserving of the title.

Others say that Marguerita went on a crusade
to free other damsels. Certainly, there were
many more damsels being freed than there were
weddings taking place, and it wasn't long
before a movement sprung up that got the
custom outlawed altogether.

Then, there were the rumours of two women who
stowed away on a ship to the Americas
together, one of whom supposedly bore a
striking resemblance to Marguerita and was
never once seen without a large, oddly sharp
looking paper knife somewhere about her
person.

Perhaps all of these stories are true, or
perhaps none are…

Whatever happened to her, this storyteller
would like to think that Marguerita found
freedom and maybe, just maybe, she lived
happily ever after.

                    END PLAY

The Vanishing Texter
By Peter Dakutis

CHARACTER
  CHARLIE - *Male, late teens-early 20s*

SETTING
  A college dormitory room.

CHARLIE

It was funny how we met. Cindy texted my
number by mistake, and it was so cute how she
kept apologizing. We kept texting and learned
that we had a lot in common. Like being
serious about school, staying pure until
marriage, wanting lots of kids. We had the
same sense of humor, too, like watching videos
of animals doing crazy things. After a while,
we swapped photos, and I knew she was the
right kind of girl for me. I could tell that
she was sweet, smart, and super cute.

We talked a few times on the phone. She was
shy about it because of an issue with her
vocal cords. When she was stressed, she wound
up talking in a whisper. So I did the same to
make her feel better. It was our special way
of communicating.

Mostly, we texted. At different times of the
day, just to say hey, I'm thinking about you.
And we both said we didn't want to get ahead
of ourselves, but the feelings were so
intense. She said she considered me her
boyfriend. I told her I felt the same about
her.

Cindy was going to be home on Halloween for
fall break. It was funny that I was going to
school down here, where she lives, and she was
going to school up where I'm from. The plan
was to have dinner with her parents and watch
a movie. She said she didn't like scary
movies, but she'd watch one with me if I held
her hand. But Halloween didn't go as planned.
She kept getting delayed, and it got late. So
no dinner and no movie. Finally, she texted
that she was almost there and I should go
ahead to her parents' house.

I was ready. I thought I was, anyway. I didn't
have trouble finding the house.

When I knocked on the door, Cindy's father opened it. Her mother was standing behind him.

"Hi, I'm Charlie, Cindy's boyfriend. She said you were expecting me."

"No, no!" Cindy's mother shouted. She ran off, crying.

"Son, you'd better come in and sit down," her father said. So I went into their living room and sat on the couch. He sat in a chair across from me. I had no idea what was going on.

He spoke quietly, in a strange voice. "Cindy died eight years ago on Halloween night. And for the past seven Halloweens, a different young man has showed up saying he's Cindy's boyfriend and she sent him here to wait for her."

I didn't know what to say. He looked sad, like he was waiting for bad news. And then my phone chimed, which made me jump.

"Go ahead and look at your text," he said. It was from Cindy. And as I was reading it, he said the words out loud.

"Tell my Mom and Dad I love them."

END PLAY

Work-Life Balance
By Emma C. R. Skinner

CHARACTER
  OFFICE WORKER - *Any age, any gender*

SETTING
  A corporate office break room.

WORKER

    I don't think she means me any harm. I think she just wants someone to talk to?

    No, that's not right. It's not about talking. She's never asked me to say a single word. She just sits there. In the corner of the office. Her face looks like paper filaments. It frays at the edges. I never see the rest of her - what the dead bones might look like beneath the sandpaper skin, the black-and-white suit. I try not to look too hard at her, if I can. It feels disrespectful. And kind of scary...

    You know, most people walk into their workspace and don't find a corpse. Right? In fact, I'd say everyone does that! Almost every person who gets a new job arrives at that job to not find a corpse. That's a pretty well-set standard. It's so taken for granted that we don't even think about it...

    I've tried emailing HR about it. Twice, in fact. But they don't respond. One instance of ignoring me could be an accident. Two is starting to feel like it's on purpose. And it's okay, honestly. I don't mind all that much. There's no smell, and she's not mean.

    She just sits slumped behind the door all day, staring at me. Sometimes it looks like she's listening to my phone calls, or has opinions on my emails. I try not to listen. But I can't discount her too much.

    "Uncomfortable scenarios are good for personal growth."

    That's what they told me, on the first day of my orientation. There's even a poster that says it, right over my desktop computer...

Having a dead woman haunting your desk is pretty uncomfortable. So it's got to be a great growth opportunity. Right?

Maybe I can put it on my resumé.

END PLAY

ABOUT
DRAMATIC CHAOS PRODUCTIONS

We are a London-based Theatre Company with an aim to portray honest perspectives and create an emotional response.

We love creative people and everything they dream up. We want artist's work to be seen! Too much gets hidden away in forgotten folders unsuitable for submission anywhere. Maybe it's too short, maybe it's always the wrong topic or maybe it questions those at the top.

Well, we're interested!

This is our first Anthology and we're so excited to create more in the future. We are honoured by the many writers who have trusted us to share their work.

Some of these pieces are also available to be seen on our YouTube Channel - @DramaticChaosTP

P.s.
Next time you find yourself wondering if you can write something…

You can! You can do it!

Printed in Great Britain
by Amazon

36133458R00275